# Continental Dash

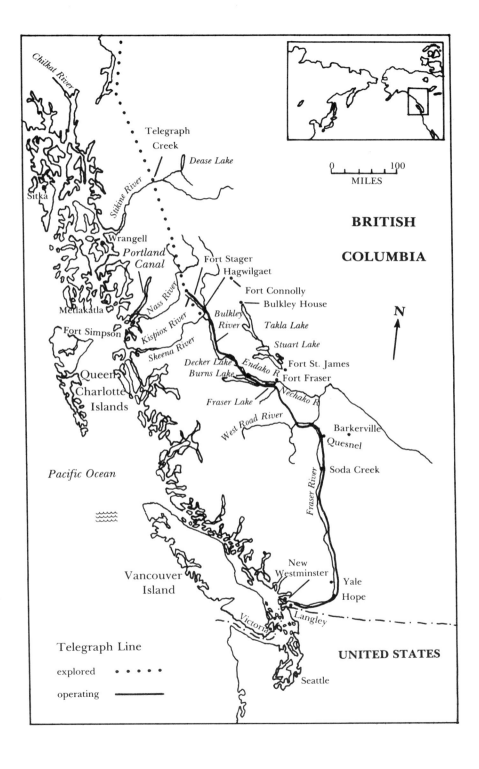

Chilkat River

Telegraph Creek

Dease Lake

0          100
MILES

Sitka

Stikine River

**BRITISH**

**COLUMBIA**

Wrangell

Portland Canal

Fort Stager

Hagwilgaet

Fort Connolly

Bulkley House

N

Metlakatla

Nass River

Bulkley River

Takla Lake

Fort Simpson

Kispiox River

Stuart Lake

Skeena River

Decker Lake

Endako R.

Fort St. James

Queen Charlotte Islands

Burns Lake

Fort Fraser

Fraser Lake

Nechako R.

West Road River

Barkerville

Quesnel

Pacific Ocean

Soda Creek

Fraser River

Vancouver Island

New Westminster

Yale

Hope

Victoria

Langley

**UNITED STATES**

Telegraph Line

explored    • • • • •

operating   ———

Seattle

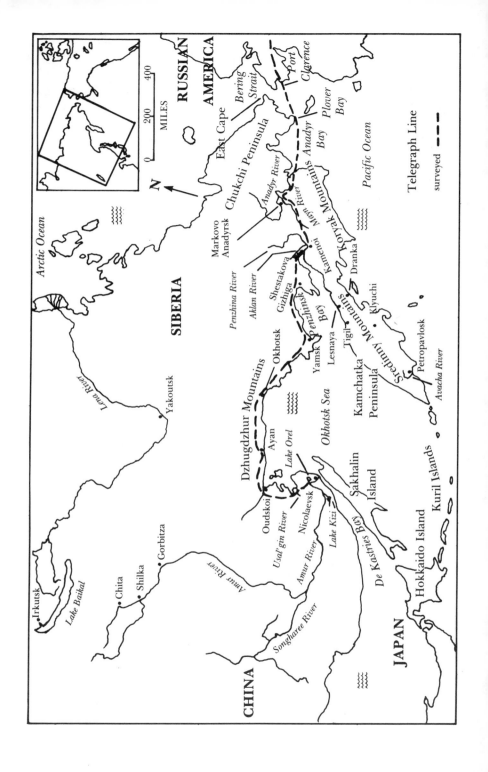

RUSSIAN
AMERICA

Bering Strait
East Cape
Chukchi Peninsula

Port Clarence
Plover Bay
Anadyr Bay

Pacific Ocean

Telegraph Line
surveyed ·····

Anadyr River
Moyn River
Koryak Mountains
Kamenoi
Dranka
Klyuchi
Petropavlosk
Avacha River

Markovo
Anadyrsk

Penzhina River
Aklan River
Shestakova
Gizhiga
Penzhinsk B(ay)
Yamsk
Lesnaya
Tigil
Sredinny Mountains
Kamchatka Peninsula

Arctic Ocean

SIBERIA

Lena River

Yakoutsk

Dzhugdzhur Mountains
Okhotsk
Ayan
Lake Orel
Oudskoi
Usal'gin River
Nicolaevsk
Amur River
Lake Kizi

Okhotsk Sea

Sakhalin Island

De Kastries B(ay)

Hokkaido Island
Kuril Islands

JAPAN

Irkutsk
Lake Baikal
Chita
Shilka
Gorbitza
Amur River
Songharee River

CHINA

N

MILES
0   200   400

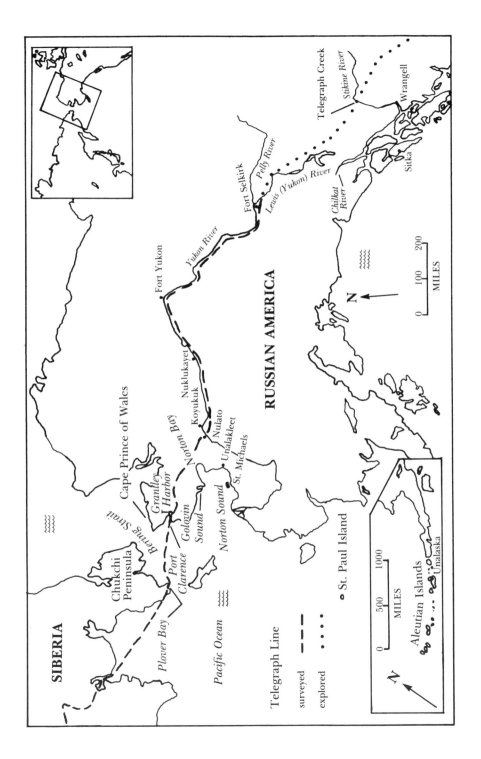

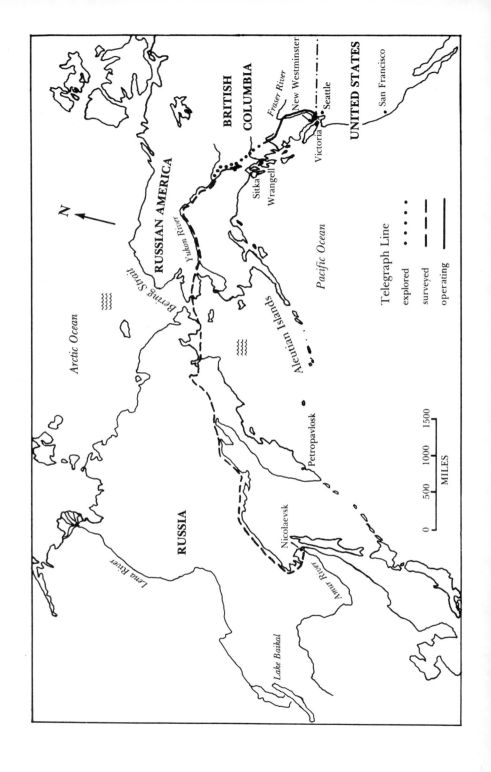

# Continental Dash

## The Russian-American Telegraph

by
Rosemary Neering

HORSDAL & SCHUBART

Horsdal & Schubart Publishers Ltd.
Box 1
Ganges, BC, V0S 1E0

The cover painting is from the sketchbook of John C. White, a former Royal Engineer who was an official artist for the telegraph expedition: watercolour on paper. It is in the collection of the Provincial Archives of British Columbia (pdp 2923) and is reproduced with the permission of the PABC.

Maps by Kathleen Moore, Vancouver, BC.

Chapter-head drawings by Tim Williamson, Ganges, BC.

Design and typesetting by The Typeworks, Vancouver, BC. This book is set in Galliard. Printed and bound in Canada by Hignell Printing Limited, Winnipeg, Manitoba.

**Canadian Cataloguing in Publication Data**
Neering, Rosemary, 1945-
    Continental dash


    Bibliography: p.
    Includes index.
    ISBN 0-920663-07-9


    1. Telegraph lines - United States - History.
2. Telegraph lines - Canada - History,   3. Telegraph
lines - Europe - History.   I. Title.
TK5122.N43 1989        384.1'09'034        C89-091005-7

# Contents

Illustrations from Whymper's *Travel and Adventures in the Territory of Alaska* appear with the permission of John Murray (Publishers) Ltd.; those from Bush's *Reindeer, Dogs and Snowshoes* with the permission of Macdonald & Co (Publishers) Ltd. Quotations from Adams' *Life on the Yukon 1865–1867* are used with the permission of Richard A. Pierce, those from Vevier's introduction to *Siberian Journey* with the permission of The University of Wisconsin Press, and those from Kennan's *Tent Life in Siberia* with the permission of The Putnam Publishing Group.

# Introduction and
# Acknowledgements

It's almost impossible to conceive now of how important, how revolutionary, the telegraph was then, 130 years ago. We take instant communication for granted; the telegraph that has been completely supplanted by modern telecommunications was the very first instrument of rapid communication. How visionary, yet how necessary, it seemed then to build a Russian-American telegraph, a globe-encircling line that would link east and west, old world and new.

And how astonishing it is to us, who think we invented the concept of Pacific Rim, to realize that American entrepreneurs of the mid-nineteenth century had a vision of North America as east of Europe via the Pacific Ocean and Russia, not west across the Atlantic—and that they saw America's destiny as firmly tied to the countries that surrounded the Pacific. In that world view, the United States and nineteenth-century Russia had twin and joint destinies to dominate the Pacific world.

Nineteenth-century entrepreneurs dreamed great dreams, then through leaps of faith and other people's money tried to make them come true. Some succeeded; some failed. The Russian-American telegraph was one of these massive attempts to conquer the world through the emerging technologies of transportation and communication—to span continents by rail, or oceans by wire.

The project of a book on the Russian-American telegraph line was conceived by Allen Wright, author of *Prelude to Bonanza,* a history of the pre-Klondike Yukon, who did a great deal of preliminary research before his death in 1983. Copies of that research are now in the Yukon Archives. Thanks are due to the staffs of the Yukon Archives, the Provincial Archives of British Columbia, and the special collections divisions of the University of British Columbia and the University of Washington. Special thanks also to Joe Thompson, Sharon Sterling, Jim Cooling and Cliff Bancroft, for reading and commenting on the manuscript. And thanks, of course, to Marlyn Horsdal, editor, publisher and shepherd.

Rosemary Neering

CHAPTER I

# Lightning Speaks

The newly invented Leyden jar was the talk of Paris in 1745. Just imagine: touch the jar and receive an electric shock that could throw you to the ground! The distinguished scientist Abbé Jean Antoine Nollet even shocked an entire company of the king's guard. Then Nollet made his way to a monastery, where he arranged the monks in a circle two miles around, joined them with pieces of wire and introduced a series of Leyden jars into the circuit. When the circuit was closed, with one accord the monks jumped and contorted.

The good abbé's procedure was bizarre, but his scientific curiosity was leading him in the direction of the future. His experiment with the monks proved that an electrical current travels with extreme speed over a circuit. It opened a scientific door on the possibility of sending messages by using electric current passing along a wire of unlimited length.

What Nollet and other eighteenth-century experimenters were seeking was eventually realized in the telegraph. In the 1830s, scientists in the United States and Europe almost simultaneously developed the first working telegraphs. For the first time in the history of mankind, a message could be received the instant after it was sent.

It took almost as little time for governments and businesspeople to recognize the importance of this new invention. Since it could tell commanders at once the whereabouts of the enemy or the results of battles, the telegraph permitted more efficient deployment of troops. The businessman could buy and sell according to prices received in a second instead of in weeks or months. Rail dispatchers could be aware in a moment that a train was ahead of or behind schedule and direct the engineers of other trains to speed up, slow down or pull in to a siding. Newspapers could use dispatches a few hours, rather than weeks or months, old. The telegraph marked the beginning of the age of rapid communication.

In Europe and North America, thousands of poles were erected and thousands of miles of line strung between cities and towns. Operators with flying fingers sent message after message in the dot-and-dash code named for telegraph pioneer Samuel Morse. Yet by 1845, there remained one basic and frustrating gap in the rapidly expanding network of telegraph lines. The lines ended where the water began, because seawater corroded telegraphic cable. Telegraphers tried using rubber to insulate the cables, but rubber rapidly broke down. Then experimenters rediscovered gutta percha, the coagulated latex from trees grown in the Malay peninsula, known for years in Europe but thought useless. Gutta percha had excellent insulating qualities for wires and was little affected by water.

Using cables wrapped in layers of gutta percha, telegraph companies set to work bridging the gaps in the telegraph system. In 1850, telegraphers successfully connected Dover to Calais with a cable along the floor of the English Channel. Messages were received for a short time, then ceased. The halt was puzzling—until a fisherman came ashore in France with a piece of the cable. He had caught it with his anchor, hauled it up and been amazed at this remarkable type of seaweed with a gold core. Despite the setback, a second, much heavier cable was laid, and the continent once more connected to Britain. In 1855, British engineers spanned the Black Sea, establishing rapid communication for the British in the Crimean War. Engineers also tackled the Mediterranean Sea and the Indian Ocean.

One major gap was more frustrating than any other—that between Europe and North America, the two busiest commercial regions in the world. Messages from Europe to America still had to travel by ship, as much as a month in the passage from one side of the Atlantic to the other. In 1857, American entrepreneur Cyrus Field determined to raise money to tie Europe to America—more precisely, Ireland to Newfoundland—by trans-Atlantic cable, and reduce the distance between the continents from a month to a second.

The seventh son of an old New England family, Field early on departed from the comfortable family bosom, determined to succeed on his own. At 15, he left home with—so the surely apocryphal story goes—eight dollars in his pocket and ambition in his heart.

In New York, he became an errand boy, paying as much for board and lodging as he received in wages. After two years, he gave up on this job and went to work for his brother's paper-making business. Soon afterward, he formed his own company, then with others started a paper-manufacturing company that went broke, worked long and hard hours to clear that company's debt and his own honour, and achieved remarkable success with his new paper-making company, Cyrus W. Field Inc. By the age of 33, he had made a quarter of a million dollars and announced his retirement.

With his wife, he toured England and the European continent; with a friend, he trod the paths of South America, bringing back with him an Indian boy and a jaguar.

But travel was not enough to satisfy his need for adventure and risk. In 1854, he met a Canadian telegraph engineer, who told him about a new scheme to run a telegraph line from Newfoundland to New York City. Newfoundland lay five sea days closer to Europe than did New York; messages sent by ship to Newfoundland, then by telegraph to New York, would arrive five days earlier than messages sent by ship from Europe to New York.

This was, thought Field, a good idea, but why think small? Looking closely at the globe in his office, he traced a 2,000-mile line along the shortest route between Europe and America—from Valentia Bay, Ireland, to Hearts Content, Newfoundland. Why not a submarine cable between the two?

His timing was superb. In 1853, an American navy survey of the North Atlantic had discovered a plateau between Ireland and Newfoundland. Commented naval lieutenant Michael Maury, the plateau "seems to have been placed there especially for the purpose of holding the wires of a submarine telegraph and of keeping them out of harm's way."[1]

Field negotiated with the British government and got an exclusive charter for all cables touching Newfoundland or Labrador for the next 50 years, rapidly raised more than a million dollars for a company to build a telegraph across Newfoundland and went to work persuading the British and American navies that new surveys should be conducted of the North Atlantic. Though the new surveys revealed that the plateau was not as flat as the first survey had suggested, they also brought good news: at no point was the plateau more than 15,000 feet from the ocean surface. And submarine cables had already been laid in water three miles deep.

Raising enough money to have the cable made and laid was Field's next task; he accomplished that with determination and despite difficulties. He then went to three British companies, the only ones in the world with the desire and the expertise to produce the cable. Over the next six months, the Gutta Percha Company in London produced a conducting core that required the drawing and spinning of thousands of miles of copper wire for the seven strands at the centre of the cable, and the careful covering of the wire with three layers of gutta percha. Two other British companies then sheathed the wire in layers of tarred hemp and armoured it with 18 strands of iron wire, each made up of six strands twisted around a central wire. It was a monumental job, requiring 335,000 miles of wire and 300,000 miles of tarred hemp to produce some 3,000 miles of cable.

Once complete, the cable was coiled aboard the two ships that would attempt the task of laying it: the *U.S.S. Niagara*, the largest steam frigate in the world, and the British navy man-of-war *Agamemnon*. More than fully loaded with 1,250 tons of cable aboard each, the two steamed out of the Thames late in July of 1857, bound for the west coast of Ireland. The *Niagara* was to lay the cable to a point midway across the ocean; it would then be spliced to the cable aboard the *Agamemnon*, and the British ship would complete the job between the mid-Atlantic and Newfoundland.

# Lightning Speaks

As cheers resounded from the crowd gathered on the Atlantic's shore at Valentia, Ireland, on August 5, the Earl of Carlisle, Lord Lieutenant of Ireland, wound up his speech. "We are about," he declared, "either by this sundown or by tomorrow's dawn, to establish a new material link between the old world and the new. Moral links there have been . . . but this, our new link . . . is to give a life and intensity which they never had before."[2]

Dozens of small boats bright with coloured bunting and packed with excited spectators milled around the bay. American sailors attached a telegraph cable to a hawser, then hauled the cable ashore from the *Niagara*. As they came ashore, the Lord Lieutenant and his staff set their hands to the hawser and strained with the sailors to bring the cable to the land telegraph line to which it was then attached.

The following morning, the *Niagara* steamed slowly out from the bay, cable reeling slowly from the wells below deck and disappearing beneath the waters of the Atlantic. Henry Field, Cyrus' brother, later reported, "There was a strange unnatural silence in the ship. Men paced the deck with soft and muffled tread, speaking only in whispers, as if a loud voice or a heavy footfall might snap the vital cord."[3]

The men paid out the cable at a rate faster than the ship's speed, to take into account any irregularities in the ocean floor. On August 13, 300 miles from shore, the cable was unrolling too fast, six miles per hour compared to the ship's four. The ship's engineer tried to slow it by tightening the brake on the paying-out mechanism. The pressure was too abrupt. The ship's stern rose on a swell; the cable pulled taut and snapped. The crew of the *Niagara* rushed to the side of the ship to see the twisted end vanish beneath the waves.

There was not enough spare cable to make a second attempt. Chastened and disappointed, the crew brought the ship about and steamed back toward Ireland. The first attempt to lay a submarine cable below the Atlantic had failed.

The failure divided those who desperately wanted to see telegraphic communication between Europe and America. Some, undaunted, sought better cables, better methods, better ships, better crew, for a new attempt. Others were utterly convinced that the project was quixotic and ill-considered.

Field was not a man to be forestalled by a single setback. The factories went back to work making and rolling onto drums an ocean's width of cable for a new attempt. The cable would once more be divided between the *Niagara* and the *Agamemnon*, but this time, the two would meet in mid-Atlantic, effect a splice and pay cable out as they steamed, one west, one east, toward their respective destinations.

In June of 1858, the *Niagara* and the *Agamemnon* met in mid-ocean, at last in calm seas after days of churning, rolling storm that threatened to sink both ships and their precious cargo. The correspondent for *The Times* of London, aboard the *Agamemnon*, described the effects of the storm:

"The lurch of the ship was calculated at forty-five degrees each way for five times in rapid succession. . . . The coil in the main hold . . . had begun to get adrift, and the top kept working and shifting as the ship lurched, until some forty or fifty miles were in a hopeless state of tangle, resembling nothing so much as a cargo of live eels."[4]

The storm over and the rendezvous made, the crews of the two ships made a careful splice that joined the cables from each ship. Equally carefully, the ships parted company and the spliced cable was lowered into the ocean. The *Niagara* steamed westward, the *Agamemnon* eastward, tied together by a growing length of cable settling toward the seabed.

But not for long. The cable aboard the *Niagara* caught in the machinery and broke; the ships made a new rendezvous and a new splice. They moved apart once more. Aboard each ship, telegraphers kept a constant watch on monitors that indicated a current passing along the submerged length of cable. A second break, for reasons not understood, forced a third splice. On this third attempt, 200 miles of cable sank to the floor before the current stopped and the ships closed back together. This time, the break had occurred just 20 feet from the *Agamemnon's* stern. Not enough cable remained for a fourth attempt and efforts to grapple the sunken cable and bring it to the surface failed. The captains ordered their ships back to port.

Still undaunted, Field ordered another attempt. Later that same year, the two ships met once more in mid-Atlantic. This time, care and determination were rewarded: on August 5, exactly one year after the first cable had been made fast to Ireland's shore, the crew of the *Niagara* hauled their cable ashore at Trinity Bay, Newfoundland. That same day, sailors for the *Agamemnon* brought to shore in Ireland the eastern end of the cable.

# Lightning Speaks

Messages flashed across Britain and the United States, and between the two countries, celebrating the expedition's success. Poems were written and songs sung to the glory of this "loving girdle round the earth." Cyrus Field was the toast of New York.

Four weeks later, he was the city's fool. The cable, never a reliable transmitter of messages, fell silent. No word passed between the two continents. Critics declared that Field's dream was over, and that the man had been foolish ever to believe that the Atlantic could be spanned. Millions of dollars and the efforts of hundreds of men had been poured into the attempt. Now, said the wise men, the futility of the project had been proven once and for all. Crossing the Atlantic by cable was not feasible.

One American listened to the debate with more than ordinary interest. Like Field, Hiram Sibley was a New Englander who had left home at an early age; he too had amassed the beginnings of a fortune by the time he was 31. Telegraphy fascinated him. He worked with Samuel Morse to help Morse obtain congressional grants to support his telegraph experiments in the 1840s, and by 1851 had bought a small telegraph company and erected 100 miles of line in the eastern United States.

He watched the proliferation of small telegraph companies in the United States, each owning a few hundred miles of line, each battling for a share of the business. He decided that telegraph company consolidation, not competition, could make him a fortune, and set about acquiring and merging small companies until he and a partner headed a new giant, the Western Union Telegraph Company.

Sibley, too, saw the need for a telegraph connection between Europe and America. When the trans-Atlantic cable failed in 1858, he was ready to consider other ways of effecting the link. In 1861, he met a man who could dream dreams equal to his own—Perry McDonough Collins.

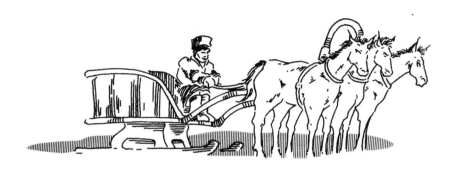

## CHAPTER 2

# Overland to the Amur

Perry McDonough Collins was born in Hyde Park, New York, in 1813, the son of parents who were, from all reports, affluent and well connected—and also patriotic, for they named their infant son after the American naval heroes, Commodores Perry and MacDonough. He wasted little time with formal schooling, choosing instead to move to New York City, where he took a job, probably as a clerk, in a law office. Little is known about his early life beyond the fact that he worked for six years on a fruitless lawsuit, hoping to wrest property or money from a large church for the heirs—himself included—of a New York pioneer.

By the time he reached his early thirties, he had concluded that the city, his law-office job and the east coast offered small reward and less excitement. In 1846, he moved on to the rapidly growing port city of New Orleans. There he took a job in the branch office of a major shipping company and met William McKendree Gwin and Robert J. Walker, later the secretary of the American navy. Both men believed fervently in America's manifest destiny to dominate the North American continent; they quickly converted Collins to their faith.

Gwin, a Democrat, was an ambitious man who wanted to become a United States senator. But there were others ahead of him in line in New Orleans, and he was unlikely to realize his political ambitions there. When news of the California gold rush reached New Orleans, Gwin decided that the territory would soon become a state, and took ship for the west coast with the primary aim of becoming California's first senator.

Collins was equally eager to see what opportunities this new golden land offered. Like 80,000 others in that hurly-burly year of 1849, he abandoned his job and headed for the goldfields. He tumbled into San Francisco in the midst of the turmoil and frenzy that the gold discoveries had created.

Most of the stampeders were after gold; they shovelled through the muck of every creek and hillside, built flumes and sluice boxes, dug tunnels and destroyed thousands of trees in their eagerness to find the glittering metal. Ramshackle shanty towns sprang up wherever rumour declared gold had been found. Men fought each other, with their fists and in hastily convened courts, over claims and pokes and cards.

Collins, like many others in that golden year, came to mine not gold but miners. He saw a fine commercial future for California that would last much longer than the gold rush, and he wanted to find a role for himself in that future. As soon as the first courts were organized, he tried his hand as a lawyer in the town of Sonora—though not with notable success. Records reveal that he took part in seven cases, lost six and won one by default. He was indicted in a claim-jumping case, not an unusual occurrence in those days of ill-marked boundaries and avaricious goldseekers, but released when the district attorney, as uncertain of the truth as was anyone else in the case, refused to prosecute.

Law was obviously not Collins' forte. He turned to business in Sonora, buying and selling lots in the rapidly developing gold town. With partners, he built a hotel, constructed a short local telegraph line and developed a gold mine. He invested time and possibly money in a bank and in companies that supplied water to the mining towns. He became a partner in a gold brokerage firm, and linked up with Gwin to launch the American Russian Commercial Company. This latter company, started with the opportunistic aim of shipping ice from the north to San Francisco, planned to set up several seaport farming and sawmill colonies in Russian America (the territory that would become Alaska). Neither plan was fulfilled.

Collins had a bombastic, frontier-American speaking style; coupled with his friendship with Gwin, who rose rapidly in local Democratic circles, his style made him a natural for politics. He helped organize the Democratic Party in Tuolumne County and was a delegate to the first Democratic state convention. Local newspapers quoted at length and with approval from his speeches outlining California's great future. When Gwin was named one of California's first two senators, Collins had a pipeline to Washington.

For Perry McDonough Collins did not intend to spend the rest of his life as a small-town developer and rabble-rouser. He saw farther than California, farther indeed than the boundaries of the United States. American expansionists such as Gwin did not think that American influence and power should end at the shores of the Pacific. Looking west to the confused affairs of nineteenth-century China and the expansionist policies of Russia, they envisioned magnificent commercial opportunities for Americans.

In 1843, in the aftermath of the Opium War forced on China by Britain and France, the Chinese were required for the first time to open some of their ports to foreign trade—trade that many American businessmen wanted to share. They were not alone. The Russian Tsar, Nicholas I, feared that increasing French and English trade with China would severely damage Russia's own overland trade with its southern neighbour in Asia. In 1847, he appointed Nikolai Muraviev governor-general of eastern Siberia, charging him with protecting and expanding Russian interests in the Far East. Energetic and visionary, the 38-year-old Muraviev was determined to expand Russian trade and contact across the Amur, the river which flowed east from central Siberia towards the Pacific through Russian and Chinese territory.

As Americans flocked to California in 1849, Muraviev was suggesting where Siberia's own gold lay: "I may state," he noted, "that whosoever controls the mouth of the Amur would in turn dominate all of Siberia. . . . The more it [Siberia] grows in population and wealth, the more it would become subject to the influence of the power controlling the mouth of the Amur."[1]

From his base at Irkutsk in Siberia, Muraviev designated bands of peasants as Cossacks in the service of the Tsar, and sent them to settle and fortify the Amur. In 1850, his emissaries founded the town of Nicolaevsk near where the Amur River meets the Tatar Strait. Men under his command annexed the island of Sakhalin and established posts along and to the north of the Amur. His policies were based on his desire to have Russia wrest control of the entire length of the Amur River from China, so that the river could be used to link Russia on the north Pacific with the rest of the country.

Gwin and William Seward, ex-governor of New York and seeker of the Republican presidential nomination, watched this expansion and convinced themselves it parallelled America's own expansion westward to California and Oregon. They persuaded Congress to finance a survey of the North Pacific Ocean and coastline, as a preliminary to American commercial expansion into those areas. When Commodore John Rodgers, the officer commanding the survey, returned to San Francisco in 1855, Perry Collins was among the eager residents who read of the voyage and considered how his own plans and thoughts fit into the overall picture.

Collins had already read the account written by Danish explorer Ferdinand von Wrangel of his travels in Siberia. The information and news brought by the expedition members backed up his own views on the potential of Siberia. Five years later, he wrote about the events of 1855:

> For several years previous to 1855, while residing in California, I had given much study to the commercial resources of the Pacific side of the United States, especially in connection with the opposite coast of Asia. I had already fixed in my own mind upon the river Amoor [Amur] as the destined channel by which American commercial enterprise was to penetrate the obscure depths of Northern Asia, and open a new world to trade and civilization, when news arrived in 1855 that the Russians had taken possession of the Amoor country, and formed a settlement at the mouth of the river. Greatly interested by this event, the important consequences of which my previous speculations enabled me fully to

comprehend, I proceeded to Washington in search of accurate information on the subject.[2]

He decided he must travel to the Amur to test its commercial possibilities for himself. "I wished to have the honor of being the first American explorer of a country and of a great river which I thought must before many years become of much interest as well as a source of advantageous commercial interest to the United States,"[3] he wrote.

Collins believed that Russian expansion eastward was part of the same great movement of peoples as the United States' expansion westward to the Pacific. Americans and Russians, he declaimed, were possessed of twin and parallel destinies to bring civilization to the lesser peoples of the Pacific—including the Chinese—and, not incidentally, to develop great trading enterprises in the process.

Collins could not afford to charter a ship to take him to the Amur, nor could he expect permission from Russian authorities for his journey if he appeared as a private citizen. On January 5, 1856, he left San Francisco for Washington, ready to use all the political influence he could muster to have himself named U.S. commercial agent to the Amur.

His friendship with Gwin presumably opened important doors: he met with President Franklin Pierce, who was impressed by the oratorical skills and expansionist vision Collins presented, with Secretary of State William Marcy and with Russian ambassador Edward de Stoekl. On March 24, he was named commercial agent for the Amur. On April 12, he sailed from New York for St. Petersburg, resolved to travel overland through Russia to the Amur's headwaters, then to descend the river to the Pacific.

Five weeks later, he landed at Kronshtadt, the port for St. Petersburg, aboard the first vessel that year to brave the ice floes of the Gulf of Finland. He sent the books and papers he would need for his Amur-mouth consulate off aboard a Russian man-of-war that was part of a fleet expected to reach the Amur, via the Atlantic and Indian oceans, in the following spring. Collins then made the short trip to St. Petersburg (now Leningrad) with his personal luggage and an American flag he planned to plant at the mouth of the Amur.

In St. Petersburg, he met Muraviev and explained the purpose of his journey. Muraviev was most enthusiastic and invited Collins to travel with Russian officials who would be returning to Irkutsk in November.

It was now close to the end of May and thus too late, he explained, to reach the Amur and proceed downriver this year, since winter would set in and the river would freeze up before the trip could be completed.

Delighted with Muraviev's co-operation, though disappointed at the delay, in August Collins took the train to Moscow, where he attended the coronation of Tsar Alexander II and made plans for his trip. It was his first encounter with the slow, cumbersome, tsarist bureaucracy, and he waited with mounting impatience for the permits that would allow him to travel through Siberia. The permits obtained, he continued to wait, this time for cold weather to set in and for Muraviev's party to get underway. Finally, on December 3, he set out along the post road for Irkutsk with a Russian member of Muraviev's staff and a fellow American, John Lewis Peyton. Though they left in the evening, in accordance with Russian custom, Collins did not sleep as they travelled east.

"My mind was busy with the future," he wrote, "and I saw that night, as if by inspiration, the deep snows open before me; the forests waved and toppled; long and beautiful vistas stretched out in the dim distance; great rivers, with broad and gentle currents, invited me on, and a great ocean seemed to bound the extended horizon. I dreamed, but my eyes were open; I saw, though the night was dark."[4]

Once free of the narrow, constricting confines of the Muscovian bureaucracy, Collins blossomed. By all accounts, he charmed everyone he met with cheerfulness, optimism and energy. In turn, he was impressed by Russia. The articles, letters and book he produced on his travels expressed his admiration for things Russian and his unbounded optimism in the commercial potential to be found along the overland route he travelled. Throughout, he drew parallels between Russia and the United States. "Collins' account of his days in Siberia and on the Amur," noted Charles Vevier, who prepared a new edition of Collins' Amur book in 1962, "is really a book about his own country. . . . Collins floated on a current of American frontier history, and scanned the banks of the stream for signs of Russia's manifest destiny in the East."[5]

In the mid-nineteenth century, travel in Russia was by a system of post roads set up and maintained under government order. These roads stretched from Moscow to the far east, dotted with post stations where government officials, messengers and travellers who carried the proper government permits could obtain fresh relays of horses and, if desired, stay overnight. Collins and his companions travelled some 3,300 miles to Irkutsk, on Lake Baikal. They stopped at 210 stations, at each acquiring a fresh troika to pull their sleigh onward. The party passed through an amazing total of 500 towns and villages.

In Irkutsk, Collins met up with Muraviev once more. He went south, to the Russian frontier town of Kyakhta, where he made further acquaintance with Russian hospitality, which seemed inevitably to consist of toast after toast in vodka, wine and champagne. He also discovered *podkeedovate*, the jolly Siberian method of indicating great respect for a visitor. Peyton was the first to suffer: he was seized by half a dozen stout merchants who tossed him repeatedly up toward the ceiling. "I stood half-aghast," he reported, "looking at the figure Peyton was cutting, a man six feet high and well proportioned, going up and down like a trap-ball, his coat-tail flying sky-high, and his face as red as a brick." Collins was congratulating himself that the merchants had chosen Peyton; then came Collins' turn. "Up I went and down I came, only to go up again, until my friends were satisfied that if I was not drunk before, my head would certainly swim now."[6]

He continued with Russian officials to the Chinese frontier town of Maimattschin, twinned with Kyakhta. There, he took part in and related in great detail the Mongol New Year celebration of the Feast of the Lanterns.

Invited to join in the feast, he and his Russian companions gulped down innumerable tiny cups of tea, hot wine and spirits, ate an infinite variety of tasty morsels conveyed on the chopsticks of the Mongol chief, and consumed several whole pigs. "The number, kind, and quality of the dishes, or rather bowls, which were constantly being served, was absolutely beyond computation. . . . After these innumerable courses, the table was cleared, when from the upper end of the room, came attendants bearing tables, on which were several whole pigs, roasted in the most approved style, and approaching quite to the front of the chief, exhibited to the guests this crowning glory of the 'feast', all smoking hot. The chief bowed approvingly to the cook, and the pigs disappeared by a side door. Then came clean saucers and more soy, and soon followed well filled bowls of the aforesaid pigs, all finely cut into thin strips, with pieces of the crisped skin broken into small squares. Finally, small bowls of plain boiled rice, perfectly dry, were served, and the feast closed in honor of the Russian guests with sparkling champagne."[7]

Musicians played, actors performed and danced, 3,000 Chinese men (no women were allowed to live in the frontier town) streamed into the streets, to eat, drink, listen to music and set off fireworks and fire-crackers against a backdrop of coloured-paper street decorations and lanterns.

Peyton now turned back to Moscow and Collins left Irkutsk on March 9, continuing east by horse and sleigh to Chita, on the Ingoda, a tributary of the Amur, where he planned to begin his river journey.

Collins wrote vividly of the entertainments and the people he met en route, never missing an opportunity to describe the beautiful women he encountered. But he rarely lost sight of his primary purpose, an investigation into the commercial possibilities of Siberia and the Amur. For, as chronicler Viljhalmur Stefansson notes, "Collins the nineteenth-century Marco Polo, and Collins the poet of coal, timber, opals, sables and steamships, railroads and rubies, were never allowed to interfere with Collins, the strict man of business."[8]

Waiting for the ice to break up on the Ingoda, he visited nearby mines, one of which was "the richest mine in Asia—perhaps in the world. The walls of this chamber were of solid silver ore. To say how much silver is contained in that mountain. . . would test too strongly human credibility. . . it was the first time I had ever been walled in with bright, sparkling, massive silver walls."[9] Not only were the mines rich, he reported admiringly, but they were worked by a trim, well-organized force of convict labourers.

Collins was equally impressed with the agricultural prospects of surrounding trans-Baikalia, describing it as good grazing country for cattle and sheep, with bountiful fish in the rivers, soil that produced good crops of grain, vegetables, flax and hemp, forests filled with game and mountains stuffed with valuable minerals. Though he did not say so, it was obvious he itched to test the trade possibilities of the resident population.

On May 18, the river ice finally broke and Collins set out downstream with Admiral Furnhelm, the Russian *ispravnik* or governor of Ayan, a Siberian province, and five other travellers bound for the mouth of the Amur. Eight oarsmen propelled their covered barge, amid a flotilla of the barges and rafts occupied by a hundred prospective settlers on their way to the river mouth.

The group reached the main stream of the Amur on June 4. "It must be confessed," wrote Collins, "as I stepped on shore I felt a high degree of exultation. I had not been the first to discover this river. . . but I was the first live Yankee who had seen it, and as the road had been a pretty long one, and some of it rather hard to travel, I felt, I must admit, a little proud of the American people, inasmuch as I had perseveringly set my face towards it two years since, and had never, for a moment, turned my back upon it, and had confidently looked, with hope and faith, as well as works, to the day when I should stand at the head of the Amur."[10]

Collins and company arrived at the town of Shilka, having travelled 440 miles downstream in less than six days. He waxed rhapsodic over the signs of commerce at Shilka, calculating that each resident along the Amur could buy five dollars worth of foreign goods a year—for a total of twenty million dollars in trade.

At Shilka, the party switched to a new barge 30 feet long and six feet wide, prepared on the orders of the area governor—luxurious transport indeed. "This was much better than I had anticipated before I left the United States, for I had made up my mind to the probable necessity of paddling my own canoe down the Amoor to the ocean,"[11] Collins related.

The group set out on their new boat on June 12, through forest and farmland suddenly decked out in the colours of a Siberian spring, "gay with flowers . . . and the air at times filled with fragrance."[12] At the town of Gorbitza, they left Russia. A treaty between Russia and China had placed this section of the river in Chinese territory. Despite misgivings about entrusting himself to the Tartars and other Chinese tribes, Collins pushed on.

Throughout the trip, he continued to note as much as possible of the inhabitants and commercial capabilities of the country. Wherever he sighted a good location for a settlement or possibilities of trade, he listed it in his diary, often comparing the countryside favourably with that of California. The more he saw, the more unhappy he was with the actions of a Russian ambassador who, 200 years earlier, had conceded this territory to the Chinese and thus denied Russia the unobstructed right to navigate the Amur and its tributaries.

However, Collins had little doubt that eventually the Russians would prevail. "Steamboats will take the place of the canoe and barge, and the swarthy tartar will view with wonder and admiration the progress of Russian power here, as his ancestors did upon the Caspian three hundred years ago. But it will be more rapid here now than there in the sixteenth century, because steam, artillery and revolvers give to civilized man an irresistible power. Commerce, navigation, the arts and sciences, will develop this stupendous country, and add, as it were, a sixth continent to the domain of civilization,"[13] he reported to the readers of his book.

Collins and company floated on downriver, under clear skies and summer warmth. At one point, the river current threw them unwilling into a deep narrow chute from which there seemed no escape. Collins consoled his comrades with a piece of Mississippi folk wisdom, that "if the current is sufficient to suck you in, it will be found sufficient to puke you out."[14] And indeed after uncertain hours travelling in what seemed totally the wrong direction, the current popped them back out into the main channel.

They drifted past the Songharee River, near the stockade that was connected to the Great Wall of China. Here, Collins surmised, trade goods from Peking were transferred to river junks for shipment onward.

On July 10, after 56 days and 2,600 miles on the river, Collins arrived at Nicolaevsk. He saw at once the potential of this young Russian settlement near the mouth of the Amur. The settlers and natives here had little of foreign manufacture, and what there was, was Chinese. Women, he noted, dressed in cloth made from fish skin or entrails; there must be a market here for American cloth.

"At Nicolaivsky must concentrate," he wrote, "the whole trade of the sea-coast of Siberia, with the incidental trade with Kamtchatka, America, Japan, China, and such other coasts, territories, and islands as may hereafter be annexed to its government. The northern overland route will be abandoned as soon as steam and post stations can be established on the river, and the whole trade of Siberia must fall into its lap. Somewhere on this coast, near or upon the Amoor, must be the St. Petersburg of the Pacific."[15]

Collins was a believer in the potential of the Amur when he embarked upon his journey, and a stalwart believer he remained. From the Amur he went north to the peninsula of Kamchatka, which he dismissed as no longer of interest now that Nicolaevsk existed. He sailed for Honolulu in October 1857, and arrived home in San Francisco on November 26. He then travelled on to Washington to unfold to government officials the wonders he had seen.

His round-the-world trip left him more firmly convinced than ever that the Russians and the Americans had great tasks to accomplish hand-in-hand.

## CHAPTER 3

# Connecting the Continents

Early in 1858, almost two years after he had left the American capital for his Russian odyssey, Perry McDonough Collins arrived back in Washington. He talked to his political friends, who talked to their friends in Congress. As a result, on the orders of Congress, Collins' account of the resources, tribes and prospects of Siberia was printed and widely distributed. Collins also asked that Congress reimburse him for his expenses, a request that seems to have been ignored.

By now, Collins was a complete convert to the idea of linking American commercial expansion in the Pacific to Russian expansion along the Amur. For centuries, Collins said, the land of the Amur had been locked up, unexploited, dormant half the year, like "one of its own quadrupeds, sucking its paws to sustain life."[1] Siberian governor-general Nikolai Muraviev had awakened it with his plans and his actions. Now Collins had seen it and was eager to help bring the land to life.

In St. Petersburg, he had talked with Muraviev about linking Asia, Europe and America by way of a great rail and steamship system that would traverse three continents and two oceans. Now he tried to convince senators and congressmen that such a plan was physically feasible and economically exciting.

The scheme seemed perfectly in line with developments in the United States and Russia. Since the early days of the gold rush, Californians had been lobbying and agitating for a transcontinental railway from the Mississippi River to San Francisco. As a network of rail lines spidered out across the United States, it was surely only a matter of time and money until California had its wish.

Russia, insisted Collins, was as enthusiastic as the United States about railways. Had they not already built one of the world's best lines, from St. Petersburg to Moscow? Were there not plans to extend that line deep into Siberia, as far east as Irkutsk? An international commercial railway and water network linking Europe, Asia and North America would benefit the United States more than any other partner in the scheme, Collins argued, since the United States lay at the centre of the route. Therefore, the project should be the goal of both private enterprise and the government.

Collins' fervour was contagious. Senators and government officials expressed interest. Caught up in his own enthusiasm, Collins proposed that he should once more visit Russia, this time travelling into Central Asia. He suggested that the United States government should sponsor this trip, down the Volga to Astrakhan and on through Tashkent, Georgia and Circassia, possibly as far as Tibet.

The government demurred and Collins did not make the long trip he had envisioned. He did return to St. Petersburg, however, in the fall of 1858. There, he met with the American representative at St. Petersburg, Francis W. Pickens, who was delighted to see him. Pickens' view of the unfolding world saw an even more grandiose role accruing to the United States through exploitation of the Amur. Pickens predicted that American commercial trade with China, by way of the Amur, would give the United States control of the "world and all the power that has ever belonged to the nation that holds its position."[2]

Collins was convinced that this great dual Russian-American project would produce a new order of Asian civilization, with European trade, commerce, manners and customs. "Russia with giant strides approaching from the North, while England and France are pushing from the South must soon meet in China," he wrote, promoting rapid American involvement in the area. With the acquisition of California, the United States no longer lay to the west of Russia. It lay to the east, across the Pacific, he declared, and those who saw this truth could lay claim to an almost incredible future of expansion and prosperity. "The problem of a North-western passage to India . . . which has occupied the great minds of Europe for some centuries, has been solved by the continuous and onward march of American civilization to the West. . . . The commerce of the world will find its path across this continent."[3]

Yet many roadblocks of terrain and finance lay in the way of a trans-Siberian railway, and Russian officialdom would not move with the speed Collins desired. Eventually, the Siberian Committee of the Russian government conveyed to Collins "in the most polite and flattering terms that the government had found his undertaking premature."[4]

If there could be no railroad at this time, could there not be another method of communication that would lead from America to Russia to Europe? In the United States and Europe, telegraph companies were busy creating a network of telegraph lines that linked city to city, country to country. "In traversing the whole extent of Northern Europe and Asia, the idea was strongly forced upon my mind," wrote Collins, "that . . . a telegraph communication could be constructed . . . uniting Europe with America."[5] Given his preoccupation with the Pacific Rim and with the relations between Russia and America, and the recent repeated failure of the Atlantic cable, the route he chose for this projected telegraph was inevitable.

Americans, he insisted, must build a telegraph line through the western United States into British Columbia, then through the northern British territories, across Russian America (Alaska), under the Bering Strait, south through Siberia, then along the Amur River to Irkutsk and eventually European Russia and all the countries of Europe.

Success of such a scheme, Collins foresaw, would deliver all intercontinental communication into the hands of the Americans. Commerce would thrive because of rapid communication; relations between the countries so connected would improve.

The project, Collins insisted, was not at all the quixotic endeavour it might seem. True, only the European, American and part of the British Columbian lines lay through occupied territory. True, reports of the weather and terrain in Russian America and Siberia were not encouraging: freezing cold, tundra, muskeg, storms, snow, ice. But what, he asked, was the alternative? Twice now, plans to lay an Atlantic cable had failed. It seemed unlikely that such a scheme would ever succeed. The difficulties of submerging a cable under 2,000 miles of rough Atlantic water were simply too great to be overcome by existing technology. Long telegraph lines had been successfully erected on land, and there was no known technological barrier to building even longer ones through colder regions. An overland line, even this one which was to be 5,000 miles long, was a much better proposition than a submarine cable under the Atlantic.

In 1859, Collins visited Montreal, seeking backers for a line from Montreal to British Columbia, one possible stage in this intercontinental connection. Sir George Simpson, North American governor of the Hudson's Bay Company, listened politely and said he would allow Collins to use his name to obtain a Canadian charter for his telegraph company. But his response was lukewarm, and the Canadian line was stillborn.

Collins returned to Washington, where he approached Hiram Sibley, head of the Western Union Telegraph Company and promoter of a transcontinental telegraph line across the United States. Sibley studied the scheme carefully and decided to back Collins. If the line was completed, it would make Western Union a world power and Sibley would bask in the glory that would come from such a mammoth and useful project.

In February 1861, under intense lobbying from Collins and Sibley, the U.S. House of Representatives Committee on Commerce voted in favour of a bill allocating $50,000 for a new navy survey of the North Pacific coasts, in preparation for the telegraph. Outdoing even Collins in purple prose, Milton Latham, the California senator presenting the bill, declared, "we hold the ball of the earth in our hand, and wind upon it a network of living and thinking wire till the whole is held together and bound with the same wishes, projects and interests."[6]

Although the bill was never voted on by Congress, the future looked bright. In October of 1861, Sibley, by now completely won over to the idea of the intercontinental telegraph, wrote to Collins:

Our men [Sibley's Western Union line builders] are pressing me hard to let them go on to Behring's Strait next summer, and as you say to me 'If I had the money' I would go on and complete the line and talk about it afterwards.

If the Russian government will meet us at Behring's Strait and give us the right of way, etc., through their territory on the Pacific, we will complete the line in two years and probably in one. The work is not more difficult than we have already accomplished over the Rocky Mountains and plains to California; and, in my opinion, the whole thing is entirely practicable, and that, too, in much less time and with much less expense than is generally supposed by those most hopeful. No work costing so little money was ever accomplished by man that will be so important in its results. The benefit resulting to the world will pay the entire cost of the line every year after completion while the world continues to be inhabited by civilized man; and it is to me a matter of surprise that any intelligent person, at all familiar with the building and working telegraph lines in the West should doubt the practicability of the successful working, after built, of a line to Behring's Strait.[7]

Eight days after he wrote to Collins, just four months and 11 days after construction began, Hiram Sibley and his cohorts completed a transcontinental telegraph line linking California to the eastern states. His fellow Western Union directors had refused to support the transcontinental line that Sibley wanted to build, so Sibley had undertaken it on his own, with government support. Once the line was complete, it was amalgamated with Western Union in 1864; the amalgamation saw Western Union lines stretch across the continent.

Early in 1862, the Senate Committee on Military Affairs recommended that $100,000 be spent in surveys and preparations for the overland line to Russia. But no appropriation was voted, for the events of the times weighed against Collins and his project. In 1861, the Union and the Confederacy had gone to war and Americans turned their energies to fighting one another. Sibley stood firm: "Let this not be called an improper time to present this subject to Congress, because we are engaged in a war for our national existence," he wrote to Collins.

"Let us rather say that the United States is not only able to suppress rebellion at home, but able also to extend her great commercial and scientific power over the earth."[8] He pleaded in vain. The request for money was turned down; the Civil War was too immediate, Siberia too far away. For much of the Civil War, the U.S. government had no time to spare for Collins' scheme.

Western Union was to some degree preoccupied with the war, helping to build and run lines for military communications, but Sibley took advantage of the dislocation and economic hardship brought by the war to continue his drive to bring small American telegraph companies under the Western Union umbrella. As he manoeuvred and bought, Western Union's profits soared. Soon investment in the company was considered a sure route to riches: between 1857 and 1864, cash and dividends from the stock made many a fortune.

Though the United States government was not thinking about the Russian-American telegraph line, Collins was still intent on the project. Despite the fact that William Gwin had lost his senate seat some years before, Collins still had friends in government. In 1863, he secured appointment as American vice-consul in St. Petersburg with the primary purpose of obtaining imperial permission and co-operation for the line. After two and a half months of negotiations in Russia, representing his own company rather than the American government, he signed an agreement with the Russian government on May 23, promising that his company would establish telegraphic communication between North America and the mouth of the Amur within five years, provided that the company had exclusive telegraphic privileges on the route for 33 years. Russia, in turn, promised to extend its own telegraphic system to meet the American line at the Amur.

The line was to pass through California, Oregon, Washington, the British colony of British Columbia, and British North America north of British Columbia. Collins needed and now sought co-operation from the British government. In the autumn of 1863, he was ushered into the presence of British Prime Minister Lord Palmerston, to whom he explained his plans. Palmerston passed him on to the colonial secretary.

British government officials were at first suspicious of this energetic American with the bombastic turn of phrase and world-circling plans. Who was this man, they enquired in diplomatic circles, and what credentials did he have? By coincidence, while Collins was in London, a

British government representative met with General Guerhard, director of Russian telegraph communication, who was in London on an unrelated matter. Enquiries about Collins and his overland line were met with Russian enthusiasm. Guerhard assured the British that the overland line could be built with little expense and without a time-wasting preliminary survey.

Both Guerhard and Paul Reuter, head of Reuter's news agency and a man with a strong vested interest in telegraphic communication, opined that the overland line was a better bet than the trans-Atlantic cable. Collins promised the British that because it would be the location for a crucial part of the line, British Columbia would become the focus of the world's telegraphic system.

Now Colonial Secretary Newcastle waxed enthusiastic, and the British government seemed inclined to give all assistance short of money. In January 1864, Collins' company was granted permission to use unappropriated Crown land in British Columbia and to cut timber thereon. His work parties could land supplies along the coast in remote areas, roads could be built where they were needed to bring in telegraph supplies and men (at the company's expense, not the government's), supplies for the line could be brought in free of duty and houses to be used as supply and service depots could be built along the route of the line.

The government refused, however, Collins' request for 33 years' exclusive telegraphic rights through the territory. They also insisted that all privileges would be revoked if the line were not completed within five years. British and colonial messages were to receive equal treatment with those of Russia and the United States.

Collins now returned to Washington, to continue his campaign. His publisher reissued Collins' book on his Russian journey down the Amur, adding to the already unwieldy title the words, "with Map and Plan of an Overland Telegraph around the World via Behring's Strait and Asiatic Russia to Europe."

Having accomplished most of the preliminary work, Collins was now prepared to take a back seat. On March 16, after negotiations between Collins and Sibley, Sibley recommended to the Western Union board of directors that WUT buy all of Collins' rights and set up a subsidiary company to build the intercontinental line. Collins received a cash payment of $100,000 as recompense for eight years of work promoting the line, mostly at his own expense, and one-tenth of the stock in the new company, the Western Union Extension Company.

Western Union directors were enthusiastic about Collins' figures: two wires transmitting 1,000 messages every 24 hours at $25 each would bring in more than nine million dollars a year. The company issued 100,000 $100 shares, offering up to 50% of the shares to Western Union stockholders who need pay only a five per cent assessment (five dollars per share) at the time of purchase, with the rest to be called on as needed. Western Union officials predicted that no more than 20% of the total assessment would be needed to complete the line.

News of the deal sent Western Union stock spiralling upwards, and a stock dividend of 100% was declared two months afterwards. Suggests one commentator, "pianos, furniture of various kinds, mortgages and homesteads were converted into cash to purchase Western Union stock."[9] The extension company stocks were snapped up. Within two months the shares that had cost their owners only five dollars to date were selling for $60.

In the minds of politician and promoter alike, the telegraph line began to look more and more like reality. On July 1, 1864, President Abraham Lincoln signed the bill that gave a permanent right-of-way through the United States to the line, together with permission to take possession of the timber, stone and land required for telegraph stations. The navy would provide a steam or sailing ship to render any assistance required in such matters as surveying the proposed route or laying cable. The United States government was to have priority for transmission of messages; telegraph rates would be decided on by representatives of the three countries involved: Britain, Russia and the United States.

Less than seven months later, the British Columbia colonial assembly passed a bill approving the 1863 deal reached between Collins and the British Colonial Office. Their agreement was almost a formality. By that time, the Russian-American Telegraph expedition was well underway.

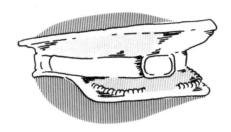

## CHAPTER 4

# On Your Mark: The Dash Begins

"I would give $50,000," said Hiram Sibley to Cyrus Field in 1864, "to know whether you are going to be successful."[1] Foreknowledge of whether the Atlantic cable could ever be successfully completed would have been worth that much and more to Sibley and his co-directors at Western Union. A trans-Atlantic cable completed before their own overland intercontinental telegraph line would, at worst, make the overland line redundant, at best cut severely into its profit.

But it was six years since the last trans-Atlantic attempt had failed abysmally, and Sibley and Western Union considered the possibility of a successful cable remote. Nonetheless, they wanted to get their own overland line completed as soon as possible, and wasted no time getting their preparations underway.

One of their first acts was the hiring of the overall operating head of the project. In August 1864, they appointed Charles S. Bulkley as engineer-in-chief for the overland line.

Bulkley came to Western Union on leave from the United States army, where he was a lieutenant-colonel and superintendent of military telegraphs in the southwest. The outbreak of the Civil War had increased vastly both the traffic over telegraph lines and the usefulness of those lines. Calls for troops, orders for troop movement, offers of money and credit, pages of war news in the newspapers of the day: all travelled by telegraph. The Union government and army commanders quickly realized the worth of this type of communication, and a military telegraph system was organized.

Little is known of Bulkley's early life or background, and no clear picture emerges of his character though obviously he had impressed his army superiors and the directors of Western Union with his conduct of military telegraph affairs. "His duties were discharged in the most satisfactory manner, and by his ingenuity, untiring perseverance, and complete knowledge of telegraphy, the greatest perfection was attained in this branch of our war effort,"[2] wrote Western Union Telegraph Extension Company (WUTEC) secretary O.H. Palmer.

One of Bulkley's first tasks was to set up the rules for the overland telegraph expedition. The telegraph builders would be travelling through wild country thousands of miles from American civilizing influences, and meeting with the natives of those regions. Bulkley decided that the expedition should be run with military precision: army discipline would keep the men in line and create a necessary cohesiveness within the company, and military uniforms would impress upon the natives that these were not men to be trifled with.

He set up a quasi-military structure for the entire expedition. Each man had a military rank: Bulkley, as head of the expedition, would be a colonel; other company members would carry ranks from major down through second lieutenant. At all times while on company service, each expedition member would wear a uniform, cut from dark blue wool and closely resembling the uniform of the Union infantry with their single-breasted coats and gold-striped trousers. Each rank would have its own insignia. The shoulder straps on Bulkley's uniform were of dark blue velvet and displayed a silver globe with silver flashes of lightning darting to each end, symbolizing the uniting of the globe that would become reality with the Russian-American telegraph. A second lieutenant, for example, wore a shoulder strap marked with a silver snowshoe, and a cap fronted with a silver canoe.

Bulkley drew up a seven-page outline to govern the organization of the company. An engineer corps would be responsible for exploring the country and determining the best route. A chief who would report directly to Bulkley would command the corps. "Its duties necessarily being unexpectedly varied and arbitrary, special rules will be prescribed for its use."[3]

Once the route was determined, working divisions would move in to erect the telegraph line. Each working division would be commanded by a superintendent and subdivided into construction parties led by foremen. The construction parties were to be further divided into four squads, with a foreman in charge of each squad.

Paperwork was not forgotten. Bulkley listed in detail the returns, employment roll, vouchers, property lists and abstracts he expected each superintendent to make out each month. "All returns are to be made out in triplicate,"[4] he declared, perhaps not anticipating the problems that such bureaucratic demands might create in freezing cold and ill-equipped wilderness.

Bulkley considered trouble on the expedition might come from mutinous men and native peoples. To avoid mutiny or disorderly conduct, he forbade the use of alcohol, declared that all work must be suspended on Sundays (a rule stated in capital letters), and prescribed the utmost care with firearms, which were to be used for defence only. Anyone beginning, joining or inciting a mutiny would be discharged forthwith, as would anyone stealing from the company.

Any native peoples encountered were to be treated with utmost kindness and consideration, and employed wherever possible on line construction. "Their interest in the work will be best secured by understanding that the success, good condition and permanency of the line will result in continual profit to them. The most scrupulous system and exactness must be observed in paying them for service of any kind."[5]

No spirits or intoxicants were to be given to the natives, and company employees could under no circumstances trade with them—a prohibition laid down to avoid the howls of protest that would follow trade not authorized by the chartered companies in the regions, the Hudson's Bay Company and the Russian-American Company.

Bulkley was aware that these precautions might not be enough.

Guards must be on duty day and night, working parties must be properly picketed to prevent surprise attacks, Indians were not to be allowed to loiter about the camps and employees could not leave the camps without their foreman's permission.

The basic rules of organization laid down, Bulkley set about hiring the men who would explore the routes and prepare for the construction of the line. In normal times, given the relative newness of the telegraph, it might have been difficult to fill positions that demanded men experienced in locating and building telegraph lines. But by the summer of 1864, some 15,000 miles of military telegraphs had been built, and hundreds of young men had gained valuable experience building and running these lines. As the pace of line construction slowed, Bulkley quickly snapped up those men he felt would be good additions to the overland expedition.

He purposely chose men in their twenties, saying that they had greater endurance and perseverance, and that they deserved the honours and benefits that would shower down on the men who forged the line. By the autumn of 1864, he had hired most of the men who would explore the route, and those who would command the working parties. He had also made a start, with the help of the Smithsonian Institute, at putting together a Scientific Corps to collect specimens and write reports on the people, geography, flora and fauna of the territories through which the expedition would pass.

Since the line would be built around the North Pacific rim, Bulkley chose San Francisco as his headquarters. In the summer and fall of 1864, working out of temporary headquarters in New York, he arranged for shipments of insulators, brackets, instruments, tools, carts, wagons and other telegraph supplies to be sent round Cape Horn to San Francisco. He ordered cable from the cable works in England to span the Bering Strait and Anadyr Bay, the two bodies of water that lay on the route.

Bulkley was aware that his exploring parties in British Columbia, the Yukon, Russian America and Siberia would be widely separated, both from each other and from Bulkley himself. It would be necessary to convey men, material and communications from San Francisco around the North Pacific rim and between each of the exploring parties. Such conveying could be done only by ship. Bulkley bought for the expedition two ships that would carry the bulk of the supplies, and hired seamen to man them. He bought also a brig, two large, fast schooners, two ocean steamers and one smaller river steamer that could travel on the deck of one of the largest ships. The U.S. navy contributed the services of a fully armed naval vessel to protect the fleet and represent the American government as needed.

*The Telegrapher*, a newspaper started and run by the members of the National Telegraphers' Union, watched these proceedings with approval. The paper's editorialists noted in October 1864 "the number of maps, charts, books and other printed matter it has been necessary to pore over, compare, and to make notes and extracts from. . . . A large map on the polyconic scale has been executed. . . to be used by the expedition, which contains portions of the two hemispheres never before placed on paper in this shape. It is considered by competent judges a chef d'oeuvre of draughting."[6]

Bulkley had, noted *The Telegrapher*, hired an interpreter and obtained a book on Chinook jargon. A surgeon had been attached to the expedition. Further, "the very best optical and astronomical instruments will be needed. These have been carefully obtained, and many of them prove to be of rare merit, many satisfactory tests having been done in this city by night and day. If these instruments prove so satisfactory in this climate, subject to the fog and smoky exhalations of this great city, they will most certainly be found to possess the most admirable properties, claimed for them by their makers, on being tested in those regions where the smoke of civilization disturbs not the rarified atmosphere so freely inhaled only by the white bear, the walrus and the adventurous whaleman."

Overall, said *The Telegrapher*, prospects were excellent.

By the above outline, the intelligent reader can easily comprehend the vastness of the enterprise undertaken, and will easily discern that a master mind is at the head of the expedition, which grasps at once the various difficulties to be encountered, and provides thoroughly the means of surmounting them. That success to the fullest extent will crown the toils, the dangers, the hopes, the fears and the grand anticipation of the projectors of this stupendous work, there can be no doubt; and through the blessing of Divine Providence, brought down upon the exertions of this little band in those far-off Arctic regions, by their own prayers, united with the holy aspirations of the dear ones at home, we all, in common with the enlightened community in which we dwell, shall listen eagerly for the first click of the instrument, announcing that space is annihilated, and that the two greatest nations of the globe are indissolubly united in fact, as they have been for years in fraternal feeling.[7]

With much of the preliminary work completed, Bulkley sailed in December for San Francisco. He was sped on his way by a letter from Western Union Extension Company secretary Palmer, who wrote, "You undoubtedly fully appreciate the magnitude and great importance . . . of the undertaking committed to your charge. While the duties may prove trying and severe, and tax to the utmost your strength and energies, there is this compensation: You are entering upon a work which if successful will give you a name and reputation, not only in the history of this country, but in that of all the civilized nations of this earth. . . . Much depends on you. You will not fail for want of material aid and moral support on the part of this company."[8]

Bulkley's reply was equally complimentary: "More courage was exhibited in the determination of those who said 'this shall be done—we will do it,' than is requisite in your engineer to accomplish the task."[9]

By this time, the overland telegraph project had taken on truly grandiose proportions. Buoyed by the expansionist rhetoric of Secretary of State William Seward and the commercial ambitions of Collins and Sibley, the intercontinental telegraph line appeared no longer simply as the Western Union extension linking America and Europe but also as the means by which Western Union and the United States would dominate the communication and therefore the commerce of the entire world. In a letter to the chairman of the U.S. Senate Committee on Commerce, Seward saw the overland line leading inevitably to communication between the "merchant, the manufacturer, the miller, the farmer, the miner, or the fisherman" of every small American community and producers and consumers on the Amur, in Japan, in China, in Western Europe, with Alexandria, Cairo and Suez. Only "transient wars" delayed connecting systems to Havana, Panama, Quito, Lima and Buenos Aires, among others. Russian telegraph lines connecting to the overland line must soon stretch out to the islands of Japan, deep into China to Peking and beyond, to Afghanistan and thence to India, to Persia and Baghdad. Western Union sent representatives to China to propose a Chinese Extension telegraph, and to Central and South America to explain the proposed extension south.

"It seems impossible to over-estimate the direct effect of this new application of the national energy in producing a rapid yet permanent development of the agricultural, forest, mineral and marine resources of the United States," wrote Seward. "Nor is it any more practicable to assign limits to the increase of national influence which must necessarily result from the new facilities we should acquire in that manner for extending throughout the world American ideals and principles of public and private economy, politics, morals, philosophy and religion."[10]

Today Russia, tomorrow the world, would have been a succinct statement of Seward's dreams in 1864.

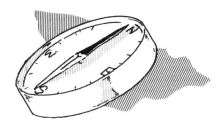

## CHAPTER 5

# Get Set:
# Headquarters, San Francisco

Between November 1864 and April 1865, the overland telegraph expedition shifted its headquarters from New York to San Francisco. Bulkley set up his new office in January 1865 in the Cosmopolitan Hotel at the corner of Bush and Sansome streets in San Francisco. His arrival and the scope of the new project resulted in columns of newsprint, and inflamed the imagination of every young adventurer in the town, quiet now after the excitement of the gold rush. Too young for the civil war—or too poor to pay for their transport east—hundreds of them besieged Bulkley's office, begging to be taken on the expedition.

Twenty-year-old George Adams was one of those besiegers. He read the long articles that detailed the project in the San Francisco newspapers and burned to trade his pointless life of drinking, cards and billiards for the glory and purpose of this grand expedition to unite the world through wire. He scurried around important friends and relatives to get letters of introduction to Bulkley, then went to visit the great man. Bulkley was friendly but discouraging: every young man in San Francisco had been to see him and he had already made up the bulk of his parties in New York. He did, however, give Adams a note of introduction to Robert Kennicott, head of the Scientific Corps and of the expedition to Russian America, and told him to try his luck there.

Kennicott was equally discouraging. He already had his quota of 12, he told Adams, and needed no more. Adams went back day after day, hoping for a chance. Kennicott tried to dissuade him, telling him that great hardship would be ahead for those who went on the trip, and enormous fortitude would be required. The man who goes on this trip, he said, will need the guts of a man I know who pushed a burning cigar into the flesh of his arm just to show his great willpower. Nothing daunted, Adams lit a cigarette and applied it to his arm.

Horrified, Kennicott called him nine kinds of a fool and said he could have been badly infected, but agreed to take Adams on if a vacancy came up. Adams immediately rushed out to find an impressionable member of the party, and bribed him to stay behind with promises of a job in San Francisco and Adams' own new suit of clothes. Then Adams persuaded his friend, Fred Smith, to do the same, bribing a current member of the expedition and taking his place.

A little older, a little more cynical, William Ennis had more to offer Kennicott. Ennis had served for five years as an American naval officer, then spent five months travelling overland from the east to the Pacific coast, arriving with neither friends nor money. He sent for money from home, then spent it enjoying "the world and all its pleasures" in San Francisco. He hired on with Kennicott, for the adventure, the Arctic and the chance to see "the Esquimaux." He scoffed at others on the expedition as they walked around the town "dressed in full uniform of the company and doubtless captivating many of those young ladies who had an eye for Brilliant objects. . . . There was more brass than brains encompassing their persons."[1]

Bulkley also made final plans for the deployment of his fleet. In early 1865, the schooner *Milton Badger* and the barque *Clara Bell* were en route from New York around the Horn to San Francisco, carrying telegraph supplies. The steamer *George S. Wright* was destined for coastal service in Russian America and Siberia. The barques *Palmetto* and *Golden Gate* would ferry men and material around the shores of the North Pacific. The *U.S.S.Shubrick*, the American naval revenue cutter on loan to the expedition, would assist along the North American coast, while the Russian corvette *Variag* was to be made available on the Russian coast, primarily to help in laying the submarine cables across Bering Strait and Anadyr Bay.

Early in April, those members of the expedition who had not yet made their way to San Francisco left New York aboard the steamer *Ariel*. With their departure, *The Telegrapher* acquired a regular correspondent, who identified himself only as Electron. Electron and his colleagues had a pleasant trip to Aspinwall, on the Panama coast, despite "the total disregard of the comfort and safety of passengers on this line."[2]

Electron thoroughly approved of the railroad that carried the group across the isthmus of Panama in less than three hours—a decided contrast to the insect-infested boat trip and steaming mud and stench of the mule trip that was the normal experience for gold-rushers 15 years earlier. Although marvellously crooked, the railroad was well built and ballasted, with fine bridges. A telegraph line parallelled the railroad, and Electron took note of its peculiar construction:

> The telegraph posts... [are] composed of cement, moulded around a slender scantling of wood three or four inches in diameter. The latter is set in the ground, and a wooden mould, consisting of staves and hoops, somewhat like an upright churn, is placed around it, filled with cement, and allowed to dry. The mould is then taken apart and removed, leaving the post ready for the insulator and wire. These posts are about eighteen feet in height, one foot in diameter at the base and six inches at the top.[3]

Reaching San Francisco by steamer, this group joined the rest of the party who had left New York a month earlier, and met with Bulkley in his hotel.

Although the original promoter of the line, Perry McDonough Collins, had turned ownership and leadership of the project over to Sibley and Western Union, he still had a role to play, especially in continuing negotiations with his friends and colleagues in Russia. Over the winter of 1864–65, Sibley and Collins travelled to St. Petersburg to work out the final details of co-operation with the Russian government. American ambassador Cassius Clay got them an audience with the Tsar and with Prince Gorchacov. Some sources suggest that for his efforts, Clay was rewarded with $30,000 worth of paid-up stock in the WUT extension company. Clay also introduced them to Serge Abasa, a young Russian nobleman and gentleman of the Tsar's bedchamber who had lived in the United States and who was immediately enthusiastic about the project. Abasa introduced them to other important Russians and threw his support behind the line. He was offered and accepted the position of head of the Siberian expedition, and made his way to San Francisco to join up with Bulkley and his crews.

Western Union had told prospective investors that the line would be complete by 1867 at the latest. To meet such a rigid timetable, Bulkley wanted his crews in place by the beginning of summer, 1865. Yet delay after delay thwarted his plans. For reasons never fully explained, the company ships could not be made ready in time. Telegraph supplies and provisions were likewise late. Bulkley fumed, but could not hurry the pace. The men who had been hired to carry the line forward waited in their San Francisco lodging places, amusing themselves as best they could. Only the crew that was to build the line through the settled parts of British Columbia made an early start that summer of 1865.

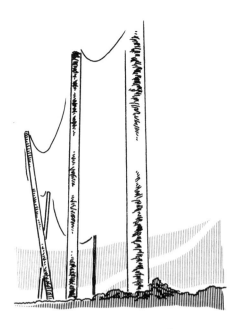

CHAPTER 6

# Go! British Columbia, 1865

Though the land had been roughly cleared for a few hundred yards back from the river front, tree stumps still littered the ground in ugly profusion. Along Columbia Street, parallelling the Fraser River and the wharves, stood a line of white clapboard two- and three-storey hotels, stores and government offices. Behind them were scattered the houses of the town's 200 permanent residents.

New Westminster, 1864, capital of the Crown Colony of British Columbia. The colony itself had existed for only six brief years. The first explorers for the fur-trading companies had entered this region in 1793; for the next 65 years, the only white men here had been traders seeking new routes and new riches. In 1858, gold was discovered in the sandbars of the Fraser River, and just as in California in 1849, goldseekers had transformed a placid and barely settled domain, as thousands of prospectors took ship from San Francisco to taste the new prospects of the British territory north of the 49th parallel.

The influx of mostly American prospectors and merchants prodded the British government into creating the colony of British Columbia on the mainland, separate from that established in 1843 on Vancouver Island. New Westminster, founded in 1859, became the new colonial capital. But by 1864, though millions of dollars worth of gold still filtered out of the colony each year, the excitement of the gold rush had shifted north to the Cariboo, and New Westminster had become little more than a stopping point for steamers bound upriver.

When new colonial governor Frederick Seymour arrived at his capital in 1864, he found the town both depressed and depressing. "I had not seen, even in the West Indies, so melancholy a picture of disappointed hopes as New Westminster presented on my arrival," he wrote to a friend at home in England. "Thousands of trees had been felled to make way for the great city expected to rise on the magnificent site selected for it. But the blight had early come. . . . The largest hotel was to let, decay appeared on all sides. . . . Westminster appeared, to use the miners' expression, played out."[1]

Western Union Captain Edward Conway, the officer in charge of telegraph line construction in British Columbia, arrived at this unprepossessing town in November 1864. Conway was a Canadian telegrapher who had left his post with the Grand Trunk Railway in Montreal in 1861, to seek his fortune in the United States. On the strength of excellent references praising his proficiency, efficiency, perseverance and temperate habits, he was hired to build and maintain telegraph lines in the New Orleans division of the United States military telegraph, part of Charles Bulkley's district. Bulkley was sufficiently impressed with his work to hire him for the overland telegraph project.

Conway was the first member of the telegraph expedition to leave New York, in the fall of 1864. He arrived in San Francisco in October, and waited impatiently for orders from Bulkley. On November 7, a telegram arrived, instructing Conway to make his way to New Westminster, where he would negotiate with the colonial government for concessions that would make it easier and cheaper to build the telegraph line. Conway would have left on the instant, but the banks were closed November 8 because of an election, and he was forced to wait until the next day. On November 9, he obtained funds for his journey and embarked aboard a steamer that would carry him north.

When he arrived in Victoria, on Vancouver Island, he gave an interview to a reporter from the Victoria newspaper, *The British Colonist*, promising that soon through the overland line "an electric belt will encircle the globe."[2] He then proceeded on to New Westminster, arriving on November 23.

In his Victoria interview, Conway outlined the telegraph route, one that had been determined by the directors of the telegraph company and engineer-in-chief Charles Bulkley. The line would strike north from Salt Lake City through present-day Idaho and Washington, cross the American-British border along the Okanagan River, then continue to the Thompson River and the goldfields of the Cariboo to the north, avoiding the Pacific coast completely.

Late in 1864, however, circumstances changed. In December, Hiram Sibley and the directors of Western Union, still busily expanding their telegraph business, took over the California State Telegraph Company. California State had already completed a telegraph line north from San Francisco to Portland, and planned to extend it through Seattle to New Westminster. Early in 1864, the president of California State had visited British Columbia, seeking and obtaining permission to build this line. When Western Union purchased California State, it took possession of the coastal telegraph. Now, instead of having to build 800 miles of new line inland from Salt Lake City to the American border, the Western Union Extension Company could use the almost-completed line along the coast.

Governor Seymour was delighted about this ray of light in a gloomy colonial picture. He told the opening session of the British Columbia legislative council in January 1865, that "the subject of telegraphic communication is the only one to which I can refer with altogether unmixed satisfaction."[3]

Conway and Seymour held lengthy talks about the telegraph, the results of which were conveyed back to Bulkley in secret code. Happy though he was with the idea of the telegraph, Seymour was concerned with the dwindling government revenues in the colony he administered. He refused Conway's request that the company be permitted to bring in all its construction material and supplies duty free. Seymour and the council compromised: Conway could bring construction and

*New Westminster, BC. An illustration in* Harper's Weekly, *1865. (Courtesy of the Provincial Archives of BC. HP 41631.)*

telegraph material in duty free, provided the company employed as much local labour and as many native people as possible in the construction of the line. Seymour refused a blanket exemption for supplies, for he feared employees of the company would abuse the privilege and bring in goods for resale. Instead, he agreed after some months of negotiations that he would grant exemptions on each individual shipment.

Early in 1865, the legislative council passed and the governor signed the International Telegraph Ordinance. Since the original negotiations for the telegraph had been between the British government and Perry McDonough Collins, the bill gave to Collins and his assigns the right to survey, build and maintain that part of the line that would pass through British Columbia, and the exclusive right to telegraphic communication in that area. Construction was to begin by January 1, 1867, and to be completed no later than January 1, 1870. Upon completion of the line, New Westminster was to be kept "in complete and continuous communication with the whole telegraphic systems of the United States and Russia,"[4] not a minor accomplishment for a six-year-old town in the colonial wilds. The legislature also transferred the rights it had given a year earlier to the California State Telegraph Company to Collins or his successors. After some initial confusion over the fact that Collins had sold his rights to Western Union and hence to the Western Union Extension Company, a new ordinance and an amendment to the old legislation were signed by Governor Frederick Seymour on February 25, 1865, and Conway had the legal permissions he needed to begin work.

That same day, John Robson, editor of the New Westminster newspaper *The British Columbian* and a future premier of British Columbia, editorialized happily over what the telegraph line would mean to the young community on the banks of the Fraser. The coming connection with the rest of the civilized world would cement New Westminster's deserved place as the centre of activity on the west coast of British North America, displacing once and for all its hated rival on Vancouver Island, Victoria.

> Those of us who came here six years ago to plant a city where then stood an unbroken forest of gigantic firs, proudly waving their towering tops as if in defiance of the puny efforts of man to conquer them, will hardly be able to recognize to the full extent the new era bursting upon us. A Government of our own, direct steam communication, direct trade with the great marts and electric connection with the civilized world, each following the other in such quick succession, are considerations calculated to bewilder the mind. And yet it is all real tangible fact. In less than a year New Westminster, traduced and deceived by a jealous and grasping neighbor [Victoria], will be the centre of all these great systems—these civilizers, which must speedily make her worthy to be the capital of an important colony, and the great centre of commerce on the British Pacific.

"We understand," he concluded snidely, "that it is not in contemplation to establish a [telegraph] branch in Victoria."[5]

Victoria made its own small riposte. The same edition of the *Colonist* that carried news of the route change also noted that the telegraph line from San Francisco to the east was out of order again; the break, a frequent occurrence, was once more blamed without proof on hostilities of the Indians.

Conway and his WUT agent, J.W. Pitfield, set up shop in the Columbia Hotel, choosing this almost vacant hostelry on Lytton

Square, just above the river wharves, in preference to more opulent lodgings that boasted a new billiard saloon "in which will always be found the best drinks and cigars."[6]

Underlining his support of and fascination with the telegraph line, Governor Seymour lent Conway his personal steam yacht, the *Leviathan*. Conway used the steamer to explore eastward on the Fraser and to visit parties working on the line between Seattle and New Westminster. Writing to Bulkley on March 4, 1865, he suggested that this line would be working within two weeks—an estimate he quickly revised to four weeks when essential material was slow in arriving and extremely cold weather put a brake on progress.

On March 6, the first telegraph message was sent and received in British Columbia, along a line Conway had built between the telegraph company office and the governor's residence a mile away. The connection, built at Seymour's request, ensured the governor's continuing good will and assistance. Conway gave Seymour lessons in the use of the telegraph and recorded that the governor was more than anxious to send telegraph messages to the governor of Newfoundland and of the Canadian provinces, presumably to demonstrate the entry of British Columbia into the world of modern communication.

On March 13, with the end of the telegraph line just 25 miles from New Westminster, the American navy cutter *Shubrick* sailed into New Westminster from San Francisco. Colonel Bulkley was on board, together with James Gamble, Bulkley's second-in-command for the line through British North America and the superintendent of the California State Telegraph Company, and other expedition members. More important, perhaps, the *Shubrick* brought the underwater cable for the Fraser crossing. Noting the ship's arrival, the Victoria *Colonist* suggested rather wistfully that Gamble might look at some means of connecting Victoria, now in a telegraphic backwater, with the transcontinental line.

Bulkley and Conway discussed the supplies and provisions that would be needed in British Columbia over the next year. Bulkley planned to buy most of the provisions needed for the expedition in San Francisco and ship them north by steamer. Telegraph insulators, wire and other material, shipped around the Horn from New York the previous winter, would also come north by steamer.

The arrangements made, the *Shubrick* and its passengers sailed for the

North Pacific, so Bulkley could select appropriate bases for the expedition in Russian America and Siberia. Conway turned his attention to laying the underwater cable. The *Leviathan* and her crew made a first attempt to lay the cable from the south shore to New Westminster, but were stymied by strong winds. On March 21, they tried again. The governor steered his ship as the American flag waved from the main peak and the British flag from the stern. The cable unreeled sedately across the river and was successfully connected to the line on the north bank. The crew tested the cable by means of a battery that a work party had taken to the south shore, and the first message was tapped out, announcing to *The British Columbian* that the cable had been laid in seven minutes and was working well.

On April 18, California State crews reached the south bank of the Fraser and hooked up the trans-Fraser cable to the rest of the telegraphic world. The first news to arrive in British Columbia by telegraph was that of the assassination of President Abraham Lincoln four days earlier. *The British Columbian* began a new column in its pages, filling it with news received by telegraph. Seymour immediately sent off a message to the Colonial Office; it arrived via telegraph and ship in the remarkable time of 17 days, a lightning-fast contrast to the three months it usually took for messages to pass between British Columbia and London. New Westminster rejoiced, but neither Bulkley nor Conway was confident that communication would continue. "The California line cannot be depended on. It is down the greater part of the time,"[7] Conway wrote to Bulkley, who decided that at some future time the company would have to build a new connection, north from Salt Lake City, well east of the Pacific coast.

The day after the submarine cable was laid, Conway headed east by canoe, horse and foot to determine a route for the line onwards from New Westminster. He had two sections of the route to survey. The first section, east with the Fraser to Hope, then north to the head of navigation at Yale, would follow the river along a yet undetermined path. The second section would be built between Yale and Quesnel, the point where gold miners turned east for the Cariboo gold mines.

Between 1861 and 1864, at the behest of the colonial government, a contingent of Royal Engineers and an assortment of private contractors had built a wagon road, known as the Cariboo Road, from Yale as far as Soda Creek on the Upper Fraser. Passengers or freight bound from

New Westminster for the Cariboo must still, however, travel to Yale by canoe or by steamer. A road from New Westminster to Yale would serve both the colony and the telegraph company. "It will obviously be to the interest of the Telegraph Company that their line should be built along the highway," wrote Robson, "and the advantage may be reciprocated by having the two schemes conjointly promoted." Robson also suggested that it would be best for the road and telegraph to follow the north bank of the Fraser, on the same side as New Westminster. A northern route would take the road through the best agricultural land and, more important, could be more readily protected in case of "trouble with our neighbours (quod avertat Deus)",[8] he remarked, blithely overlooking the fact that the line itself would be controlled by those same neighbours.

Robson felt no need for consistency, for he also wrote an editorial praising the Americans for building the line. "If the world is indebted to American ingenuity and skill for the electro-magnetic telegraph, we are indebted to American enterprise for its early application in British Columbia. . . . Without an effort on our part, without the expenditure of a single dollar of the colonial revenue, we enjoy what would have cost many thousands were it not for the enterprise of our neighbours."[9] Robson's affection for things American was not unusual in the colony, since many of the gold-rush prospectors and merchants who now populated British Columbia were American, and many New Westminsterites felt a stronger connection to the United States than to either Britain or Canada.

Late in March, Conway set out with a work party and a government surveyor to explore for the best route between New Westminster and Yale. Less concerned with the grandiose plans of New Westminster and more with logistics and efficiency, he chose to run the line along the south bank of the river, a choice seconded by the government when it came to building a wagon road. He now determined to accomplish as much as possible before spring floods raised the level of the Fraser and made it difficult to transport materials, men and supplies up and down the river.

He traced the proposed route overland to Yale, reporting by letter to Bulkley on April 28 that he had found no obstructions between New Westminster and Hope that could not be overcome. The government had already cut a road six miles towards Langley, and work could begin on that section immediately. There were narrow trails the rest of the way, with some small problems of river flooding and snowslides, but Conway saw no real difficulty. Between Hope and Yale, the high mountains closed in, but there was still room for a road and a line. The cedar trees that predominated below Yale were too large for telegraph poles, but they could be chipped to the proper size and would last ten years in the ground. In some places, snowslides posed a problem, since snow could push across the line and break it. In those areas, the line should be raised higher than usual on extra-tall poles or masts.

Conway sent E.B. Libby, a new member of the expedition recently arrived from San Francisco, to Yale to begin work from that point north. Libby was to hire small work parties to cut poles 22 feet high, eight inches wide at the base and no less than four inches at the top, and pile them ready for use at the rate of 30 to the mile. He also sent a man to Yale to establish an office there, to pay the men who would be hired and to look after supplies, provisions and routine company affairs.

By May, work above Yale was proceeding well, though a continuing shortage of good workmen for hire in New Westminster and Yale plagued Conway and Libby. Mark Wade, the historian of the Cariboo Road, described the procedure:

> A perfect system was adopted to ensure rapidity. One set of men went ahead of the others to mark and measure the line, driving pegs to indicate where the poles were to be erected. Others followed and felled trees of the proper size for the poles; after them came another gang whose duty it was to trim and peel the poles and then came the teamsters with horses and chains to haul the poles to the places marked for them. Next in order came the labourers to dig the holes for the poles and even this gang was divided into two parts, the first beginning the hole while the other part finished it ready for the pole. Another lot erected the poles, still others followed whose sole duty it was to fasten on the brackets and they in turn were succeeded by men who put on the insulators and last of all came the linemen who strung the wire.[10]

Below Yale, Conway could only wait for the government to complete the road from New Westminster to Yale, so that the line could follow apace. He sent out axe parties to cut poles and erect them where the road was complete, cautioning that the poles must be set 63 paces apart and particularly solidly in areas where the rivers were likely to flood the ground in spring runoff. He left no detail to chance, sending constant instructions to each of his foremen about such things as line location—straight but never out of sight of the government road—and workmen—useless men or grumblers were to be fired forthwith.

He wrote frequently to Bulkley and to company headquarters in San Francisco, asking that supplies be sent more speedily, that money be arranged for, that teamsters be sent since there were none worthy in British Columbia to drive the teams of horses he was buying, that spikes and insulators be dispatched. He concluded an agreement with the government that gave the telegraph company a right-of-way along the road 20 feet wide and 30 feet high. The governor agreed that workmen hired by the government to build the road would also brush out any trees that could conceivably fall on the right-of-way and endanger the telegraph line.

*The Cariboo Road and the telegraph line. (Courtesy of the Provincial Archives of BC. HP 10228.)*

By May 20, 75 men were at work and 2,000 poles laid out. Bulkley had instructed Conway to use the provisions sent from San Francisco, and to buy only fresh meat and produce in British Columbia. When provisions did not arrive on time, Conway had a problem, and he nagged Bulkley repeatedly for more rations. "You cannot bring too large a supply of rations,"[11] he wrote. He told Bulkley that the amount of food specified for soldiers in the United States army, the measure adopted for use on the telegraph line, was not sufficient: hardworking men ate far more in these northern climes. Beans were cheap and eminently suitable; also in demand were pork, bacon, flour, salt and sugar. Why didn't you send enough cable, he asked; please send more. We need more wire, where's the *Milton Badger*, how can I move quickly without wire and insulators? Send me 75 mosquito bars, he pleaded, a comment unwritten on new problems facing his work parties.

By May 23, the advance parties working north from Yale had cut poles and prepared the route for 80 miles. In the Fraser Canyon where the rock walls closed in tight upon the river, Conway had decided he would not use poles. Instead, workmen would fasten the line to the rock with iron brackets. By mid-June, almost 300 miles of poles had been erected, from Yale well up the Fraser, and Conway was promising a reporter from *The Cariboo Sentinel* in Barkerville that the line would be finished to Quesnel by the end of the month. He also pledged a line from Quesnel into Barkerville and the gold-rush country.

Conway and his men were moving so fast that they were quickly outstripping the supply of insulators and wire, and Conway feared he would have to discharge the work parties he had hired with such difficulty. Then, on June 17, the company schooner *Milton Badger* tied up at New Westminster with 200 tons of material and stores, including line, brackets, insulators and submarine cable to replace the original and inadequate cable across the Fraser. Within 48 hours, crews were stringing wire east from New Westminster. Ten days after the ship's arrival, a new cable had been laid from the south shore to New Westminster, the line was complete to Matsqui and Governor Seymour spurred on the crews working on the government road to Yale.

Trying to juggle men, material and supplies from his base in New Westminster, Conway began to reveal that the strain of command was eating away at him. He fired his agent at Yale, for extravagance and poor management, then gave him a letter of recommendation to Gamble at the California State Telegraph Company, saying the man had left of his own accord. He nagged Libby to stop working his horse teams so hard, and pestered Bulkley and Gamble with telegrams asking that money be sent on time. Unnamed "others" had placed him in a very delicate financial situation that would reflect very badly on the company and himself, and perhaps destroy the company's credit in British Columbia, he averred.

Whatever the cost to his peace of mind, his harrying bore fruit. On August 17, the first telegraph message from Hope to New Westminster was transmitted. The telegraph agent at Hope sent the message to the hotel at New Westminster, directing that a bottle of champagne be delivered to Conway at the New Westminster telegraph office. Nine days later, another bottle was on its way to Pitfield, to celebrate the completion and opening of the line as far as Yale. Conway wrote to Gamble in San Francisco, announcing that the construction parties were racing ahead at the rate of ten miles a day, and that he expected to have 400 miles of line working by the end of August.

By September 2, workmen had completed the line almost the full length of the Cariboo Road, as far as Soda Creek. At 3 P.M. on September 14, barely six months after construction began, the line was completed to Quesnel, 450 miles from New Westminster, "great enthusiasm prevailing."[12] If the rest of the line was completed with as much dispatch and energy, the hopes and dreams of Perry Collins would be well on the way to fulfillment.

CHAPTER 7

# British Columbia, 1865:
# Into Unknown Territory

From the American border to Quesnel, the telegraph passed through known territory, the larger part of the line twinned with government roads. Thousands of prospectors, government surveyors and settlers had already passed over the trails along the Fraser River, the most efficient route to the interior. From Quesnel north to the Yukon River was a different story. Here lay a land known only to the Indians and to the men of the Hudson's Bay Company who had established fur-trading posts and trade routes through the northern interior. But the Indians did not use compass and map, and the men of the H.B.C. were not concerned with reaching the Yukon. North from the Cariboo, the overland telegraph parties were breaking fresh ground.

On May 17, 1865, Franklin L. Pope and several companions left San Francisco by steamer bound for Vancouver Island. Pope, then 25 years old, had been a telegraph operator in his native Massachusetts from the age of 17. In 1864, he fell ill and was advised to take up outdoor, physical work. He joined the Russian-American telegraph expedition, and was named chief of explorations in British Columbia, with the rank of major.

Pope and his companions reached Victoria on May 25. The capital of the Crown Colony of Vancouver Island was vastly different in 1865 from the small fur-trading post it had been a decade earlier, before prospectors and merchants flooded in, drawn by the mainland gold rush. Pope noted it was now a maritime port of call and supply depot, with a population of four or five thousand, including representatives from almost every nation on earth, English and Americans predominating.*

Pope and the men with him went almost immediately to the Hudson's Bay Company store "for the purpose of being fitted out with the necessary supplies and provisions for our proposed campaign through the upper country."[1]

The group left Victoria as soon as they had their supplies and provisions, and arrived at New Westminster on board the steamer *Enterprise*. Unlike Governor Seymour, Pope was much impressed by the Fraser River town, with its well-built wharf, geometrically laid-out streets, its public buildings—a courthouse, two or three churches, treasury, library and hospital—and the view from the town along the river.

Pope's immediate task was to explore north from Quesnel, laying out a route for the telegraph line from Quesnel to the Yukon River, where it was to join the line being built by work parties sent to Russian America. He left for the interior on May 31, with 25 men hired in San Francisco and Victoria, on board a sternwheel steamer bound for the head of navigation at Yale. They chugged upriver against the strong spring current, past Hope, which he described as the prettiest town in British Columbia, next to New Westminster, and into the rapids between Hope and Yale.

---

*Much of the information about Pope's sojourn in British Columbia comes from a manuscript in the possession of the Western Union Telegraph Company archives; the manuscript bears no author's name, but evidence within makes it clear it was written by Pope, who probably hoped to have it published as a book. It remains unpublished, possibly because of Pope's stilted writing style and fondness for cliché.

The rapids, "frequently too powerful for any steamer", astonished Pope with their ferocity. "Below the engineer could be heard stirring up his fires . . . for the ensuing struggle between the forces of steam and water. . . . 'All forward!' shouts the skipper and the passengers rush to the bow of the boat and gather in a little crowd on the deck. Then the steamer slowly glides forward for a few moments and the bar is passed."[2]

At Yale, the group found trains of pack animals and heavy wagons coming and going to and from the Cariboo. They took possession of the 30 mules that Conway had bought for their exploring expedition, loaded on their supplies and headed north along the Cariboo Road, through the "overpowering and terrible grandeur" of the Fraser Canyon between Yale and Lytton. "Looking down into a narrow gorge," recalled Pope, "many hundred feet below, the whirling river, white

*A steamer on the Fraser River, at Soda Creek, BC. (Courtesy of the Provincial Archives of BC. HP 10268.)*

with foam, is seen rushing along with fearful speed."[3] Pope and his companions had only admiration for the men who had built a road through such difficult terrain.

The mule train made its way across a wire suspension bridge that hung high above the river, across the face of a precipitous cliff known as Jackass Mountain and into dry plateau country that replaced the coastal rainforest. The town of Lytton was windy, dusty and disagreeable; with no reason to stay, they left as soon as possible. Now the road followed the Thompson River, through rolling, scantily forested country, where crops could be grown only with the help of irrigation. They continued on away from the river, past the roadhouses, stables and ranches of the Cariboo country, seeing an increasing number of cattle and horses grazing the bunchgrass hills. At Lac La Hache, they left half the group behind, to make beef pemmican to feed the exploring parties over the winter.

The Cariboo Road ended at Soda Creek, 360 miles north of Yale, once more beside the Fraser, and the group embarked with its freight by steamer for Fort Alexandria, 80 miles north. The steamer, another *Enterprise*, had been built here before the Cariboo Road was complete. The boilers and machinery came in small sections via mule from the head of Harrison Lake to Lillooet, and were put back together at Fort Alexandria; the planks and timbers were cut from local forests.

The group left behind at Lac La Hache caught up at Fort Alexandria; the mule train was sent ahead by a narrow trail along the river while the passengers and freight reached Quesnel aboard the steamer. They arrived at Quesnel on July 3, and paused briefly to consider their course of action. Electron, *The Telegrapher's* pseudonymous correspondent*, described Quesnel as the most northern town upon the American continent and the jumping-off place of civilization. In the town, which consisted of a single street of log buildings, the "principal business done here by the inhabitants consists of asking each other to 'take some-

---

*Electron never identifies himself, but was probably Pope himself. The correspondent consistently refers to Pope in the third person, and on one occasion *The Telegrapher* prints an article signed F.L.P., in which reference is made to "your regular correspondent", indications that Electron was someone other than Pope. However, some of Electron's reports to *The Telegrapher* are identical to parts of Pope's letters to his brother Henry, at home in Great Barrington, Mass. A third brother, Ralph, joined the telegraph expedition later in 1865 and spent the winter of 1865 as quartermaster in Quesnel.

thing,' and of playing 'three card monte' and other moral and instructive games. They are 'laying on their oars' at present, waiting for the 'fall trade' when the miners go down the country from the Cariboo to winter below with their pockets heavy with 'dust,' when a rich harvest will doubtless be reaped by these worthy 'artists'."[4]

The men celebrated the fourth of July at their camp, named the Last Chance, with salutes, a good dinner, speeches, toasts and songs. The next day, they started off on horseback with their mule train, over a narrow Indian trail. Originally, they had planned to move north by river, using large wooden boats similar to those in the service of the H.B.C. But the river was extremely high, swollen with spring runoff, and river travel was difficult and dangerous. Instead, they decided to follow the trail northwest toward Fort Fraser and Fraser Lake.

They were led by a native named Kel-sun, who blazed the trees as he passed. Then came the axemen, who widened the trail through standing and fallen timber, and built bridges across swamps and streams. Bringing up the rear was the mule train, laden with blankets and provisions. En route, one of the men, James Butler, disappeared so completely that several days' search could not find him. "We have since heard," reported Electron, "that he strayed from the trail while chasing a deer, and climbing a tree to ascertain the direction of the camp, a limb broke, precipitating him to the ground a distance of thirty feet and injuring him so severely he was unable to move for three days. In this disabled condition he finally managed to return the entire distance to Quesnelle after twelve days of most intense suffering and exposure, being reduced to a skeleton and being hardly able to move. Had he not been a man of unusual strength of constitution, he must have perished in the wilderness."[5] Butler must have recovered, however, for he continued to work for the telegraph expedition for at least another year.

Some of the trail was easy; some was not. The descent was so steep down one hill that "the poor mules were unable to keep their feet and rolled down the hill one after the other with their cargoes in the greatest confusion."[6] In places, they had to cut the trail through fallen timber. They met and followed the West Road River, then cut across country to the Chilako and eventually the Nechako River and Fraser Lake. En route they met various groups of Indians, either in their villages or spearing salmon along the rivers.

They soon discovered that the only maps that had been made of the region were frequently inaccurate, showing streams flowing the wrong way and reaching the sea at the wrong place. A Nechako Indian woman, Too-gum-a-hen, drew for them a much more accurate map, sketching the entire country between Fraser Lake and Bella Coola, at the head of Bentinck Arm on the Pacific coast. Too-gum-a-hen located the rivers, lakes, mountains, Indian villages and trails on her map, and described the arduous ten-day portage necessary to reach the source of the Nechako River.

Pope quickly discovered that travel in this country was not the major problem; transporting supplies was. Within a week, he sent ten of his men back to Quesnel so that he could save enough provisions to feed the rest of the group. On July 29, the remaining men reached Fort Fraser, built in 1806, the first fur-trading post in British Columbia. The buildings of the post were arranged on three sides of a square, within a log stockade; also within the fence was a large field where potatoes, peas and turnips were grown. Outside grazed the horses and cattle belonging to the H.B.C.

Pope called a council of the native groups in the area and explained the telegraph to them. He set up a telegraph line several hundred yards long, strung on small poles, powered by a small battery and completed by a pocket telegraph instrument at each end. "Major Pope then arranged a revolver at the farther end of the line in such a manner that it could be fired from the opposite end by closing the circuit. Everything being in readiness, Major Pope requested the chief to place his finger upon the key, which was followed by an instantaneous report of the pistol at the extremity of the wire. This performance excited the utmost wonder and admiration. . . . "[7]

Following the demonstration, Pope told the natives that the completion of the line through their country would enable them to know in advance when the salmon were entering the river, so they could set up their weirs and nets ahead of time. Convinced by the revolver shot, the promise of swift communication and by gifts of tobacco, powder, shot and red cloth, the Indians promised every co-operation.

The group moved on the short distance to Fort St. James, a Hudson's Bay post at the southern end of Stuart Lake. Pope noted that the fort, large and commodious, housed ten to 15 employees.

Pope now turned his attention to preparations for the winter. He sent botanist J.T. Rothrock north along Stuart Lake to find a location for a winter post, while he considered how the men would obtain provisions that would sustain them over the winter. Almost everyone in the region, white or Indian, lived solely on dried salmon in the winter, but Pope wanted more for the telegraph expedition. He sent the pack train back over the trail to Alexandria, obtained an additional boat from the H.B.C. and embarked with Peter Skene Ogden, the chief factor at Fort St. James, for Alexandria, where he planned to obtain a load of provisions to bring back up the river. The trip down—the Stuart River to the Nechako, the Nechako to the Fraser, the Fraser to Alexandria—with the river current, was extremely rapid; the 300 miles took less than three days. The trip back, with loaded boats, was "toilsome and arduous", 18 days in length, as the Indian paddlers tracked the boat (hauled it by walking along the shore) and poled upriver. Once they arrived back at Fort St. James, Pope dispatched the boat for another load of supplies.

Pope's return to Fort Alexandria disgusted Edward Conway, who was eager to plot the telegraph route north of Quesnel. Conway's line would soon reach Quesnel, and Conway wanted to keep building north at a speedy pace. He considered that Pope was wasting his and the expedition's time by dashing back and forth with supplies instead of establishing the route west and north from Quesnel. "Owing to the failure of Pope's Exploring Expedition," he wrote to Gamble in August, "I am compelled to stop my work and commence exploration myself. Of course, this causes great delay."[8] Conway then left New Westminster and headed to Quesnel.

He left Quesnel September 20 with four men and ten mules; the mules proved of little value and were soon sent back. He followed the trail to Fort Fraser, and characterized the country as very favourable for the telegraph line. The country in general was open, with beautiful prairies, lakes and plentiful meadows for pasturage and hay, he reported. There should be little trouble in wintering stock over, provided the animals arrived in time. Timber for poles was abundant and convenient. The line need cross only two rivers, the West Road and the Nechako. In most places, the telegraph could follow the trail, but cutting out some of the twists and turns of the trail would save some 25 miles. The line to Fort Fraser would be about 150 miles long.

From Fort Fraser to Fort St. James, Conway wrote to Bulkley, the route was not as favourable. Two 3,000-foot mountain ranges impeded passage, much of the land was heavily timbered and swamps would make it difficult to build the line along some of this route.

The company would have to bring in its own labourers for there were no settlers here and "No dependence whatever can be placed on Indian labour. They will work, when they are out of food, but prefer being idle, as long as they have sufficient to keep them alive."[9]

At Fort St. James, he met Pope returning from the winter camp established by his men to the north and the two continued by boat along Stuart Lake. They decided that the high bluffs tight to the lake north of Fort St. James would make a lakeside route impossible. They followed the Tachie River north, battling rapids and a strong current for 16 miles between heavily timbered banks, to Trembleur Lake, where Conway reported the line could be built along the beach. Another short river journey, on the Middle River, brought them to Takla Lake, 60 miles long.

The trip from Fort St. James to the north end of Takla Lake took them six days. There, they found Rothrock and the rest of the telegraph party in winter quarters they had built and named Bulkley House. With difficulty, Pope and Conway obtained an Indian guide and pushed on 60 miles northwest to Fort Connolly, another post of the H.B.C., arriving after "rambling six days in the woods." Conway was encouraged by the weather, reporting that "they have never had a man frozen in the vicinity of Connolly's lake, though they often camp out in the middle of winter."[10] Pope and Conway stayed at the lake six days. Conway reported they returned to Bulkley House because they could not get a guide who would take them to the Stikine River. Pope wrote that there was no point continuing on, as winter had already set in, the deep soft snow in the mountains made it impossible to travel by dog team and there were no snowshoes to be had.

In a column in *The Telegrapher*, Electron/Pope described the miserable trip, where "we had to carry our blankets, provisions, axes, frying pans, guns and forty other traps on our backs, and the whole forest, from here to there, has been burnt and blown down and the logs are piled 'criss-cross' in every direction, several feet high, like a pile of matches thrown on the floor. . . .

"Then we had to wade a [large] river . . . about daylight one morning, with the ice running down. That was snug and comfortable! . . .

*The exploring expedition to Fort Connolly. From Pope's sketchbook. (Courtesy of the Provincial Archives of BC. pdp 1451.)*

We got snowed in up in the mountains and had to stay there until all our 'grub' was eaten up . . . [and] had to travel back with nothing for three of us to eat except two dried woodchucks and four dried fish. We used to scramble over the logs all day and sit down at night and eat our piece of dried woodchuck . . . a good deal tougher than gutta percha, with first-rate appetites. O yes, and we had tea too; made it out of a plant that grows here in the swamps which makes first-rate tea."

Overwhelmed by his own hardships, Electron was astonished to see Indian children running around naked in the snow "never seeming to care about the cold."[11]

In October, Conway retraced his steps to Quesnel. There, he instructed Libby to send 30 head of cattle to Fraser Lake, to get muskets and revolvers for a construction party that would tackle the route north, and to have a pack train distribute materials and provisions along the probable route of the line to Fort Fraser before the worst of the winter snows fell. Conway then went south to his headquarters at New Westminster.

In November, Pope dispatched a report to Conway, probably sending it out with a passing Indian or trader from the Hudson's Bay Company. In it, he described the country north and west of Takla Lake. To help him with areas where he had not been, Pope persuaded Indians to draw rough sketchmaps. These he pieced together into a single map. This map was very reliable, he said, for showing how lakes and rivers connect and the relative locations of waterfalls, rapids and portages. It was, however, of little use for measuring distance or setting compass bearings, for compass bearings were scarcely relevant to the Indians in their travel, and they measured distance by the time it took to traverse it, not by actual space.

Pope said that the rivers were in general navigable from June to December. Travel by land was almost impossible in December and January because the snow was soft. Once a crust formed on the snow at the end of January, men could travel by snowshoe. Dogsleds were useless, he continued, because there was nothing along the route that could be used for dogfood.

The scarcity of game—occasional bears, beaver, game birds and fish were all he saw—was balanced, he noted drily, by the superabundance of "mosquitoes, blackflies, gnats, with which the whole country literally swarms during the summer time."[12] Although it might be possible to grow turnips, potatoes and cabbages, he concluded that the wise man would bring his own provisions.

Early in 1866, a report from Electron appeared in *The Telegrapher*, a copy of a letter that Pope had sent to his brother in Massachusetts. Electron was grateful for the latest letters received; "although our nearest post-office is over four hundred miles, and only two houses between here and there, our letters come through with considerable regularity. . . . We generally send our mails by some stray Indian, going through the wilderness, who is pretty sure to deliver them safely, for he knows he will get a potlatch [present] of tobacco."

Electron told *The Telegrapher's* readers that his party was living in a beautiful place at the head of Takla Lake, with a view 30 miles down the lake from their winter quarters, which were about as large as the kitchen of his house at home. (Perhaps something of an exaggeration: the log building erected at Bulkley House was 20 feet by 35 feet, with two rooms on the ground floor and a second storey for storage.)

He finished his epistle with a description of life at Bulkley House:

Probably you folks at home would be interested to know how we live and what we live on here; and I can assure you that there's many a hotel in the Eastern States not so well kept as Bulkley House. I have a cook who takes care of the house, chops the wood, and runs the establishment. We have plenty of good bread, bacon, beans and dried salmon; tea, coffee, chocolate and sugar; also dried apples and rice once or twice a week. When we are on a trip we live on bread and bacon, with tea and sugar. We get a good many ducks and partridges, and some fresh fish once in a while. Fresh woodchucks are excellent, and we have them often.[13]

He then announced, news undoubtedly to Bulkley, that he expected to leave Bulkley House by the following June and be home by fall.

Boredom was the greatest enemy of the men at Bulkley House, and they determined to relieve it with a mammoth Christmas celebration. Finding little in the larder, the fish not biting and the partridge and grouse cleaned out for miles around, two hunting parties set out into

*Bulkley House. From Pope's sketchbook. (Courtesy of the Provincial Archives of BC. pdp 1450.)*

new territory across the mountains. They returned with a "noble fat beaver, some rabbits, a splendid bag of mountain grouse and ptarmigan."[14]

Christmas dawned cloudy and cold, but the ten men at the post were not deterred. After breakfast, they welcomed gaily dressed natives who came to pay their respects and take part in sporting competitions. Shooting matches over 100 yards were followed by foot races "to keep up the circulation of blood and fun."[15] Novice snowshoe races drew a large entry. The climactic event of the day, attended with hot and heavy betting, was a women's 500-yard race over unbroken two-foot-deep snow. Betting favourites among the six entrants were a 12-year-old, a 20-year-old and what Electron described as an 85-year-old, all in peak physical condition. The 20-year-old outran her rivals in the final 100 yards, swept through the course in four minutes and won the prize of a red handkerchief.

Sports were followed by Christmas dinner, prepared by a volunteer *chef de cuisine* who transformed the contents of larder and hunting bag into grouse pie, roast beaver, apple and bread sauce, plum pudding, cheese and mince pies. Then came speeches and toasts drunk in coffee and the reading of Christmas carols written for the occasion. The chronicler of the celebration suggested Charles Dickens had better look to his laurels. A noisy, energetic dance, aided by a small keg of rum brought by a native visitor, concluded the festivities and cemented the friendship between telegrapher and Indian.

While Pope, Rothrock and Conway led exploring parties overland through the interior, another group was venturing into British Columbia by water. Late in the summer of 1865, Conway sent Captain Horace Coffin, in command of the steamer *Union*, north up the coast. The ship left New Westminster August 30, arriving at the mouth of the Skeena River two weeks later. The *Union* then churned 90 miles upriver, to the head of steamer navigation. Coffin had his men offload provisions and telegraph supplies, and continued the journey in two canoes. They landed supplies 185 miles from the river mouth, at the Indian village of Hagwilgaet, which was located at the junction of the Skeena and a river they named the Bulkley. The supplies would serve Conway or Pope whenever their construction parties arrived.

The *Union* then chugged back downriver and north along the coast to the Nass River. Coffin was able to take the ship 45 miles up the

Nass; the party went another 40 miles by canoe. By then it was mid-October, too late in the season to attempt the Stikine, so Coffin took the *Union* back south, leaving his remaining material and supplies at Fort Simpson, on the coast, for next year's explorations.

Many of Coffin's notes about the rivers were dispatched overland, to be carried from Indian to Indian to Conway, somewhere in the interior, but they never arrived. Conway speculated they were destroyed by Indians who were determined that these interlopers would not take over the lucrative native trade routes. Conway noted proudly in a letter to Bulkley that Coffin's entire trip had cost just $2,860, including $1,325 for steamer rental and the fees of the captain and engineers.

To anyone acquainted with the conditions under which Conway and his men had worked, his achievements in 1865 must have seemed remarkable: 450 miles of line built and working, country to the northwest explored, supply routes determined and supplies delivered along the rivers inland from the Pacific. But far from congratulating himself, Conway was beset with increasing frustration. He had been working for 12 months straight now with not a single day's break. A perfectionist who expected no less from his men than from himself, he was constantly disappointed with what he viewed as the intemperance, extravagance and laziness some of them displayed. Supplies, materials and money were consistently late in arriving, and he could not push the line north as rapidly as he intended or as he had thought possible. Bulkley, usually on the move around the North Pacific rim, rarely answered Conway's letters; when he did communicate, he said little to soothe Conway's injured feelings or dispel his fears.

In December of 1865, Conway cracked. After dispatching three routine notes to Bulkley—not an unusual number of daily communications to his chief—Conway wrote a fourth curt note. "My resignation goes down by first mail. Will take me two months to settle my accounts." The following day, he explained himself to Bulkley. "I can no longer hold my position with credit to myself or justice to my employers," he wrote. There was too much to do, and too few good men to do it with. The limits on pay would not allow Conway to hire more good men. Furthermore, Pope's failure to explore as rapidly as Conway expected had forced Conway to explore for the route as well as building the line. I cannot, he wrote, "explore, construct, organize and manage a line in my rear." Nor could he bear to keep working for the company and see things go wrong. "I have but little peace of mind and no patience whatever when things do not go to suit me."[16] He could not save a penny, given the cost of living in British Columbia, nor could he support the family he had left behind in the United States. Most important, he could no longer put a smooth face on what was in fact a very rocky road.

Once he had dispatched his resignation, Conway continued to do his job, dealing with routine matters, and sending a brusque reply to Bulkley when the latter questioned his expenses and mentioned bad press reports about the expedition in British Columbia. He sent Bulkley a long report on the Hudson's Bay Company in British Columbia, recommending that the telegraph company was better off acting independently rather than relying on the co-operation of the H.B.C.

"We know the country better than the H.B. Co. having been over all that they have seen and a great portion of it that they know nothing whatever about. They have no right whatever for trading in New Caledonia, as their charter for the place has expired. They have charged us the most exorbitant prices for all that we have received, as you will perceive by the vouchers. We can secure a number of their employees whose time expires early next season."

Then, in one of those about-faces increasingly characteristic of the man, Conway concluded, "I am on the very best of terms with all the employees and officers of the H.B.C. and shall continue to be so. I merely express my opinion."[17]

Of Conway's precipitate resignation, neither man made a mention. Bulkley ordered Conway to San Francisco; Conway refused, then changed his mind. Late in December, Conway left New Westminster, bound for San Francisco and some resolution of his difficulties with the Western Union Extension Company.

## CHAPTER 8

# Siberia, 1865: First Sight

Through the spring and summer of 1865, Edward Conway and his men built the long thin line of posts and wire north through British Columbia, and Franklin Pope's explorers ventured into the lesser-known territory beyond the Cariboo Road. British Columbia was the easiest reached of the regions the line would traverse. In San Francisco, Charles Bulkley considered how to tackle the remaining portions of the line.

The company planned to join Russian America and Siberia via submarine cable beneath the Bering Strait, an underwater distance of 178 nautical miles that engineers promised would present no difficulties. A short land line would lead to a second, 209-nautical-mile submarine cable under the Gulf of Anadyr that would surface at the mouth of the Anadyr River, west of the Bering Sea. From there the line would cut overland some 500 miles behind the Koryak Mountains, then parallel the Okhotsk Sea coast southward another 1,500 miles to the Amur River and the planned Russian line to Irkutsk, Moscow and the European world.

This was all theoretical. Few explorers and no Americans had ever travelled through Siberia, and Bulkley had only the most general idea of the lay of the land. The first task of the Siberian contingent of the telegraph expedition would be to chart the land and determine the best route for the line.

Since the Siberian line would link up with the North American line at the Bering Strait, Bulkley initially planned to concentrate on the route from Anadyr Bay south. He wanted to land an exploring party at the mouth of the Anadyr River, with directions to explore and begin building as soon as possible. But the Russian consul at San Francisco warned against any such move. The land bordering the Bering Strait, he told Bulkley, was 1,000 miles from any known settlement. If men from the telegraph company were landed by ship on the Anadyr, they would be forced to rely on the supplies and canoes they brought with them. They could not expect to get dogsleds or reindeer from the natives for transportation, nor would the natives have any food to sell them. Their problems of transport and supply would be compounded by their total ignorance of the country. Instead, said the consul, Bulkley should send his men to one of the Russian ports on the Okhotsk Sea, where they could set up a supply base and obtain information, dogs, sleds and horses.

Bulkley saw the force of the consul's arguments, but still wanted to link the Siberian line to America as soon as possible. In the spring of 1865, he decided to mount two offensives, one west from the mouth of the Anadyr and a second skirting the Okhotsk Sea far to the south. Six men would be dispatched to the Anadyr, four to the Okhotsk.

The decision made, Bulkley was eager to get his Siberian expeditions underway. But none of the ships he had bought or leased was yet ready for service; in any case, all would be needed to move men and supplies to Russian America and to the Anadyr and none could be spared to take men to the Okhotsk Sea. Fortunately, the Russian trading brig *Olga* was about to leave San Francisco bound for ports along the Okhotsk Sea and Bulkley immediately booked passage for his four young adventurers aboard her.

The group was commanded by Major Serge Abasa, the Russian nobleman selected to oversee exploration and construction of the line in Siberia. With him would go George Kennan, Richard J. Bush and James Mahood. Bush, a young soldier just returned from three years' service in the Carolinas, came from Massachusetts; Mahood was a California civil engineer hired in San Francisco.

Kennan, barely 20 in 1864, was nervous, excitable and adventuresome. Although he had been turned down for civil-war service because his constitution seemed too weak for the privations of war, he had no doubt that he would thrive on the difficulties to be encountered in the wilds of Siberia. He was working as an operator in his father's telegraph office in Ohio when he heard of the overland project; he invested his savings in the Western Union Extension Company, then "led by a desire of identifying myself with so novel and important an enterprise, as well as by a natural love of travel and adventure which I had never before been able to gratify,"[1] applied to join the expedition. Bulkley was impressed by his verve and his telegraph experience and hired him.

The four men loaded themselves up with blankets, heavy shoes, flannel shirts, rifles, revolvers, bowie knives, pots of arsenic for preserving specimens, alcohol, butterfly nets, snake bags and pill boxes. They also packed a library that included Danish explorer Ferdinand von Wrangel's descriptions of his travels in Siberia and the most up-to-date works on botany. "Before night," wrote Kennan, "we were able to report ourselves ready—armed and equipped for any adventure, from the capture of a new species of bug to the conquest of Kamchatka."[2] On July 3, 1865, the *Olga* sailed from San Francisco, to the accompaniment of waves, cheers and a parting admonition from the Scientific Corps: "God bless you! Keep your eye out for land snails and the skulls of wild animals."[3]

Bush later described the group as "young, stout, healthy and ambitious"[4] but neither youth nor ambition made the 47-day crossing of the Pacific more bearable. The sea voyage quickly disabused the men of all romantic notions of ocean travel. "Never again will I pin my faith to poets," declared Kennan from the miserable depths to which monotony, perpetual seasickness, roaring nor'westers and chilling fogs had sunk him. "[I would] look with complacency upon a sand bar and two spears of grass, and would not even insist upon the grass."[5]

Forty-six days of sailing brought the *Olga* within welcome sight of the Kamchatkan peninsula. In preparation for landing, the crew scrubbed everything in sight, including the two little pigs brought along on board. On August 19, the 47th day out of San Francisco, the *Olga* entered Petropavlosk, a snug harbour near the southern tip of the Kamchatkan peninsula, surrounded on three sides by narrow, high cliffs. Flocks of children, blue-shirted Russian peasant settlers, dark-haired Kamchatdal natives and barking dogs gathered at the quay to welcome the sea-weary travellers.

Petropavlosk was one of the oldest Russian settlements on the Pacific coast, established in 1740 to underline Russia's claim to the coast and named for the *St. Peter* and *St. Paul*, the two ships that explorer Vitus Bering built on the Okhotsk Sea. When Petropavlosk was the military headquarters for the coast, it had been home to 1,000 settlers and soldiers. During the Crimean War, ships of the French and British navies attacked the inoffensive town; when Kennan saw its simple bark-covered, straw-thatched houses, he was aghast at the military mentality that had ordered an attack on a town so far from the battlefronts. "It could not possibly have any direct or indirect influence upon the ultimate result and only brought misery upon a few inoffensive Kamchat-

*Petropavlosk. (From Whymper,* Travel and Adventures. . . . )

dals who had never heard of Turkey or the 'Eastern Question'."[6] By 1865, after Siberian governor-general Muraviev established Nicolaevsk on the Amur far to the south and transferred the Tsar's military forces to that town, Petropavlosk had been reduced to 300 residents.

As soon as they arrived at Petropavlosk, the exploring party began to realize some of the problems they would have on their journey. Only Abasa spoke Russian; few of the natives or settlers knew any words of English. Tormented by the difficulty of learning the multiple Slavonic syllables, Kennan speculated that the Russians must have built their side of the Tower of Babel higher than anyone else to have been punished by such a dreadful and unintelligible language. He asked Abasa to teach him the words for "I need food", so that he would at least be saved from starvation. "He coolly replied," reported Kennan, "that whenever I wanted anything to eat, all that I had to do was to say, 'Vashavwesokeeblagarodiaee veeleekeeprevoskhodeetelstuoee takdalshai.'. . . I frankly told the Major that he might print out this terrible sentence on a big placard and hang it around my neck; but as far as for learning to pronounce it, I couldn't and didn't propose to try."[7] The news that Abasa had only been joking and had given him some of the longest, toughest words in the Russian language did not raise Kennan's spirits.

Abasa looked for help and was delighted to discover a young, enthusiastic American merchant, known to history only as J. Dodd, who had been at Petropavlosk for seven years as a trader. Dodd, bored by what had become routine, happily agreed to accompany the telegraph explorers as guide and interpreter. Abasa also hired Vushine, the first of many Cossacks who were to act as guides, interpreters, *aides de camp* and intermediaries. Many of the Russians in the area were Cossacks— ex-soldiers, settlers or traders in the service of the Tsar.

Because they had been delayed by the long weeks spent waiting for supplies and transport in San Francisco and by the lengthy sea voyage, Abasa and his crew had not reached Kamchatka until mid-August, far too late in the season to accomplish much of worth in 1865. In his letters to Bulkley, Abasa now began to give vent to his doubts about the company's commitment to the Siberian portion of the line. Revealed in his letters as a worrier and a pessimist, Abasa now questioned whether Bulkley or the company directors had any idea of the potential problems entailed in building through Siberia.

"It has been generally thought," he wrote soon after his arrival, "and a very great error it was, that the work on the Asiatic side would be comparatively easy. . . . Our task will be difficult, hard and require an immense amount of energy and labor. In stating this I do not mean to say that the construction of a telegraph line through the country is impracticable or impossible, but I consider it my duty to expose the real state of things frankly and honestly."[8]

Bulkley expected Abasa and his men would receive full co-operation from the local settlers and government officials, as promised by the Russian government. But, noted Abasa, no one at Petropavlosk had ever heard of the expedition, and small wonder, since no mail had been delivered to the town in the past three years. Any new delays such as that inflicted on them in the summer of 1865 would be fatal to the expedition's success: ships carrying supplies and reinforcements could navigate the Okhotsk Sea only from June through September. Abasa had little money to hire men or animals or buy supplies, because the company's arrangements for such things as letters of credit were unworkable in a land where messages passed between towns perhaps two or three times a year.

If the company replied to Abasa's complaints, that reply has not survived. Despite his growing scepticism, Abasa prepared for the task of finding the best route for the telegraph line. He decided to establish his headquarters at Gizhiga, beyond Kamchatka on the protected north coast of the Okhotsk Sea. It was, he wrote to Bulkley, the logical choice, for it was close to the midpoint of the proposed telegraph line and was a seaport convenient for loading supplies. The Russian governor of the territory lived at Gizhiga, along with Russian merchants who could supply provisions, and Abasa understood that several American merchants planned to set up shop at Gizhiga in 1866 to trade with the local natives and settlers. Nearby coal mines could provide fuel for the expedition's steamships.

Wanting to go to Gizhiga and getting there were two different propositions. Abasa tried to persuade the captain of the *Olga* to take the group there, but the captain refused, since it was late in the year and the ship could be caught by the autumn ice. He chose instead to sail to De Kastries Bay, near Nicolaevsk, where he could sell his cargo to local traders. Abasa decided to break his Siberian exploring party into two groups. Mahood and Bush were to depart with the *Olga*, to explore north from the Amur to Ayan, midway along the west coast of the Okhotsk Sea, and thence if possible to Okhotsk. Abasa, Kennan and Dodd would strike north towards Gizhiga by land and sea. Once there, Abasa could explore southwards towards Okhotsk while Kennan and Dodd could move north towards Anadyrsk, a Russian settlement some 300 miles north of Gizhiga.

"All minor details, such as means of transportation and subsistence, were left to the discretion of the several parties," reported Kennan. "We were to live on the country, travel with the natives, and avail ourselves of any and every means of transportation and subsistence which the country afforded. It was no pleasure excursion upon which we were about to enter. The Russian authorities at Petropavlosk gave us all the information and assistance in their power, but did not hesitate to express the opinion that five men would never succeed in exploring the eighteen hundred miles of barren, almost uninhabited country between the Amoor river and Behring's Strait. . . . The Major replied simply that he would show them what we could do, and went on with his preparations."[9]

*Church at Petropavlosk. (From Bush,* Reindeer, Dogs. . . . )

The six men spent the following week preparing for their journeys. They also sought out clothing to protect themselves against the Siberian cold. There were no bargains to be had, for a generation of traders had taught the Kamchatdals that furs from their peninsula were the best and warmest to be had. The Americans bought *kuklankers*, knee-length parkas made from two thicknesses of reindeer skin with the fur left on, with hoods bordered by long soft dog or wolf fur and embroidered in silk or patterned with reindeer skin of different colours; *torbassa*, long boots made of the tough skin from reindeer legs, where the hair grew shorter and coarser; *chazees*, fur socks; *malachis*, fur bonnets; and *archaniks*, black tippets of Siberian squirrel tails, to be carried between the teeth and protect the face as the owner fronted the wind.

They did have time to investigate the social life of Petropavlosk. They made their first acquaintance with the *samovar*, that essential urn that produced "Siberian nectar"—the tea that would sustain the Americans throughout their travels. They rode wildly through meadow and wood, watched with amazement as Russian ladies lit up *papyrosa* (Russian cigarettes) and made diary notes on the bears, dogs, berries and wildflowers they saw. Bush, Mahood and Dodd rode out to visit a Tartar exiled to Kamchatka by the Tsar. The Tartar was a deserter from the Russian army and convicted member of a band of robbers "among whom he had distinguished himself for his desperation and cruelty."[10] Seventy-six years old, he had spent 46 years in Kamchatka. Like many Kamchatkans, he lived in a house overrun with cockroaches so numerous and so hardy that they could be killed off only in winter by opening doors and windows to freeze the insects to death or so stupefy them with cold that their unmoving bodies could be swatted.

At length, their preparations complete, the two groups took leave of each other, one headed south for the Amur, the other north for Gizhiga.

CHAPTER 9

# Siberia, 1865:
# North from the Amur

A scant seven days after they arrived at Petropavlosk, James Mahood and Richard Bush departed once more aboard the *Olga*, bound for the mouth of the Amur. They sailed south through the Kuril Islands, then threaded the passage between Hokkaido and Sakhalin, and moved north through the Tatar Strait to De Kastries Bay. The 15-day voyage was on the whole serene, marked by drama only once, when tides swept the *Olga* rapidly towards the rocks. Disaster was averted at the last minute when a fast-rising wind caught the ship and blew it back off-shore.

Since the *Olga* drew too much water to penetrate through the strait to Nicolaevsk, near the mouth of the Amur, the ship's captain anchored in De Kastries Bay along with five other trading ships. Mahood and Bush had been told a small steamer would be at De Kastries to convey them onward, but no vessel awaited and none was expected for several days. The rough telegraph line to Nicolaevsk was, not unusually, out of order, and there was no quick way to summon help. Instead, Mahood, Bush and the *Olga's* captain struck out overland, with three Russian soldiers and three horses for company. The soldiers walked; Mahood, Bush and the captain rode.

They set off at a slow pace through pouring rain over swampy trails. Twenty miles along the trail, they arrived at Lake Kizi. They stopped for the night, and for a meal: "The hospitable keeper had brushed the cockroaches from a rude table, and spread an array of brimming tea-cups . . . around a ten-pound loaf of brown bread, near which was an old-fashioned, gayly-figured china plate, containing about equal amounts of butter and besmeared cockroaches. 'Did we eat?'. . . . Tea, bread, butter, and I don't know but the cockroaches too, were soon 'things that were'."[1]

All boarded an undersized scow to sail the lake, but when choppy waves slopped over the edge and threatened to sink the craft, the captain, one soldier and Bush decided to walk along the shore, preferring the certainty of being soaked to the knees to the probability of capsizing the overloaded boat. At the far end of the lake, the group obtained a larger, barge-like boat from a German merchant and sailed up the Amur River by hoisting their two tents to the wind. Reclining and smoking on mattresses of fresh hay, Mahood and Bush listened to the Russian boatmen-soldiers sing melancholy Slavonic airs.

After two days on the river, the rain descended again, and the group took shelter for the night on shore in a tiny cabin already occupied by a detachment of soldiers. Mahood, Bush and the "great fat Dutch sea captain" slept in one bunk. Bush, on the outside, was prey to the wind and rain that penetrated the cabin's flimsy wall; Mahood, on the inside, spent the entire night with one foot wedged against the opposite bunk. The captain, in the middle, monopolized the covers, gave forth an astonishing range of snores and declared in the morning that he had slept most excellently indeed.

Five days after they left De Kastries Bay, Mahood and Bush arrived at Nicolaevsk, on a *prasnik*, one of the many saints' days, notables' death days, Sundays, birthdays and other holidays that cluttered the Russian calendar. It would have been more surprising had it not been a *prasnik*, for, as Bush noted, sometimes there were eight *prasniks* in a seven-day week. The 5,000 local residents, mostly military personnel and convict-exiles, marked each holiday by going to church in the morning and to one of the town's 75 bars in the afternoon.

Bush and Mahood were forced to spend six weeks at Nicolaevsk, first waiting for the *ispravnik* (the local governor) Admiral Furnhelm, to arrive, then waiting for Furnhelm to arrange for reindeer to convey them north. They spent the time acquiring supplies and joining in the life of the town. The lower end of the town, founded by Governor Muraviev mainly as a Russian military outpost, housed government foundries and sawmills. At the upper end were the log houses of the residents, two schools, a barracks, two photographic galleries and other businesses including the offices of merchants who traded vodka, other spirits, cigars, tea, sugar, flour and salt for furs. Officers and grey-coated soldiers promenaded along the two-mile main street, keeping to the narrow board sidewalks, out of the way of the hay-laden drays pulled by small horses.

Mahood and Bush were welcomed by the acting commercial agent for the United States on the Amur, who served as their interpreter as they moved around the town. Under instructions from Abasa, Bush and Mahood examined the Russian telegraph line that led from De Kastries Bay to Nicolaevsk. Russian engineers had failed in several attempts to bring the line across the Amur. Instead, a small steamer conveyed messages from Harborofka, on the south side of the river. Mahood reported that the line was well-built, with good poles well barked and firmly set in place, and good stations along the line. Nonetheless, the line worked poorly and service was erratic. Mahood couldn't say why, though he suspected incompetent operators and indifferent repairs, but forebore to make the obvious comment, that problems on the Russian portion of the line boded ill for the eventual success of the entire intercontinental overland line.

Abasa had instructed Mahood to buy or copy maps of the territory through which the pair planned to travel. Mahood did his best, but was unable to get detailed maps or much information. Though he was given a map of the seacoast provinces to copy, and a rude map showing the reindeer route from the Amur to the Okhotsk coastal town of Ayan, the maps showed nothing of the country between the coast and the mountain range that parallelled it, and no information at all was available on the region north of Ayan. Mahood quickly realized that the maps would be of little use, either in deciding where to go or in describing where they had been. He would have to rely on the compasses they carried for direction and their common sense for distance as he made his reports. He was, however, able to persuade a Pole named Swartz, who worked for the Russian-American Company and who had done some travelling by sea and on land in the region, to join the expedition.

Bush, the studious diary-keeper of the trip, took note of the local natives. He was not overly impressed by the Gilaks, a settled people who lived from fishing along the lower reaches of the Amur, though he was startled by their easy ability to wander half naked in weather that sent him seeking a heavy overcoat. He chose not to spend much time in their platform dwellings, raised on posts, where hundreds of curing fish hung in the rafters above a smoky central fire. He clearly preferred the Tunguse who lived farther inland, dark-skinned, nomadic hunters and trappers of Tartar origins, who used reindeer as their beasts of burden and who dressed in fur coats and skin pants.

Governor Furnhelm told them they would be best advised to travel after freezeup, which would occur between the end of September and the first of December. He suggested a roundabout route to Ayan, one that would take them far back behind the mountains but would assure them of easy travel along known trails and Russian post roads. Mahood disagreed: the telegraph, he said, must go as close as possible to the sea, so that supplies and materials could be brought upriver to the workmen. He decided that he and Bush would seek a more direct route, closer to the Okhotsk Sea, even though it might involve more hardship and danger.

He planned to lead the telegraph party some 50 miles along the north bank of the Amur as far as Lake Orel, then strike north to Oudskoi, on the Okhotsk Sea. The governor ordered a group of Tunguse to come to the end of Lake Orel with reindeer for the trip. He also ordered Yakov, a Cossack who spoke Tunguse and Yakout and who had travelled a great deal in the area, to accompany the explorers as far as Oudskoi, a month's journey away.

On October 21, Mahood, Bush, Swartz and Yakov started off on their explorations north, travelling by steamer along the river and then the lake. On October 26, reindeer and guides arrived at the far end of the lake.

Before they could set off on reindeer-back, Bush, Mahood and Swartz had to learn to ride the beasts. With their cow-like heads, narrow bodies, toes that struck together as they walked to produce a continuous rattle, slight legs and large antlers moulting long strings of bloody velvet, the reindeer seemed unlikely steeds to the Americans. They were much more practical than horses or dogs for prolonged winter travel, however, since they could forage through snow to find their own food, and their broad hooves spread as they walked, making it easier for them to move through snow and marsh.

Bush and Mahood spent some time learning how to deal with these creatures. Sled animals had one antler removed so they could be harnessed side by side. Riding animals usually had both antlers chopped off, since otherwise they could skewer the riders. The reindeer's backs were weak, so they bore both riders and packs on their shoulders. A saddle made of two buckskin pads stuffed with moss or hair and about a foot wide, joined by curved deerhorn links, was placed high on the animal's shoulders; there were no stirrups. A would-be rider took in his left hand his *polka*, a five-foot staff with a small loop fastened at one end to keep it from sinking into the snow. Placing his right hand on the saddle, he leapt into place, dividing his weight between his hands. On his first attempt, Swartz jumped completely over his deer; Mahood touched the saddle with his foot as he jumped, and his steed immediately moved ahead, leaving him sprawled in the snow; Bush failed to raise his leg high enough to reach the saddle and had to be lifted onto the deer by a native guide—all much to the amusement of the Gilak children who gathered around to see the strange sight.

Their next task was to stay aboard the loose-skinned deer. With each step, the saddle swayed alarmingly; unless the rider counterbalanced by swaying in the opposite direction, he headed for the ground. With some bravado, Mahood declared in his next report to Abasa that reindeer riding was "rather an agreeable means of locomotion, in many respects preferable to horseback riding."[2]

Their lessons finished, they rode off on October 26, falling off their new steeds about once every mile or so. The two Tunguse guides each led a dozen packed reindeer; each reindeer carried about 70 pounds of supplies and provisions packed in special reindeer-freighting boxes.

Mahood had decided that the most likely route for the telegraph line was overland across the tongue of land that projected into the Okhotsk Sea, then along the coast to the village of Ayan. He knew there were no roads, no government stations and few Russians living along his route, but expected little difficulty until he tackled the section beyond Ayan.

Winter set in quickly; in a matter of days the temperature dropped from 30° F. to −11° F. Bush welcomed the colder temperatures since they promised an end to the misery of man and beast slogging through icy swamps, with water up to their knees. On November 6, following closely along the coast, the group was halted by the Usal'gin River, 200 yards wide, 12 feet deep at low tide, "whose mad waters, aided by the retreating tide, were rushing furiously onward, winding through the barren plain, and carrying on its bosom large sheets of ice, crashing and grating together, and undermining the steep mud banks. Now and then tons' weight of this mud would fall in the seething tide, crushing the thin ice, and causing the stained waters to boil and foam like a cauldron."[3]

The guides hoped to meet natives nearby who might have a boat, but they found no one near the river. Unable to cross near the coast, they battled upriver 30 miles to a narrower stretch, where they built a raft to

*Reindeer in Siberia. (From Bush,* Reindeer, Dogs. . . . )

carry their cargo across, and swam their deer to the far bank. The Americans and their companions rode on, noting that barren stretches of land alternated with trees the right height and shape for telegraph poles. In his report, written later for Abasa, Mahood also described grasslands where cattle could be grazed, to supply beef for telegraph construction parties.

Now the group entered on the snow-covered barren tundra. The plains were dotted with lakes, each lake covered with innumerable leaf-like frost crystals standing two inches high "sparkling like a sea of gems"[4] that broke underfoot, making a sound like a thousand tiny bells. They joined up with a wandering group of four Tunguse; Bush tried to flirt with the girl and was much put out when she completely ignored him in favour of their Tunguse guide, a man Bush considered decidedly inferior in looks and sophistication. "No accounting for taste," he grumbled to his diary.[5]

In mid-November, after three weeks of their own company and that of nomadic natives, they eagerly sought a post of the Russian-American Company at the mouth of the Tugur River where they expected to find 30 employees and tons of supplies. They were disappointed: the small group of one-storey log buildings known as Captain Lindholm's whaling establishment lay deserted. For years, American, Russian and other whalers had harvested the Okhotsk Sea, killing so many whales that now few were left. The Russian-American Company came late to the slaughter; the company abandoned this and its other posts on the Okhotsk just a few years after they opened them. Only a few Yakout families remained at the Tugur, waiting for the countryside to freeze over so they could travel more easily to Nicolaevsk.

It was the first meeting between the Americans and the Yakouts, whom Mahood described as the Yankees of Siberia: traders who roved from their home territory farther west near Yakoutsk on the Lena River with their trinket-laden deer along the trails of eastern Siberia, trading for furs. Mahood was able to purchase some leftover beef, good skin clothing and warm furs from the families, but at costs five times those in Nicolaevsk.

The telegraph party had now surveyed and located a route for the line from the Amur to the Tugur and was ready to continue north towards Ayan. Steep-sided mountains descended to the sea north of the Tugur, forcing the Americans to choose a route that took them inland behind

*Yakout woman, (left) and Yakout man, (right). (From Bush,* Reindeer, Dogs. . . . )

the mountains. Their Tunguse guides from the Amur region, however, refused to continue. Each year, they hunted sables along the Amur; the thick furs provided a good portion of their year's income. Sable-hunting time approached, and the Tunguse could not be persuaded to remain with Bush, Mahood and Swartz. Bush did manage to catch up with a group of hunting Tunguse, from whom he purchased new deer to replace the ones that would return home with the guides.

Somewhat fearful but undeterred by the prospect of navigating through an unknown country without local guides, the three headed inland on snowshoes, leading deer packed with their supplies and equipment. These snowshoes, five feet long and ten inches wide, Bush described as very different from the Canadian variety; soled with sealskin or the hairy skin from deer or horse legs, they glided forward in the manner of skin-wrapped touring skis, but did not slip back on slopes. Even with snowshoes, it was hard walking: the men and deer either sank to their bellies in soft snow or slid down hard-packed slippery slopes. But the weather was calm, and they soon arrived at the Arla River, where they watched the Tunguse ice fishing, using long, funnel-shaped traps under the ice. En route, they stayed in the small Yakout split-log houses, peering out through the windows of ice mortared with a snow-water mix. At night, to protect their windows from the warm breath of the sleepers inside, the Yakout stuffed deerskin pillows against each icy slab.

## Siberia, 1865: North from the Amur

With just tea, sugar and beef left as provisions, they pushed across the hills back towards the coast, to the native village of Algasee. Here, they met their first sled dogs, and were able to replace their deer with dogs and to travel by sled rather than on foot and deer-back. The sleds, eight to ten feet long and made entirely of wood except for the rawhide lashings, were drawn by Eskimo dogs harnessed in a line to a seal thong. The driver had no whip, but used an *ostle*, a four-foot wooden staff with an iron spike at the end that he used alternately as a brake or as a missile to throw at lazy or disobedient dogs and pick up again as the sled flashed by.

They had now entered a region where wolves ran freely. The Yakout showed them the pens they used to capture wolves: a double circle of palisades, with a door in the outer ring and a deer tethered in the inner ring. The wolf, entering by the door, could run only in one direction; on completing the circle, he automatically pushed the entrance door closed and found himself trapped.

Two weeks out of the deserted whaling post, the men arrived by

*Oudskoi. (From Bush,* Reindeer, Dogs. . . . )

79

dogsled at Oudskoi, on the Okhotsk Sea coast. In the glory days of whaling, up to 70 whalers at a time had anchored at Oudskoi. Now, a solitary Russian supply steamer visited once or twice a year to deliver provisions to the governor who lived at Oudskoi and collect the *yasak*, the imperial tax on furs. Between visits, the local *ispravnik* and priest gambled and drank. Bush was not impressed by the Russian priesthood, repeating a Russian saying that "he is so great a rascal they cannot even make a priest of him."

Mahood, Bush and Swartz spent four weeks in Oudskoi, staying at the priest's house high on a bluff overlooking the river and waiting for new deer to be brought in for the rest of their journey. They were pressed into the social life of the town, like it or not, whirled around in marathon dances by calico-clad ladies, treated to horses' entrails at the *ispravnik's* table, forced into godparent duty for the *ispravnik's* new child and taught the art of sledding on snowshoes down the riverbank near the church.

They left for Ayan on December 20 with a new Cossack, Ivan, and sped onwards by the good wishes and multiple kisses of their hosts. They could not obtain dogs for this stage of the trip, so travelled once more with reindeer. They had great difficulty getting any Tunguse to accompany them, since no man in the village knew this route, but finally, by showing their compasses and insisting they could not possibly get lost, they persuaded two Tunguse to go along. They loaded the deer with their supplies and new provisions—tea, beef, sugar, *ukale* (dried fish), *sukarie* (black bread dried in small cakes), and a few pounds of milk frozen in bags, from which they could hack off and thaw pieces as required.

Almost immediately, wolves killed two deer, forcing the two Tunguse accompanying the party onto snowshoes. On December 24, their way along the coast blocked by steep mountains and sheer cliffs, they turned inland, working their way up the canyon of the Gerom River, dragging their deer across smooth ice that provided no foothold for the splay-toed animals. The deer were soon bruised and sore from their frequent falls. The men were forced to walk and run alongside the deer, pushing and shoving the animals onward.

The sweat ran from their faces, freezing their hoods and beards into a solid mass of ice. They could not slow down, for if their sweat cooled, it would freeze on their skins under their clothing. Bush sprained his ankle badly; the continuous walking meant continuous pain. One Tunguse guide suffered fearfully from legs swollen and covered in sores, a frozen chin and frozen toes. At least every 30 minutes, each man scratched his nose, to make sure it hadn't frozen.

They camped each night in whatever shelter they could find. Though the weather was severe, they did not neglect the purpose of their trip, and each night, they took out their document boxes and made notes on their day's journey. Bush described his own journalizing on December 24: "His thick glass inkstand is placed in the hot ashes, to keep the ink from freezing. He dips his pen in the ink, and proceeds to record some brilliant idea or incident in his journal; but in the midst of the sentence the ink thickens on his pen and refuses to make a mark, when he thrusts it into the blaze of the candle and thaws it out to complete the sentence."[6]

It was Bush's task, too, to keep a temperature record on their journey. He tried valiantly to record temperatures throughout the day, but soon found the constant battle against the land and the weather made this impossible. He brought out his thermometers, a small Fahrenheit and a large Reamur (a temperature scale now rarely used), only twice a day, in the morning and the evening. After Swartz stepped on and broke the Fahrenheit thermometer, he could record temperatures only in Reamur.

Now, in the last week of December, they were steadily ascending the Dzhugdzhur range, the divide between Okhotsk and Arctic waters. They made their painful way up one branch of a river, but were turned back by ice and steep cliffs, and had to cast around for a new route through the mountains. On December 30, they stood at the summit of a pass through the mountains, looking east to the Okhotsk or west to continental Russia. Bush described the scene:

> Here all signs of vegetation ceased, and we were confronted by a high barren ridge . . . the view from the top was grand, but our hearts failed us when we saw that the ridge dipped abruptly on the western slope, and disclosed a deep basin or gulch, beyond which was another range to be crossed. . . . We were standing on the summit of the highest range of mountains in Eastern Siberia, confronted by a deep, wild chasm, in which the large trees resembled straws. Back of us the gorge we had been following six

days wound its way for miles among lofty bald peaks, the dark woods thousands of feet below becoming more and more indistinct as the distance increased. On all sides towered still above us other peaks in their solemn majesty, while a silence that was deathlike hung over all.[7]

Then they began to descend again, down the ridge which was compacted with snow that made walking difficult for man and beast alike. Without guides, they had no real notion of where they were, where they were going or where they could route the telegraph line. The last day of 1865 found them casting about in the snow, seeking a route back to Ayan and the Okhotsk Sea.

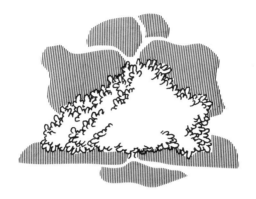

## CHAPTER 10

# Siberia, 1865: On to Gizhiga

An "inordinate quantity" of champagne poured down their gullets, followed by copious libations of every other drink available in Petropavlosk. The boat crew was reduced to happy imbecility, sang, blessed the Americans and fell overboard with regularity. Vushine hauled them back on board, rapped them on the head with a paddle, pushed the boat off sandbars, steered it down a middle course and kept the expedition from going literally in circles.

In this contented manner, Serge Abasa, George Kennan, the American trader Dodd, the Cossack Vushine and their native guides and boatmen set out on September 4, 1865, a week after their colleagues Mahood and Bush had left Petropavlosk for the Amur. Lacking any means of sea travel, Abasa planned to lead the group from Petropavlosk overland through the Kamchatkan peninsula to the north coast of the

Okhotsk Sea and the port of Gizhiga, which would become their head-quarters for telegraph exploration and construction north to the Anadyr River and south to the Amur River.

There was a cheerful unreality to the early days of this venture. Abasa, Kennan, Dodd and Vushine, with their hospitable Kamchatdal crewmen, sailed north up the centre of Kamchatka along the Avacha River by day, camping on the riverbank at night. The first morning en route, Kennan awoke from his bed of bearskins under a cotton tent to view the colossal snow-covered mountain peak of Koryakskaya crim-soning in the dawn, flanked by the neighbouring volcanic peak, Avacha. He waxed poetic, declaiming verse in the morning sun, but was brought sharply down to earth by Dodd, who summoned him to breakfast. His fit of poetic abandon was not over; as the party continued upriver, he described in his diary, fruit, flower and fauna, in terms such as those he gave to lilies, "downcast and mourning in funeral garb some unknown flowery bereavement."[1]

The group stopped for lunch that day at the Kamchatdal village of Okoota, in a log house chinked with moss and thatched with grass, looking out through windows made of translucent fish bladders

*Mounts Koryakskaya, Avacha and Koseldskai. (From Whymper,* Travel and Adventures. . . . )

stitched together with reindeer sinew. The governor at Petropavlosk had sent a special courier ahead of them, to tell the natives to stay home with their horses till the Americans arrived; at the village, the explorers mounted horses and rode away up the valley that stretched before them, singing "Bonnie Dundee." They dined that night at another native village, which Kennan named simply Jerusalem, on a pilgrim's feast of cold roast duck, reindeer tongues, blueberries and cream and wild-rose-petal jam.

"We had come to Kamchatka with our minds and mouths heroically made up for an unvarying diet of blubber, tallow candles and train-oil," wrote Kennan, but instead they were presented with celestial ambrosia made from an equal amount of white loaf sugar and alpine rose petals, with a little juice from crushed blueberries, all macerated together into a rich crimson paste. "Imagine yourself," he invited the reader, "feasting with the gods on the summit of high Olympus!"[2]

From Jerusalem, their trail led them into the foothills of the Sredinny Mountains that form the backbone of the Kamchatkan peninsula. At first, they rode through sunshine, birch and alders, crushing blueberries underfoot with every step, their only enemy the relentless mosquitoes. Then the road changed from grassy and beautiful to wet, precipitous and treacherous. The horses stumbled, the men were thrown onto rocks and into ravines, the boxes of supplies were smashed. Trail and weather improved again, and Kennan, the journey's main chronicler, who regularly plummeted into depression then swooped to exhilaration, again ascended to the heights of metaphor. He confided that his group now resembled a band of brigands, sweeping through the valleys on horse-back, Kennan adorned with a blue hunting shirt and red Turkish fez, Dodd with a scarlet and yellow handkerchief wound around his head, Vushine trailing a long streamer of crimson ribbon, all with rifles slung across their backs and revolvers belted around their waists. Just a few days into their overland journey, so little was left of Bulkley's uniformly attired military men that Kennan suggested "a timid tourist, meeting us as we galloped furiously across the plain. . . would have fallen on his knees and pulled out his purse without asking any unnecessary questions."[3]

When they reached the headwaters of the Kamchatka River, the group transferred once more to a boat, this time a raft softened with a six-inch layer of flowers and hay. As they floated downriver Kennan

*Riding near Mount Avacha. (From Bush,* Reindeer, Dogs. . . . )

once more grew lyrical. Perhaps if he had drifted down the Rhine or seen the Alps, he might not have been so overwhelmed, he wrote, but he had never seen such beauty as this.

The raft, made of three dugout canoes lashed together and covered over by a platform, floated by or stopped at a dozen Kamchatdal villages on its way north. By mid-September, as hoarfrost whitened the grass each morning, they had reached Klyuchi, a settlement founded by Russian peasants sent 6,000 miles from home.

Idyllic though most of the journey was, it was of little real use in locating a route for the telegraph line, for Kamchatka lay east of the Okhotsk Sea and the telegraph line was to be built along the north and west coasts. But Abasa had no swifter way of getting to Gizhiga this late

86

in the season, since the Okhotsk would already be freezing over and ships could not safely enter the sea. Although he tried to justify the Kamchatkan trip by reporting to Bulkley that they might be able to run the telegraph line through Kamchatka if the more natural route proved impossible, that seemed a highly unlikely eventuality. Abasa wanted to move as quickly as possible out of the peninsula and onto the Siberian mainland. From Klyuchi, he had two choices. He could continue down the Kamchatka River, then head north along the east coast of Kamchatka to Dranka and cross the neck of the peninsula where the mountains were lower. Or, despite the lateness of the season and the likelihood of blizzards and deep snow in the passes, he could try to go west across the mountains from Klyuchi to Tigil, on the Okhotsk Sea coast.

Impatient, he chose to cross to Tigil via the Yolovka River and the mountain passes. The travellers transferred to Kamchatdal canoes, which would be easier to paddle against the swift current of the river. The canoes were, however, so precise of balance and easy to capsize that, Dodd told Kennan, the natives who used them parted their hair in the middle to preserve equilibrium. The banter was part of a fast-developing friendship between Kennan, the enthusiastic 20-year-old adventurer, and Dodd, still in his 20s but a seasoned Siberian traveller.

At Yolovka, they switched once more to horses. Russian guide Nicolai Bragan led them into the mountains in a cold, driving rain, through tangled undergrowth and fallen trees, along narrow rock ledges where the pack horses frequently lost their footing and their loads or cut their legs. In one jump across a stream, Kennan was thrown, knocked unconscious and, his foot caught in the stirrup, dragged through the brush until the stirrup broke—with no injurious results except a loss of dignity.

By late afternoon, tired, cold and wet, the party reached the summit. Here they entered the tundra, tableland covered by wet spongy moss, and caught sight of a bear which they proceeded to hunt with enthusiasm though without success. "Hunting a bear with a Russian rifle is," noted Kennan, "a very pleasant and entirely harmless diversion. The animal has plenty of time, after the gun begins to fizzle, to eat a hearty dinner of blueberries, run fifteen miles across a range of mountains into a neighboring province, and get comfortably asleep in his hole before the deadly explosion takes place."[4]

Once across the mountains, the group floated downriver by raft to

Tigil, having travelled the 700 miles from Petropavlosk in 16 days. Kennan had few recollections other than those of champagne, cherry cordial, white rum and vodka, of this, the trading centre of the west coast and the winter rendezvous of the northern Chukchi and Korak tribes.

At Tigil, Abasa faced another decision. North of the town lay the Samanka mountain range; beyond the mountains, 300 miles of tundra stretched to the top of the Kamchatkan peninsula. It was now the end of September and between seasons: the first winter storms had invaded the mountains, and horses would have a weary time of it fighting their way north through the snow and wind. But the tundra was not yet frozen hard; if he wanted to move north by dogsled, he would have to wait another month. Caution suggested waiting, but Abasa wanted to meet up as soon as possible with the telegraph party presumably heading south from the Anadyr.

He devised a plan with a double thrust. Kennan, Vushine and six Kamchatdals would ride and lead 20 unloaded horses through the mountains. He and Dodd would take the group's heavy supplies by whaleboat along the coast. The two parties would rendezvous at Lesnaya, and set out together across the tundra.

At first, Kennan and Vushine had an easy time of it on the road north from Tigil. Soon, however, the road, better described as a trail, turned away from the coast and became a narrow rocky ledge. By the third day, a driving snowstorm whipped pellets of snow into the faces of man and horse. Kennan wanted to turn back, but he dared not. His orders were to continue and he thought he would never be able to convince the major that Anglo-Saxon blood was as good as Slavonic if he returned so soon.

In drifts up to their waists, their caps fringed with icicles and their clothes frozen, the group drove on. Finally, the guide was no longer able to force his horse into the storm. They must turn east away from the wind, into the wilderness of mountains. Within an hour, they were lost and wandering aimlessly. Convinced they faced death otherwise, Kennan determined to head west for the coast by compass direction alone, despite the guide's scepticism: how could a compass, that had never been in these mountains before, find its way to the coast when the guide could not?

The compass—aided by Kennan—knew the way. They reached the

sea and stood on a precipice 160 feet above its thundering waves. Kennan and Abasa had planned a system of flag messages and rendezvous along the coast. Kennan now led his group to the first of these planned rendezvous, at the mouth of the Samanka River on the Okhotsk Sea, where he had instructions to wait for two days. A gale blew up, and Vushine dropped a bombshell: they were eating the last of their provisions. He had brought only three days' food because he thought they would be meeting Abasa and the whaleboat within three days.

Kennan now could not wait for Abasa. Travelling back along the route they had just escaped was not a welcome prospect. Only one alternative remained: a dash along the narrow strip of beach at lowest tide 30 miles to where they could rejoin the trail along the coast. At worst, they would have to abandon the horses to the incoming tide and climb the cliffs to save themselves. In character as always, Kennan welcomed the dash, for "there was a recklessness about this proposal which made it very attractive when compared with wading laboriously through snowdrifts in frozen clothes without anything to eat."[5]

They took off at ten in the morning, galloping south through seaweed, shells and driftwood. Halfway along, they sighted a bear on the beach, and crept up upon it, only to discover, not a bear, but people: messengers from Abasa whose boats had been driven back to shore by the storm. They took the messengers on board their horses and galloped on, reaching the trail and beating the onrushing tide by a scant ten minutes.

By the next night, they had rejoined Abasa and Dodd in Tigil. Their first attempt to move north had failed. Their horses were disabled and their guide blind from inflammatory erysipelas caused by their days in the storm. Abasa himself was ill and beset by delirium brought on by a severe attack of rheumatic fever, which he blamed partly on overexertion and overexposure, partly on disappointment. Their only choice now was to obtain dogs to carry them overland and wait for freezeup.

The temperature dropped to −47° F. Abasa lay delirious in his bed. Kennan took refuge in the headman's log cabin, reading Shakespeare and the Bible, studying Russian, occasionally venturing out to go hunting (though with little success), and helping to make fur and skin clothing and bearskin sleeping bags for the journey ahead. Dodd and Vushine were sent back along the road for provisions and a doctor, and to hire dogs for the next part of the journey. Acquiring dogs proved to be a difficult task since a disease had killed off many of the natives' dogs and they did not want to part with those that were left. Late in October, a Russian doctor arrived to steam, bleed and blister Abasa. Perhaps fearing more of the same treatment, Abasa regained his feet and set about supervising construction of sleds and snowshoes. Shortly afterwards, Dodd returned with supplies and provisions, including tea, sugar, rum and tobacco, and Vushine succeeded in collecting 200 dogs, some from each village within a day's travel.

Abasa now planned to cross the same Samanka Mountains that Kennan had tackled without success. On November 1, the men put on their furs and set out again, with 16 sleds, 18 men, 200 dogs and 40 days' provisions. The weather was clear and cold now, and two feet of snow covered the trail and made for easy travelling. Two days later, they arrived at the first camp of the wandering Koraks, a reindeer-herding tribe that inhabited northern Kamchatka.

The Koraks immediately impressed Kennan with their tall athletic bodies and frank manner. The Koraks, who travelled across the tundra by dog team, herding up to 4,000 reindeer and carrying their conical tents with them, depended on reindeer for almost everything. They rode them and harnessed them to sleds. They used them for clothes and food, covered their tents with reindeer skin, used their sinews for thread, their bones for fuel, their skin for snowshoe covers and their bodies for sacrifices to the gods. Unlike the natives to the south encountered by Mahood and Bush, however, they did not drink reindeer milk, for reasons that Kennan could not discover.

At the first Korak camp, the four adventurers entered a tent through a 12-foot-long passage, to find a large smoky interior containing a number of *pologs*—fur-enclosed compartments warmed and lit by moss burning in bowls of seal oil. They were invited to sample *manyalla*, a staple Korak food made of clotted reindeer blood, tallow, half-digested moss from reindeer stomachs and dried grass, boiled and made into loaves, then frozen for use in camp or on the trail. As he listened to their drum beats and chanting, and watched them get "drunk" by eating a native mushroom, Kennan found it difficult to believe he was travelling in the nineteenth century, with its newspapers, railroads and telegraphs.

Once across the mountains, they sent their dogs home and switched to sleds drawn by reindeer to cross the tundra. On November 23, having crossed the 62nd parallel of latitude, the explorers reached Kamenoi, at the mouth of the Penzhina River and the head of the Kamchatka Peninsula. This area was home to settled Koraks, a group who aroused in them no admiration at all. These Koraks lived in hourglass-shaped driftwood houses known as *yourts*; visitors climbed up a pole on the outside, then slid down a pole on the inside into a round enclosure with a wooden platform and a central open spot where the fire was.

The settled Koraks were unco-operative, and Abasa complained about the lack of Russian control in the area, although he tempered his criticism with the realization that the local *ispravnik* would have neither the time nor the possibility of visiting one-hundredth of his enormous territory. Finally on what would probably be part of the telegraph route, the major wanted to hurry north to the Anadyr River, to make contact with the group he believed had been landed there by Bulkley. But the Koraks flatly refused to hire out their dogs to take him there; only under pressure from the *ispravnik* did they agree to take him west to Gizhiga.

This disappointment was followed by another. A Cossack who had been travelling in the north reported there was no news at all of any party of Americans landed near the Bering Strait. Swallowing his dismay that he had only four men to explore 2,000 miles of telegraph route, from the Amur River to Bering Strait, Abasa turned towards Gizhiga.

The men travelled now in *pavoskas*, long narrow sleds covered with sealskin and mounted on runners. Kennan likened riding in one to sitting in an eight-foot coffin with a bushel basket over his head. Their Korak drivers were surly and reckless; seven times in three hours, Kennan's *pavoska* was overturned, and he was dragged through the snow upside down. Abasa was not amused. He determined that when he returned with plenty of men to build the telegraph line, he would teach the Koraks a lesson. "The settled Koraks," Kennan declared, "are unquestionably the worst, ugliest, most brutal and degraded natives in all northeastern Siberia"[6]—a not uncommon response from explorers when the local natives found their own concerns more pressing than those of the explorers. Kennan did not entirely blame the Koraks, however; he suggested they had learned to lie, cheat and steal from the Russians and other traders.

On November 25, after three months' travel from Petropavlosk, the group arrived at Gizhiga. Grimy, smoky, long-haired, their skin frozen and peeled, covered with reindeer hair, they hung grimly to their sleds as the dogs careered up to the governor's house. With no news from Russia for 11 months, the *ispravnik* could not wait for them to wash and change. He hustled them into the house, to be told of the French invasion of Mexico, the murder of Lincoln and the American civil war. Then he sent them off to wash, shave and dress in their company uniforms.

The self-designated First Siberian Exploring Party returned to dine with the governor, between papered walls and curtained windows, on china and with silver. As appetizers they ate smoked fish, ryebread and caviar, and drank brandy; for dinner, the governor presented them with cabbage soup, salmon pie, venison cutlets, game, meat pies, pudding and pastry. The assortment of food and the formal occasion made them uneasy and happy to return to their quarters, toss off their uniforms and put on their travelling clothes, to sit crosslegged on bearskins on the floor and light up their pipes.

Abasa had now been away from San Francisco for five months, and had yet to see for himself a single mile of the proposed line route. He had no supplies or provisions, and above all, no news from the com-

*Gizhiga. (From Bush,* Reindeer, Dogs. . . . )

pany. He could only hope for co-operation from the natives and the Russians of Siberia, and exhort his men to do their best.

The proposed telegraph route between the Amur and the Anadyr rivers consisted of three approximately equal sections: the Amur to Okhotsk section being explored by Mahood and Bush; the route from Gizhiga west and south to Okhotsk, which Abasa and Vushine would now explore; and the route north from Gizhiga to Anadyrsk, a collection of four Russian villages halfway between Kamenoi and the mouth of the Anadyr River. This last section he felt would give the fewest difficulties; to it, he dispatched Kennan and Dodd.

Since Abasa now believed that no exploring party had been landed at the mouth of the Anadyr, and since the country from the river mouth to Anadyrsk was desolate and unknown to Russian and American alike, he decided to leave it unexplored for this winter season.

Abasa could get little information about the country between Gizhiga and Okhotsk. "In winter," he wrote in a report to Bulkley, "the intercourse between Ghijiga and Okhotsk is very limited. The yearly mail and a dozen of sleighs with goods for some trader, are the only passengers over the distance. You may easily imagine, that there can be no regular road; travellers follow no track, but go in certain directions, guided by the environing mountains, streams, roads etc. Snowstorms, or a foggy atmosphere, conceal the signs by which a traveller is accustomed to find his way, and force him to remain stationary for days, and even weeks. A compass cannot be of much use in this mountainous country, where a false step, or a team of dogs becoming unmanageable, can lead to fatal consequences.

"Such a travel is certainly not without danger, especially as all means for making the road more practicable have been neglected through the carelessness of the inhabitants, who themselves know but little about the country, when forty or fifty versts [the Russian verst is slightly more than three-fifths of a mile in length] from their home."[7]

Half by force and half by persuasion, Abasa acquired two dog teams and set off with Vushine and native helpers for Okhotsk on December 17. To the best of his ability, he explored each route along which the telegraph line might be strung. Combining information he gathered by observation on his travels with information he obtained from Russian officials, Cossacks and natives, he made recommendations as he went about the best route. Above all, he wanted to avoid mountains and thickly wooded regions. He assessed the character of the country in different seasons, and evaluated accessibility for delivery of materials and supplies and possible modes of transport. He was particularly careful to check on the amount each river rose in the spring, noting that the Russian line along the Amur had been damaged repeatedly by spring floods. The end of 1865 found him somewhere en route between Gizhiga and Okhotsk.

Kennan and Dodd left Gizhiga by dogsled on December 13, in a tumult of howling dogs and shouting men, to follow the regular sled route—called a winter road, but in fact just a track along a route known to natives and Cossacks—to Anadyrsk. With them went a Cossack guide-interpreter, a Russian cook and a number of natives.

Winter had set in in earnest. They travelled during the three hours of daylight and under a moon that shed its blue light on the "great snowy Sahara", where mirages of tropical lake and oriental city rose on the boundless, treeless snow. Each night they built a Siberian half-faced camp, drawing three sleds into a semi-enclosure ten feet square, with one open side. The snow was shovelled out of the interior, and banked around the three sides. A roaring fire was built on the open side, the ground covered with four inches of willow or alder twigs, then with bearskins laid down before the fire. Man and dog alike ate dried fish; the men drank tea and contemplated the stars and blue streamers of the *aurora borealis*, while the dogs howled with an unearthly clamour half the night.

At Shestakova, a Korak village, the Gizhiga men and dogs returned home, and the explorers waited in a *yourt* through a howling snowstorm for fresh dogs that were to be sent to them from Penzhina, a village to the north. A Russian Cossack arrived first, having spent 39 days travelling from Petropavlosk, carrying letters for Abasa from Bulkley, who had touched at Petropavlosk on his journeys around the Pacific rim. Kennan restrained his curiosity and didn't open them, then regretted his restraint as the messenger dwindled in the distance. On December 22, sleds arrived from Penzhina together with news at last of an American party at the mouth of the Anadyr. The news, passed by bands of wandering Chukchi, said the Americans were building a shelter and planning to stay the winter.

Dodd and Kennan agreed that they must try at all cost to find the party as soon as possible. "We could hardly believe that Colonel Bulkley

*A dog team. (From Bush,* Reindeer, Dogs. . . . )

had landed an exploring party in the desolate regions south of Behring's Straits, at the very beginning of an Arctic winter; but what could Americans be doing there, if they did not belong to our expedition," he asked. Though no one had ever travelled to the mouth of the Anadyr in winter before, they were intrigued by "an adventure just novel and hazardous enough to be interesting."[8]

They packed up their tobacco, provisions, tea, sugar and trade goods on their sleds and hurried north over the great barren steppe that lay between the Aklan River and Anadyrsk, through storm and snow. Viewing the broad expanse broken only by stunted trees and the gnarled dwarf trunks of trailing pine, Kennan was struck by an increasing sense of desolation. "I had come to Siberia with full confidence in the success of the Russo-American telegraph line," he wrote, "but as I penetrated deeper and deeper into the country and saw its utter desolation, I grew less and less sanguine. Since leaving Gizhiga, we had travelled 300 versts and had found only four places where we could obtain poles and had passed only three settlements. Unless we could find a better route than the one over which we had been, I feared the Siberian telegraph line would be a failure."[9] On Christmas Day, unremarked by the travellers, a severe *poorga*, or Siberian storm, set in. The party massed the sleds together and huddled in their fur bags. Wrote Kennan:

> There is nothing so thoroughly, hopelessly dreary and uncomfortable as camping out on a Siberian steppe in a storm. The wind blows with such violence that a tent cannot possibly be made to stand; the fire is half buried by drifting snow; and fills the eyes with smoke and cinders when it burns at all; conversation impossible on account of the roaring of the wind, and the beating of snow in one's face; bearskins, pillows, and furs become stiff and icy with half-melted sleet, sleds are buried up, and there remains nothing for the unhappy traveller to do but crawl into his sleeping bag, cover up his head and shiver away the long dismal hours.[10]

The storm abated after two days and, out of dogfood, they hurried on again on December 28. Now they entered thick forest and soon lost any sense of direction. More by luck than by skill they found their way to Penzhina, a little collection of log houses and flat-topped native *yourts* halfway between the Okhotsk Sea and Anadyrsk. There, they spent the last three days of 1865, trying to explain to the natives what a telegraph line was, and engaging men to cut wooden poles 22 feet tall and five inches in diameter at the top. Their explanations fell upon uncomprehending ears: some thought the crazy Americans were trying to build a wooden road for summer travel, others suggested a huge house. The lack of comprehension was demonstrated when Kennan returned later: the natives had cut poles at least 12 inches in diameter and so heavy a dozen men could not lift one. After all, they explained, if the Americans were going to build a road high atop rows of wooden poles, they would need timbers at least this large.

As the year closed out at −53° F., Kennan found himself pondering past and present: his last New Year's Eve had been spent on muleback, riding through magnificent tropical forest from Lake Nicaragua to the Pacific coast. He could not imagine a greater contrast between that scene and this frozen, barren, endless steppe. Yet though their eyelids froze together as they drank their tea, their fur coats were covered with rime just a few feet from the fire, tin plates and spoons burned their hands, and it was a race to eat their soup before it froze to the plate, they were not downcast. In fact, Kennan and Dodd sat by the fire for two hours experimenting to see what effect the intense cold had on themselves and their possessions. Their only real problem, Kennan reported, was cold feet, for it is not Arctic cold that kills but wind, fatigue, perspiration that freezes on the skin and hunger. From these they did not suffer.

## CHAPTER 11

# Siberia, 1865: On the Anadyr

Abasa and his men left San Francisco in July 1865, to explore and plan the telegraph route from the Amur along the Okhotsk Sea and north toward Anadyrsk. Abasa expected that a second group of telegraph explorers would make its way south and west from the mouth of the Anadyr to complete the Siberian route. Once he left San Francisco, however, Abasa had no way of knowing what was happening far to the north.

Perhaps it was better for his peace of mind that he did not know. In July, Bulkley had dispatched Collins L. (Mac) Macrae and his men—Lieutenants A.S. Arnold and Alex Harder, and Mssrs. Robinson, Smith and Davis—from San Francisco aboard a company ship to Sitka, the expedition's marshalling point in Russian America. On August 19, orders arrived at Sitka from Colonel Bulkley aboard another company ship, instructing Macrae to get his group outfitted from company stores at Sitka and board the *Milton Badger*, bound for the mouth of the Anadyr.

Macrae was perhaps not the most forceful of leaders. His woes began almost at once, on the day before his party was to sail. He complained in his report to Bulkley that he was not permitted to outfit his party himself, but had to abide by the decisions of Colonel William B. Hyde, the telegraph company officer in command at Sitka, who refused to give him proper supplies. He would not, grumbled Macrae, even supply a tent, although there were many available for that specific purpose, "thinking instead that some worthless tent covers were sufficient."[1] Hyde's side of the story has not survived.

On August 21, the six men sailed on the schooner *Milton Badger*, meeting the *Golden Gate*, commanded by Captain Scammon, on September 6 at the Ounismak passage of the Aleutians. Macrae understood that if there were no native transport available for the men at the mouth of the Anadyr, the *Badger* was to take the group to Kamchatka. He asked Scammon, officer in charge of the company's fleet, to confirm Bulkley's orders. Scammon, later to be scuppered for severe alcoholism, refused. Macrae was left no option but to land at the Anadyr mouth whether or not any transport was available to take him and his men upriver.

The ship anchored at Anadyr Bay on September 20. The explorers disembarked with their supplies and faced the prospect that they might have to spend the winter at this desolate spot. According to Macrae, Captain Harding of the *Badger* refused to give them any materials to build a shelter, finally parting reluctantly with enough boards for a roof and allowing Macrae to purchase a stove from the company. The *Badger* departed, and the men set to work building a shelter. They dug a pit five feet deep, nine feet by 18, piled an embankment of sod and earth around the pit to insulate it, and roofed it with the boards and driftlogs, interweaving them with branches of trailing pine. Here, they had the help of Cook, Robinson's shaggy black Newfoundland dog, the "dog of the expedition"; Cook was put to work hauling logs from the riverbank. They also built a long tunnelway of sod, to keep the cold out when they entered or left their snug abode.

On October 2, Bulkley arrived on board the steamer *Wright*; he left again on October 13, taking Davis with him, the steamer forced out to sea by ice that was rapidly stretching out from the land. Bulkley, at least, seemed to have no fears for his men, in their makeshift encampment several hundred miles from the nearest village.

By November 1, there was enough snow for sledging, but no amount of pleading on Macrae's part could persuade the wandering Chukchi who crossed the river with their reindeer near the camp to take the party to Anadyrsk. Never heard of the place, they told him by signs, although they had marriage certificates naming Anadyrsk as the place of marriage; can't understand you; can't sell our reindeer because we need them. Macrae was able to trade tobacco, beads and needles for reindeer meat and skin clothing.

Macrae was forced to wait for O-Cargo-Cray, a Chukchi who had passed by soon after the explorers landed and promised to return to take the group to Anadyrsk. Not by nature patient, Macrae set out with Robinson one day to try to find the Chukchi at his camp 25 miles away. When they arrived at the camp, they found it deserted and silent. They turned around immediately and headed for their own camp, now travelling in the dark and plagued by intense cold. Returning was a long desperate struggle, not improved by a moment of black comedy when they finally arrived and Cook, not recognizing his master, refused to let the men into the tunnel. At length, the men inside heard the returning wanderers and called Cook off guard duty. Both Macrae and Robinson suffered from their 23-hour non-stop trip; Robinson was in bed for three weeks, recovering.

When O-Cargo-Cray finally arrived, he said he could not take the group to Anadyrsk: his reindeer were too small to carry an extra five men and their supplies. Macrae must send the Great Deer Chief a gun and some tobacco, and the chief would send reindeer and sleds in a month. Though he suspected he was being gulled, Macrae saw no choice. He gave O-Cargo-Cray a gun and sent him off with a rifle for the chief. Macrae and his men settled in to wait in the −50° F. weather. By December 31, 1865, there was still no news.

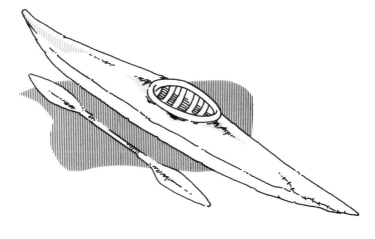

## CHAPTER 12

# Russian America, 1865: Stalemate

Facing Siberia across the Bering Strait lay another Arctic territory, its dangers and configuration all but unknown to the men of the telegraph expedition. The Western Union Extension Company planned to link Siberia to Russian America by cable under the Bering Strait, between Cape Prince of Wales on the North American side and Provideniya on the Asian. From Cape Prince of Wales, the telegraph poles would lead across Russian America to the Yukon River and thence south to the line rapidly snaking north through British Columbia.

A certain amount was known about the territory the line would traverse. Since the late 1700s, Russia had owned, and the Russian-American Company had controlled, the land from the Bering Strait south to Sitka. The Russian trading company had established trading posts, missions and schools along the coast and for a little distance inland on the major rivers. The company maintained a healthy trade with the native Indians and Inuit of the region and company ships visited the posts of St. Michaels and Sitka every year. Between 1841 and 1843, Russian naval lieutenant Lavrentii Zagoskin had explored and mapped the Yukon River between Fort Yukon and the sea.

Whalers and traders from the United States, Russia and other nations sailed the northern seas near the Bering Strait, and American, British and Russian naval officers had prepared charts and maps of the seacoast and ocean. Perry McDonough Collins had been involved in an ambitious though unsuccessful venture to export ice from Sitka to California, to compete with ice supplied from Boston around the Horn. In the 1840s, the traders of the Hudson's Bay Company had ventured west to build the posts of Fort Selkirk and Fort Yukon on the Yukon River, and every year H.B.C. brigades came and went overland east and south with furs, provisions and trade goods.

Knowing that Russian, American and British explorers travelled with relative ease in this land filled the organizers of the telegraph expedition with great expectations of rapid progress. On July 10, 1865, the telegraph explorers bound for Russian America sailed from San Francisco aboard the flagship of the expedition, the barque *Golden Gate*, and the company steamer *George S. Wright*. In charge of the party was Robert Kennicott; among his company were George Adams, the young man who bribed and persuaded his way into the expedition, his friend Fred Smith, and William Ennis.

Robert Kennicott had achieved much while still very young. Never-defined "ill health" prevented his going to school as a child, so he studied at his Illinois home and developed a great love of natural science. By the age of 17 he was in Cleveland studying natural history. At 18, he set off on a month-long collecting trip that took him to Pembina on the Red River, in British North America. By 1855, barely 20 years of age, he was well regarded as a naturalist in Illinois and had started the Museum of Natural History at Northwestern University in Chicago. He spent a year at the Smithsonian, then left in 1859 on a three-year expedition to British and Russian America, travelling with the Hudson's Bay brigade canoes across the north, collecting specimens and making notes on the natural history of the north. Wherever he went, he talked about the importance of natural history and science, showing the traders of the Hudson's Bay Company how to prepare birdskins and collect specimens. All those who knew him praised his energy and enthusiasm. For ten years after his trip, H.B.C. men continued to send specimens back to the Smithsonian.

When Bulkley sought someone who could lead the expedition through Russian America, friends and mentors of Kennicott immediately suggested the young man, then working for the Academy of Science Museum in Chicago. The job was offered and accepted. Kennicott asked only that he be allowed to hire assistants who would collect specimens en route; his group of six scientists and a volunteer assistant became known as the Scientific Corps of the expedition.

In the summer of 1865, Bulkley was more concerned with getting the Russian-American part of the expedition underway than with collecting scientific specimens. He left San Francisco aboard the *Wright*; Kennicott and his party were aboard the *Golden Gate*. The *Wright* towed the *Golden Gate* from harbour, then the two vessels headed north separately, the *Wright* bound en route for Victoria, the *Gate* for Sitka direct. At Victoria, Bulkley met Frederick Whymper, a young English artist who had arrived on Vancouver Island three years earlier, drawn by the excitement of the gold rush and impelled by his own surplus energy. Whymper immediately volunteered to join the expedition, and was just as quickly hired by Bulkley. "Doubtless Colonel Bulkley's preference for youth, activity, and 'go'," suggested Whymper, "is that of Americans generally. . . . In England, I have sometimes thought that youth was considered more of a crime than a recommendation, and that you were nowhere until you had—like an old port—acquired 'body' and 'age'!"[1]

The men on the *Gate* spent their time reading, smoking, card playing, drilling and eating. Ennis, the one expedition member aboard with wide experience in sea travel, was not altogether impressed, noting that they ate hash three times a day, bread with butter that had a tendency to "perform maneuvres over the table . . . [and] raw onions a delectable lunch about midnight."[2] They saw no land for 23 days, finally sighting the Queen Charlotte Islands off the starboard bow early in August. On August 10, they arrived at Sitka, the southernmost post of the Russian-American Company, on what is now known as the Alaskan Panhandle, pulling into harbour two days after the *Wright*.

Sitka, headquarters of the 21 North American fur-trading stations of the Russian-American Company, was a welcome haven for the seabound voyagers. Its bright yellow houses topped with red sheet-iron roofs, the green dome of the Orthodox church, the hulks of old vessels lying along the rocks at water's edge and the old fur-company buildings gave Sitka "an original, foreign, and fossilized kind of appearance."[3] Above the town rose thickly wooded hills, surmounted by snow-capped peaks. Though he liked Sitka's looks, Whymper scorned its climate, "the most rainy place in the world. Rain ceases only when there is good promise of snow. Warm sunny weather is invariably accompanied by the prevalence of fever and pulmonary complaints, and rheumatism is looked upon as an inevitable concomitant to a residence in the settlement."[4]

Though the governor was away, the 800 residents of Sitka gave the expedition a rousing welcome. The Russians introduced the Americans to the custom of "15 drops", usually a half tumbler of anything from good cognac to raw, fiery vodka, to be tossed down at a single gulp. Refusal would insult the host; the only respite was the innumerable cups of "chai"—Russian tea poured from the omnipresent *samovar*. Ennis, for one, was sorry to leave Sitka, saying goodbye with gratitude and regret to his "lady friends Madame I.A.K. and M."[5]

*Sitka. (From Whymper,* Travel and Adventures. . . . )

# Russian America, 1865: Stalemate

The two ships and the men of the expedition remained at Sitka while Bulkley collected information about the Yukon River and the Anadyr across the Bering Sea in Siberia, and made plans for his exploring parties on the Yukon and the Anadyr. On August 22, Bulkley, Whymper and Kennicott and his men left harbour, the *Gate* once more under tow by the *Wright*. The hawser joining the two ships broke on August 31, and they drew apart under cover of heavy fog. The next morning, a wild storm broke over the *Gate* and the steward's boy shouted an alarm: "Breakers ahead!" Wind and waves threw the ship towards the rocks. Ennis, who had been at sea for five years, had never seen danger to equal this. Captain Scammon set all hands to the sails and the *Gate*, "Gallant craft as she is",[6] came about just in time to avoid shipwreck.

How had the *Wright* fared in the violence of the storm? Scammon feared the smaller ship must have been sunk. When he rounded the tip of the peninsula into Norton Sound and caught up with the company schooner *Milton Badger*, en route for the western shores of the Bering Strait, Scammon ordered the *Badger* to the Aleutian Islands in search of the *Wright* or news of her. But when the *Gate* sailed into harbour at St. Michaels in Norton Sound, they found the *Wright* safely anchored, having survived the storm.

As natives paddled their skin boats around the two ships and watched the unloading of men and supplies with avid curiosity, Ennis viewed the scene before him with some amusement, noting that two years before he had been in sunny France.

St. Michaels was no Paris. Located on a small island just offshore in the sound, the fort, known as the redoubt, was the principal trading station for the Russian-American Company and its main base for explorations along the coast and inland. Founded in 1833, it resembled a Hudson's Bay post, with its picket walls and bastions enclosing dwellings and storehouses. Walls and buildings alike were constructed from the vast quantity of spruce driftwood carried down to the sea each year by the Yukon and Kuskokwim rivers. The Russians stacked the wood along the mainland shore each fall and carried it to the island by dogsled over the ice in winter, to remedy the total lack of wood for fuel and building on the island and nearby shores.

Unlike the men of the telegraph expedition, the Russian labourers at the redoubt were not there by choice; they were convicts serving their term in American exile. Most married "after the fashion of the country", and produced mixed-race children known as Creoles. The children were usually taken from their parents, educated at Sitka and entered in the service of the company. After a number of years, they could choose whether or not to continue working for the company. The average workman for the Russian-American Company was paid 50 pounds of flour, a pound of tea and three pounds of sugar a month, plus about 20 cents a day.

The crews of the *Wright* and *Golden Gate* and the expedition members who were to stay in Russian America unloaded provisions and supplies here, for later transport into the interior. They also disembarked a small steamer, the *Lizzie Horner*, which was to carry Kennicott and expedition members upriver to Fort Yukon, which the Russian explorer Zagoskin had termed the head of navigation on the river.

By September 26, the *Gate* and the *Wright* had both departed for Plover Bay, on the Siberian side of Bering Strait. The expedition engineer, Green by name, began to put the *Lizzie Horner* into working order, only to discover he had left one of the most important engine pipes on board the *Clara Bell* at Sitka. The Russian blacksmith at St. Michaels made a substitute from copper, but no amount of tinkering produced a head of steam sufficient to set the ship in motion. The *Horner* was useless. Kennicott's men could not travel upriver by steamer.

*St. Michaels redoubt. (From Dall,* Alaska and. . . . )

The failure of the *Lizzie Horner*—and of the engineer Green, who proved incompetent—was a major blow for Kennicott. If he could have reached Fort Yukon before the river had frozen, he could have moved south by dogsled in January and February and, with a moderate amount of luck, met the teams moving north from British Columbia early in spring. A second party commanded by Ennis was to seek a telegraph route west to Bering Strait. If both the explorations had been successful, the entire route of the line from Bering Strait to New Westminster would have been charted.

Without a steamer, the plan was doomed. Though Kennicott could get small skin boats from the Inuit who lived along the coast, the group could not possibly paddle to Fort Yukon before freezeup. Casting about for an alternative plan, Kennicott decided that he would try and get his supplies as far upriver as possible, to somewhere that would serve as a winter base for an assault upon the river. He and his men would take the supplies from St. Michaels to Unalakleet, a small post on the shore of Norton Sound. From Unalakleet, they could follow the winter route the Russians took to Nulato, their post on the Yukon River. From St. Michaels to Nulato along the twisting course of the Yukon River from its mouth on Norton Sound was 700 miles; the route overland from Unalakleet to Nulato was just 200 miles long.

Kennicott borrowed the Russian camp boat, a peculiar wooden craft 40 feet long and 30 feet wide, with two masts and ten oars, to convey some of the men and supplies to Unalakleet. Kennicott and the rest of the men travelled in large, open, wood-framed, sealskin-covered, flat-bottomed boats known by the Russians as *baidaras* and by the Inuit as *oomiaks*. They rowed, sailed and tracked by line along the shore of the sound through cold and swirling snow, arriving at Unalakleet, a distance of 60 miles, after three days.

Not at all sure where his best course of action lay, Kennicott temporized by sending out various parties in search of provisions and sled dogs. George Adams was dispatched to explore up the Unalakleet River to see if he could buy dogs, fish for dogfood, reindeer meat, sleds and skin boots for the men. Adams, clad in his newly acquired reindeer-skin coat and sealskin boots lined with a layer of hay, set out upriver October 2 with an Indian and a Russian companion, in a three-holed sealskin kayak called a *bidarka*, paddling, writing notes and trying to learn some words of Russian. The following day, ice began to spread

*A* baidara, *(top) and a* bidarka, *(bottom). (From Dall,* Alaska and. . . . )

from the banks of the river and they put on speed lest they be frozen in and have to walk back. Poling, tracking and paddling upriver, they reached an Indian village that same day. The next morning, Adams donned his uniform coat, a large red sash and a fancy rosette and went to trade his needles and tobacco with the natives. Persuaded by either the togs or the trade goods, the natives sold him a boatload of dried salmon for dogfood and the group headed back downriver.

They thought they had beaten the ice, but three miles above Unalakleet, the river closed in on them, and they were forced to haul *bidarka* and supplies alike home over the snow and ice.

Two weeks later, Adams and Smith set out once more along the river and across the neighbouring mountains, seeking provisions and dogfood. Adams was impressed with his native Indian companions, who packed a hundred pounds compared to his light load of pistol and rifle, yet regularly outdistanced him. On occasion, they also carried Adams and Smith through the icy water of streams that had not yet frozen. On October 22, Adams ate reindeer, watched the natives dance and wrote in his diary to his family back in San Francisco, "You are all at church. How I wish I were with you."[7]

They continued overland, staying in the smoky subterranean mound houses of the natives, or in tents when the smoke proved too much for them. Adams wrote his diary by the light of a bowl of oil, with a strip of cloth dangling over the edge as a wick. Indians at one village provided them with a breakfast of fish and reindeer meat, supplemented by expedition tea, and traded them 300 pounds of speckled trout.

Several days later, Kennicott caught up with them, and together they pushed overland towards the Yukon River and Nulato. Their native guides had returned home, and now they carried their own packs through increasingly cold days. On a night when the temperature dropped to −16° F., Smith remarked that "he should not wonder if cool weather could set in soon."[8] Kennicott was not impressed with their Russian guide, who seemed stubborn and unhelpful. "Hacherine was saucy," Adams remarked cryptically. "The major played ball with H's head, using an axe handle for a bat. This did Mr. Russian good."[9]

Their food ran low and their spirits dropped with the temperature. On November 8, they took "a light breakfast on the recollection of what we had eaten the day before." The next day, they arrived at Nulato with their cheeks, noses and hands frozen. The commander at the Russian post served them up "the best meal I have ever eaten—salt fish raw, black bread, tea and white sugar."[10] Adams gulped down 15 cups of tea.

Nulato was the farthest inland, most northerly Russian post on the river, about 700 miles west of Fort Yukon. On the north bank of the river, on flat land near the mouth of the Nulato River, it was composed of the by-now familiar picket-log square, guarding log buildings inside. Inside the buildings, the men slept on platforms two feet above the ground, and looked out into the day-long gloom of an Arctic winter through seal-gut windows.

*The fort at Nulato. (From Dall,* Alaska and. . . . *)*

Stored in buildings at the fort were enough provisions to last the half-dozen employees of the Russian-American Company through the winter. As Kennicott had discovered on his way to Nulato, the expedition could not rely on the country or on its inhabitants for food. Nor were there sufficient supplies at Nulato to sustain the telegraph party over the winter. The only option Kennicott could see was to put the explorations for a telegraph route on hold and to spend the winter bringing provisions from Unalakleet to Nulato. Kennicott headed back for Unalakleet November 15, expecting to be away for 40 days. Though he had no idea how they would accomplish their task, he instructed Adams, Smith and a third expedition member to explore on or near the proposed telegraph route from Koyukuk, a small native village above Nulato, westward toward Norton Bay, then southward toward the Yukon mouth. "I do not see how you can do any good by staying here," he told them, "but I leave you here for the bare chance."[11]

*Nulato and the Yukon River. (From Dall,* Alaska and. . . . )

Kennicott headed west and Adams northeast, though he had been told the natives at Koyukuk were starving and in no mood to welcome strangers. For reasons undisclosed but presumably on the advice of others, he left behind his warm skin clothing and moved out into −32° F. weather clad only in a thin coat and clothing full of holes and with only a blanket to sleep in. The cold forced him to rise every hour in the night to drink hot tea and keep himself from freezing to death. Bitterly, he wrote in his diary that henceforth he would take his own counsel on what to wear on his travels.

He discovered, as expected, that it was far too early to travel into the mountains, for there was not nearly enough snow cover to permit the use of dogs. A letter awaited him on his return to Nulato; Kennicott said he now planned to leave from Unalakleet for Fort Yukon on February 1. Adams started out for Norton Sound, a trip that he was told would take him 30 days now or ten days in March when snow conditions had improved. Without a guide, he was soon lost and turned back to Nulato. Just days after his return, the Russian commander of the post died. Adams' sorrow was practical in nature, for the commander had promised he would obtain proper winter clothing for him, a promise that now could not be kept. He decided to return to Unalakleet, but without a guide, interpreter or proper clothing, he was forced once more to abandon the effort.

Undaunted, he made a third attempt, with Smith. Halfway along the trail, they broke their axe handle, and could no longer even chop wood for a fire. Worn down by cold, fatigue and misadventure, they registered themselves "completely disgusted with everything",[12] a state of mind that changed rapidly when they met a group from the telegraph party who fed them coffee, sugar, soup, reindeer meat and pancakes. They completed their oft-attempted journey to Unalakleet on December 23.

The rest of the expedition party had not been idle. William Ennis, in charge of explorations west from the head of Norton Bay to the Bering Strait, had left Unalakleet on December 2 with two sleds, three expedition members and two Russians. The first two days, he travelled over good winter roads and stayed at Inuit villages. He was frustrated at his first stop and forced to lay over a day, because an important festival put a stop to any work or trading, and Ennis had to wait to get new sled runners and dogfood. Fish was becoming increasingly scarce; Ennis visited a second Inuit village, but found few fish and a festival once more in progress. Annoyed at the delay and high prices, he continued on, but found a third village deserted after 13 years of sickness and death.

Inuit and Indians he talked to on his route told him that the rivers between Golovin Sound and Grantley Harbor on the Bering Strait were not navigable even by skin boats. Intending to check this information, Ennis was halted by a gale so fierce that with seven dogs pulling and five men pushing, the sleds could make no headway. Out of dogfood and exceedingly discouraged, the group returned to Unalakleet.

Ennis reported to Kennicott that the territory he had been able to cover was very suitable for telegraphic purposes. It was moderately level with wood and water available, though there were no trees of a size sufficient for telegraph poles. He had been unable to penetrate farther west than the shores of Norton Bay but thought the country between the bay and the Bering Strait would be similar to that around Norton Bay. He had no idea about the territory between the bay and Nulato, since, lacking guides, information and dogfood, he had been unable to travel east. Perhaps, he suggested, in the spring men could be sent to Nulato, then north up the Koyukuk River and west across the mountains to a spot where provisions could be cached for later exploration and construction parties.

In March or April, men could go by dogsled west from Norton Bay towards Grantley Harbor and hope that they would be able to obtain sufficient dogfood. Alternatively, they could wait for open water and hope that the rivers were navigable.

We have done our best, he reported to Kennicott, and have gathered what information we can. One of his group had been so worn out by the trip that he had lain down on the sled and cried. Another who had been sent to St. Michaels was so badly frozen that he would have died had a Russian not rescued him and brought him to the fort. Ennis concluded that he was greatly disgusted with the Arctic.

Though Kennicott did not commit his feelings to paper, it is more than likely that he agreed. Close to a year from the time he arrived in San Francisco and four months after his arrival at St. Michaels, the Russian-American section of the telegraph expedition had accomplished very little.

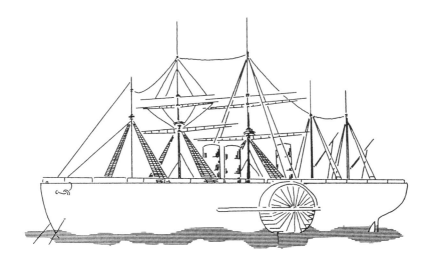

## CHAPTER 13

# Around the Pacific Rim

Every member of the land parties, be he in British Columbia, Russian America or Siberia, had harsh words for the overall organization of the telegraph expedition. Yet one look at a map of the North Pacific showed the enormity of the task that faced Colonel Charles Bulkley. From his base in San Francisco, he must ferry men, telegraph supplies and provisions to widely separated camps along some 3,500 miles of largely uninhabited coastline. At the same time, he must assess the progress being made in each region, decide what was most needed and when, make reports to his company headquarters in New York, arrange for the purchase of all necessary materials in either San Francisco or New York and assume overall direction of a steadily growing fleet of ships. The greatest irony of the project was that the very telegraph the men were building would have aided Bulkley immeasurably, for messages and requests took from a month to a year to reach Bulkley, by company ship or overland with fur traders, missionaries, Cossacks or natives.

Bulkley started well. By the early months of 1865, work had begun in British Columbia, most of the company ships loaded with telegraph supplies had made the long journey round the Horn to San Francisco, and key men had been appointed to supervise the exploration and construction parties in British Columbia, Russian America and Siberia. Bulkley set up an office in San Francisco, and left his men in charge of acquiring provisions and filling out the crews. Bulkley himself set out on a reconnaissance of the North Pacific aboard the *U.S.S. Shubrick*, loaned to the expedition by the American navy, Captain Charles R. Scammon commanding.

On this trip, he decided on the main supply bases for the expedition: Victoria and New Westminster for British Columbia; St. Michaels on Norton Sound and Port Clarence on the Bering Strait for Russian America; and the mouth of the Anadyr, Kamchatka and probably Plover Bay near Provideniya on the Bering Strait for Siberia. His exploration of the west coast of the Bering Strait convinced him that the telegraph cable must reach land at Plover Bay, more to the south than originally intended, since strong winds and shifting fields of ice farther north would destroy any submarine cable.

He returned to San Francisco, to discover that the expedition had met with its first serious check. For reasons never fully explained, the company ships were not ready to sail for points north in the spring of 1865; they did not sail until mid-July, too late in the season for much of note to be accomplished. When they did sail, Bulkley was with them, on board the steamer *George S. Wright*. He stopped briefly at Victoria, then continued north to Sitka.

At Sitka, he directed his vessels to the bases around the North Pacific, where they would land their exploring parties. He continued on board the *Wright* to Plover Bay, leaving the sounding of the Bering Strait to Captain Scammon, now commanding the company flagship, the *Golden Gate*. Plover Bay, a whaling station for several decades, would provide as secure an anchorage for the company ships as it had for the whalers. Sheltered at the southern entrance by a long spit, it contained two basins where ships could safely anchor. The Chukchi who lived in a village on the spit could provide labour and deer for the expedition members who would eventually set up a station here.

Frederick Whymper, who arrived at Plover Bay aboard the *Golden Gate* shortly after Bulkley, was half relieved, half disappointed to discover they would not meet up with the famed and dreaded pirate ship, *Shenandoah*. "The whole of the coast was strewn with fragments of vessels burnt by her," said Whymper, "and the natives had several boats and other remains of her wanton doings."[1] The *Shenandoah* had, by all reports, left these Arctic seas in June of 1865, after destroying 30 American whalers and sending their crews down to San Francisco.

Plover Bay became the ship rendezvous for the entire expedition. On this occasion, the *Wright, Gate* and the barque *Palmetto* were in harbour together, the *Palmetto* bringing a load of coal for the *Wright*. The *Wright* and Bulkley then visited the Anadyr mouth.

Bulkley reported to his principals in New York that he had carefully explored along the coast and chosen such bays and harbours as seemed safe and useful as supply depots. He found that the coast south of Plover Bay was mountainous and offered no inducement as an alternate place to land the intercontinental submarine cable. In any case, a landing farther south would only increase the length of cable needed to join the continents. He confirmed the original company plan, that Plover Bay should be linked to the mouth of the Anadyr by submarine cable, since a land line would have to cross regions that were both mountainous and inhospitable.

He left the mouth of the Anadyr River on October 13, and a week later, arrived at Petropavlosk, where he received reports brought by Cossacks from Abasa and his subordinates, sent on orders and suggestions, and expressed himself satisfied with explorations to date. "[Abasa] is pushing forward with commendable energy, and a determination to succeed, that astonished his countrymen," reported Bulkley to the company directors.[2]

Bulkley then left aboard the *Wright*, intending to steam across the Pacific farther north where the distance in open ocean would be shorter, then to return south to San Francisco via the Queen Charlotte Islands and Victoria. Eighteen continuous days of violent storms threatened the *Wright's* safety; on one night, the captain lashed himself to the deck and remained there with the seas washing over him until the storm abated. The sea drove faster than the ship, and "acted in such a manner on the screw, that in turn, it worked the engine at a greater rate than we had ever attained by steam!"[3] The captain ordered the engine coupling disconnected lest the engine be ruined. So much water washed through the deckhouse that soap stored in boxes there lathered and spread suds throughout the ship.

The storm ripped sails to tatters and swept the ship's funnel overboard. Once the wind and waves subsided, the chief engineer jerryrigged a water tank and extra sheet iron into a substitute smokestack. On November 30, 1865, the ship steamed into San Francisco harbour after a total journey of some 10,000 miles.

Back in San Francisco, Bulkley began ordering materials and buying stores for the next year's work. In general, he was pleased with prospects for the telegraph; if he had doubts, he did not express them in his reports to the Western Union management. He thought that the Bering Strait crossing presented no obstacles in either construction or operation, for the sea bottom was soft and even, the landing safe and the cables not so long that their performance was doubtful. The land lines, firmly planted in the frozen earth, should stand as if morticed in rock. There were no trees in the far north to fall upon the lines, no sleet to weigh them down. Using reindeer and dogs for transport, men could readily watch and repair the lines. The Indians, he reported, were friendly, honest and hospitable. Game was abundant in summer, reindeer and dogs would serve as beasts of burden, and the line would be located so that supplies could be transported by water as much as possible. The natural history collections were progressing well and the military organization of the expedition impressed strangers and was good for expedition members. The Russians were kind, helpful, hospitable and aware of the vital importance of the enterprise.

Bulkley indicated the expedition would require two more sailing ships to transport materials and stores to parties on both continents, and a bigger steamer than the *Wright*. The *Milton Badger* should be sold, to be replaced by a more substantial square-rigged ship. Any steamer built for the expedition should also be able to sail, in case no coal was available to fuel the engines. Bulkley himself planned to have built at Petropavlosk two small sternwheel steamers of shallow draft that could tow barges and small flat boats up the Yukon and Anadyr rivers.

The hiring and buying went without major incident, although one man hired as a doctor, in Whymper's words "showed a decided leaning towards stimulating fluids", and drank up his salary with great speed. Lacking funds to buy more drink, he discovered the wine and brandy carried in the company medicine chests; having consumed all of these, he came upon a small can of alcohol, which soon went the way of all the rest. Still adventuresome, he drank his way through the "ethers, tinctures, phial after phial, of spirits of lavender, peppermint, and sweet nitre. . . camphor and tincture of myrrh, rhubarb and aloes. . . [and] the laudanum, that also went the same way."[4] Perhaps with equal relief to both parties, the weakness of the miscreant was discovered and he was discharged.

That winter, seven ocean vessels and a variety of smaller craft made up the telegraph fleet at the wharves of San Francisco. The company bought a new flagship, the *Nightingale*, a ship that had been built as a model clipper intended for exhibition in London in 1851. She served as a slaver, was captured by the United States navy during the Civil War and used as a blockading vessel, then finally was bought by the telegraph company. Over the winter, after a season's heavy work, the *Wright* was refitted and two river steamers, the *Wade* and the *Wilder*, were built, in San Francisco rather than in Petropavlosk, for service on the Anadyr and Yukon.

As Bulkley had recommended, the *Milton Badger* was sold and replaced by the barques *H.L. Rutgers* and *Onward*. To the north in Puget Sound, shipwrights completed work on a sternwheel steamer, the *Mumford*, named for a director of the company in Rochester.

Bulkley had hoped to have all his vessels at sea by late spring, but once again was thwarted. Telegraph material needed for the various divisions was late arriving from New York, and he was unable to dispatch his boats on time. The barque *Clara Bell* was the first to leave, in May, with coal, brackets and insulators, plus four workmen, for Petropavlosk and Major Abasa's command. The *Rutgers* also left in May, for Puget Sound, to load a cargo of telegraph poles, lumber including two framed houses, wire, telegraph material, stores and 39 workmen. All of this, save one house intended for Plover Bay, she landed at Port Clarence.

The flagship *Nightingale* followed the *Rutgers* and met her at Plover Bay, with a cargo of stores and material plus the two river steamers. Bulkley himself steamed out of San Francisco aboard the *Wright*, to make a thorough reconnaissance of the coast where he had not done so before. Over the summer, he and his ship visited Petropavlosk, the Anadyr River, Plover Bay, St. Michaels, Port Clarence, the Seniavine Straits, St. Pauls Island, Unalaska, Sitka and the inner passage between the Alaskan Panhandle and Victoria on Vancouver Island.

Also on board the *Wright* were a Russian government commissioner, Paul Anasoff, and T.W. Knox, a correspondent for New York newspapers who planned to disembark at Petropavlosk and make his way across the country to St. Petersburg.

The ship, her crew and passengers had better luck now than on their return home in 1865; the weather was calm and pleasant, the steamer fitted up in almost luxurious style. At Petropavlosk, Bulkley found the Russian navy corvette *Variag* awaiting his orders. He had intended that the Russian ship help in laying the cable across the Bering Strait—but the cable still lay, unfinished, in London. Instead, he dispatched the *Variag* to help Abasa as best she could in the Okhotsk Sea.

The *Wright* arrived at Petropavlosk in late July and remained there while Bulkley sent off messengers for Abasa and made arrangements to transport supplies over the following year. The *Wright's* passengers, among them Frederick Whymper, took advantage of the delay to enjoy Kamchatkan hospitality—"three months of Russian hospitality would kill most men; and the fortnight spent on this visit was the hardest work I have ever done in my life!"[5] judged Whymper, who was not used to the constant round of drinking, dancing, smoking, singing, cheering and endless cups of tea that were *de rigueur* for any self-respecting Russian host. Fortunately for him, the ship left Kamchatka on August 6, as Bulkley prepared to visit his other camps around the Pacific rim.

## CHAPTER 14

# The Race Continues

Bulkley was not alone in experiencing the trials and tribulations of the race to link the continents by telegraph. In the summer of 1865, seven years after his last attempt to lay a cable on the floor of the North Atlantic, Cyrus Field once more put out to sea.

The intervening years had produced a mixed bag of evidence on whether the submarine cable was feasible. To the failure of the Atlantic cable in 1858 was added a second shock: a cable laid across the Red Sea fell silent shortly after the Atlantic cable died. The British government appointed a scientific commission to consider whether submarine cables could ever work.

It took the commission, composed of prominent scientists and engineers, four years to complete its investigation. Their report was cautiously encouraging. "A well-insulated cable, properly protected, of suitable specific gravity, made with care, and tested under water throughout its progress with the best known apparatus, and paid into the ocean with the most improved machinery, possesses every prospect of not only being successfully laid in the first instance, but may reasonably be relied upon to continue for many years in an efficient state for the transmission of signals."[1]

Cyrus Field had never lost faith. The cable laid in 1858 had worked for 27 days; as far as Field and his colleagues were concerned, there was no question about the feasibility of a submarine cable across the Atlantic. Theoretically and scientifically, the cable could be built. The only questions left were technological: could a cable be built that was good enough to stand the strain, and could machinery be constructed that could pay it out properly?

Field's optimism was buoyed by advances in cable-making. By 1862, 74 submarine cables with a total length of more than 12,000 miles were operating successfully under seas around the world. A cable now linked the north and south shores of the Mediterranean. England spoke to India in Morse code along a 1,400-mile cable that crossed the Persian Gulf.

In 1862, the American and British governments agreed to support a new attempt to lay an Atlantic cable. Field and his fellow directors asked Glass, Elliott and Company, the cable-making firm in London, if it would not only make the cable, but supervise its laying as well. Directors of the company, supremely confident, agreed; they also agreed to take 20% of the cost of the line in company shares. Field tried to raise the rest of the capital required in the United States, but this attempt was less successful: many applauded Field's courage, but few were willing to invest in what they considered a highly speculative venture. Persuasive as ever, Field finally managed to raise some money from American investors.

It was not enough. Field received word from England that a lack of capital meant the cable attempt would have to be put off for another year. In January 1864, Field returned to England to try again, his 31st crossing of the Atlantic in the ten years he had been working to achieve his goal. New supporters came to his rescue, Glass, Elliott merged with the Gutta Percha Company to form a company that would specialize in submarine cables, and the race was on again.

Summer, fall and winter passed, as the new company's employees invested immense care and effort in manufacturing the cable. They were determined to avoid the problems of the previous, unsuccessful cables: standards that the cable must meet were set very high and test after test was conducted on the cable as it was manufactured. The conductor core of the cable was three times the size of the previous core; the weight per mile was almost three times as great. The new insulation was formed of eight layers, compared to three in the old. The coating that covered the insulation was thicker and better, and the shore ends of the cable were made even stronger, to withstand any possible fouling by ships' anchors. The tensile strength of the new cable was two and a half times that of its predecessor.

Those who studied the previous failures were convinced that the splice between two lengths of cable aboard two ships seesawing at mid-ocean had been the source of many problems. This time, the cable was to be in one immense length. How then to carry it across the Atlantic, given that the *Niagara* and the *Agamemnon* had been severely burdened with just half the total length of a much lighter cable? The answer came from the dreams of engineer Isambard Kingdom Brunel. Brunel had envisioned an enormous ship that would carry passengers across the Atlantic, and had commissioned the ship, the *Great Eastern*. Launched in 1858, the *Great Eastern* was five times the size of the largest ship then afloat, designed to carry 6,000 passengers or 10,000 troops. Her size, however, was her downfall: not enough passengers could be tempted to travel aboard her, and she bankrupted three companies that owned her.

She might well be perfect for the cable project. Some of the men involved in the project approached her owner. He refused to sell, but offered a sporting gamble: If the project succeeded, he would take $250,000 in cable stock; if the project failed, he would charge nothing.

The coils of cables were rapidly mounting up in water-filled tanks at Glass, Elliott. The *Great Eastern* tied up 30 miles below Greenwich, the closest she could approach to the cable works. Week after week, month after month, five months in all, tug and barge brought 20 miles of cable per day to the *Great Eastern*. By the middle of June, the ship was fully loaded: 5,000 tons of cable, 8,000 tons of coal, provisions—including 120 live sheep and 500 live chickens—for the crew: a total of 21,000 tons.

So many journalists wanted to make the crossing that all were excluded. In addition to the crew, only Field, the owner of the *Great East-*

*ern*, a historian and two artists were permitted aboard. On July 15, 1865, the *Great Eastern* weighed anchor and set out to sea.

The shore end of the cable was laid near Valentia, and spliced to the cable aboard ship. On July 23, they set out westward into the evening sea and sky. Disaster struck quickly. Just 73 miles from shore, the strong signal from the shore end of the cable almost disappeared. There must be a break somewhere in the cable; the faulty section must be cut out.

Slowly, as the *Great Eastern* returned toward shore, the cable was brought back aboard. The fault was found: a piece of iron wire the size of a needle had pierced the cable. The section of the cable was cut out and the cable respliced; the ship turned west once more.

Four days later, the signal ceased again. Now the cable lay two miles below the surface; retrieving it was a lengthy, difficult process. Again, the faulty section was cut out and new cable spliced. Again, a pin was found, driven through the insulation.

W.H. Russell, the expedition's historian, depicted the scene: "An exclamation of horror escaped our lips! There, driven right through the centre of the coil so as to touch the inner wires was a piece of iron wire, bright as if cut with nippers at one end and cut off short at the other. . . . It corresponded in length exactly with the diameter of the cable, so that the ends did not project beyond the outer surface of the covering. No man who saw it could doubt that the wire had been driven in by a skilful hand."[2]

One of the crew claimed that a workman had been hired by a rival company to drive a nail through a cable that was being laid across the North Sea. The same crew had been on duty both times that a wire had been found in the Atlantic cable. Was someone aboard the *Great Eastern* a saboteur?

Guards were set to watch the cable, and the process of unrolling it into the ocean began again. The ship passed the midpoint of the ocean without further trouble, and hopes soared. Only 800, then 600 miles to shore. Then, as the cable passed endlessly into the water, a grating noise sounded from the machinery. Had another piece of wire cut into the cable? Before the crew could stop the machinery, the suspect section slipped into the ocean.

The cable was cut, and the men began to haul it back on board. But the hauling engine was not equal to the task. The ship's engines had been stopped and she began to drift backwards, rubbing against the cable. As seamen hauled the rubbed section back aboard, it snapped. The seaward end slipped over the side of the ship and disappeared beneath the ocean.

What could be done now to save the expedition? The captain decided to grapple for the cable end with five-armed anchors designed for just that purpose. From noon on August 2, when the cable broke, through the night and into the next morning, the ship crisscrossed the area where the cable had been lost. The next morning, the grapnel caught something; as the load increased, all were convinced it was the missing cable. Three quarters of a mile above the ocean floor, a swivel on the grappling machinery failed and the cable sank again, taking with it two miles of wire rope.

The crew was set to try again. Three days of fog intervened; on August 7, the grappling continued until the cable was caught. Again, the lifting mechanism failed and the cable sank back to the ocean bed. On August 11, the cable was caught again—and lost again. With each failure, two miles of wire rope sank out of sight. Too little rope remained to make another attempt.

The *Great Eastern* turned back for home. Field was distressed, but not destroyed. The cable itself had been successful as far as it had been laid; either sabotage* or accident had been the cause of failure. Field was easily able to persuade the directors of the company that they were on the verge of success. All that was needed now was more money to try again.

The directors of the Western Union Extension Company found cause for cautious hope in this fourth failure of a trans-Atlantic cable. As long as no submarine cable connected the continents, the Russian-American Telegraph could yet conquer the world.

---

*The question of whether the cable aboard the *Great Eastern* was sabotaged has never been satisfactorily answered. The same group of workmen was on duty each of the three times that the cable failed; certainly, those on board the *Great Eastern* at the time were convinced that human hands had inserted the wire that broached the insulation. However, Russell points out that on the third break, there were broken armouring wires on the cable lying below the section that proved faulty, and that these might have pierced the section above. Similar broken wires might have been responsible for the two previous problems.

## CHAPTER 15

# British Columbia, 1866:
# "This Infernal Country"

In British Columbia, telegrapher Edward Conway entered 1866 with his resignation presumably still on Charles Bulkley's desk and the line he had built clattering away between New Westminster and Quesnel. The strange matter of his unacknowledged resignation remained in limbo despite Conway's prolonged visit to San Francisco in January of 1866. Probably Conway met frequently with Bulkley and with other officials of the Western Union Extension Company while he was in San Francisco, yet somehow no one seems to have mentioned his decision to quit. If the matter was discussed, evidence of the discussion has not survived.

On March 1, Conway arrived back in Victoria from San Francisco, and announced to enthusiastic response that the company ships *George S. Wright* and *Clara Bell* would soon be in town with cable that would link Vancouver Island telegraphically to the mainland. The cable did indeed arrive and was laid; on April 25, the first messages were sent, from Victoria to New Westminster offering good fellowship, and from New Westminster to Victoria, accepting. The mayor of San Francisco sent cordial greetings to Victoria, and congratulated her most heartily upon "the accomplishment of an enterprise which cannot fail to respond to our mutual benefit", and the British consul in Victoria wired the vice-president of Western Union in California, "Have wired the tail of the British lion to the left wing of the American Eagle. They work peacefully in harness."[1]

Conway moved on to New Westminster, and once more began writing to Bulkley, asking the latter to acknowledge his resignation. By April, presumably in response to the complaints, Bulkley raised Conway's pay and made the raise retroactive, allowing Conway to settle his affairs at home. In another of his emotional reversals, Conway thanked Bulkley and apologized for the trouble he had caused.

"You are aware," he wrote on May 1 from Quesnel, "my stock of patience was never very extensive, it has all been driven out of me in this infernal mining country, where one encounters nothing but heavy timber, [?] mills, broken miners, [?]lug operators, English aristocrats, loafers and swindlers, all of which tends to drive a man crazy. Punishment in Siberia is a Paradise in comparison to this place."[2]

Conway had, temporarily at any rate, forgiven Bulkley, but he was now upset with Pitfield, his agent and trusted right-hand man who seemed to have turned against him, though he does not specify where the disloyalty lay. "I am too *honest* and faithful ever to succeed in telegraphing," he lamented. "I shall soon leave it in disgust."[3] He wrote angry letters to Pitfield, but made no further move to leave the company.

Perhaps he had no time to make plans for his future. From the day of his return to New Westminster, he was hard at work once more, laying out the schedule for the coming season. Conway had now been put in charge of both explorations and construction for the forthcoming season, and he wanted to make good use of his men and his time.

He had not been impressed by the country he had seen the previous year north of Fort St. James, considering it too barren of game, too rough and too far from the Skeena, Nass and Stikine rivers which he planned to use as supply routes for telegraph materials and provisions for the workmen. Winter expeditions made by Rothrock and Pope from Bulkley House into the wilderness to the north and west added to his determination to find a better route.

In January, Rothrock and several companions decided to test the weather and practise winter travel by heading south to Stuart Lake, taking letters and reports to be mailed and seeking news that might have filtered through to the post on the lake. Their trip was horrendous, the problems of deep snow and slush compounded by the fact that they took insufficient food for their journey and could find no game along their route. By the third day of the trip, they were ready to give up more than the trip: "Freezing to death, quiet bliss;" wrote Rothrock in a reminiscence ten years later. "We were not cold, we were not anything, except sleepy. It seemed as though each eyelid had an immense weight that we could not shake off, and we only wanted to be left alone in a nap that would have no waking."[4] The Cree Indian with them realized their danger of falling into an eternal sleep, and kicked and dragged the falling men along the trail until they were close enough to a trader's cabin that he could go for help. The men survived and returned to Bulkley House.

Pope and three companions, two of them natives, left Bulkley House February 19 seeking a route for the telegraph northwest to the Stikine River, a journey of some 300 miles into "a country which has hitherto been a terra incognita even to the adventurous explorers and fur-traders of the Hudson Bay Company." A sled drawn by four dogs carried the 400 pounds of provisions and supplies the group required for the trip. Each man slogged through the deep snow on snowshoes "without which one could not move ten rods from home. . . . We set out on our journey into the unknown wilderness, with no guide but the compass and the certainty that the River Stekine lay at an unknown distance to the northwest."[5]

Day after day, the men travelled below a brilliant sun and blue cloudless sky. The dogs were frequently mired in snow ten feet deep; sometimes they would struggle through an entire day with only their heads above the surface of the snow. At those times, the men pulled the provision-laden sled, sometimes even carrying the exhausted dogs on their backs. On March 23, the group reached the headwaters of the

Skeena River. "Matters thus far had been anything but encouraging," Pope reported to *The Telegrapher*. "After a month of protracted and very exhausting labor we had accomplished but one hundred and fifty miles, and our dogs were all nearly 'used up'."[6] They killed one dog that day and feared they must soon put the rest out of their misery, leaving

*A camp on the journey to the Stikine River. From Pope's sketchbook. (Courtesy of the Provincial Archives of BC. pdp 1348.)*

them with no transportation for their provisions. Nonetheless, they decided to go ahead.

Now the snow firmed up, and the men and the three remaining dogs continued on with much less difficulty. They crossed a divide and began following what turned out to be a tributary of the Stikine. On April 15, they met an Indian family, who had just killed what Pope described as a reindeer that they shared with Pope and his men. They spent several days resting with the family, enjoying the unexpected comfort of spruce-bough beds in a dwelling made from fir branches.

They reached the grand canyon of the Stikine, 80 miles long, 300 feet wide, from 300 to 2,000 feet deep, and bypassed the worst sections by means of a 40-mile portage. Pope was greatly impressed by the canyon, whose walls were "in most places perpendicular and wrought by the hand of nature into the most curious colors and forms. Through the bottom of the canon the river rushes furiously along, filling the whole space between the walls."[7] Though the ice in the centre of the river had broken, firm ice still clung to the canyon walls; Pope and his companions travelled over this ice for 30 miles, clambering up and down the cliffs where no ice existed, hauling up dogs and baggage with ropes.

They reached Buck's Bar, where gold had been discovered in 1862, and were amazed to encounter two other telegraph explorers, who had been dispatched from the "lower country" to explore for a possible route between the Stikine and Lake Babine to the east. Pope and his companions saw these men off into the wilderness, then built a boat from the remains of old miners' sluice boxes and other lumber that the prospectors of 1862 and 1863 had left behind. On April 28, with the river almost free of ice, they set out. In three days, the swift current and their own efforts with the oars propelled them the 160 miles to the mouth of the Stikine, along the river's winding course through a pleasant valley walled by steep mountains. Anchored there, by great coincidence, was the *Otter*, the H.B.C. steamer based at Victoria, on her semi-annual trading trip up the coast. They rowed out and climbed aboard, delighted to see other faces after their 70-day journey. Pope and his companions arrived at Victoria on the 24th of May, then continued on to New Westminster. Pope then returned to the United States.

Rothrock set out again in March, exploring north and west, though where he went neither he nor we know. "When I was there," he explained years later, "the country was unnamed—no one knew, except by conjecture, where any of the small streams went, further than that they went East or West. I had no means of fixing my position astronomically, except approximately and crudely by the altitude of the pole star."[8] He conjectured, however, that he probably came within 70 miles of Dease Lake, probably not far from the Stikine River.

Rothrock's reports confirmed Conway's opinion that he must find a better route between Fort St. James and the Yukon. By the time Pope returned to New Westminster, Conway had already decided to abandon the proposed route by way of Bulkley House. On his earlier trip, he had talked to native and trader, to glean as much information as possible about the country between Fort St. James and the Yukon River. From them, he gathered that a possible route led northwest from Fraser Lake along the Bulkley River to its junction with the Skeena, near Hagwilgaet. From Hagwilgaet, the route turned north along the Kispiox River, then overland to the Nass River and eventually to the Stikine.

In May and June of 1866, two of his men had explored this route from Fort Fraser along the Bulkley River to its junction with the Skeena. Their reports were favourable, and Conway immediately sought work parties to cut trails and poles along the route.

The task was not simple, for labourers were scarce in the British Columbia spring of 1866. In 1865, prospectors discovered gold on the Big Bend of the Columbia, and now the out-of-work miners who had clustered in the Cariboo deserted it for the excitement of the Big Bend rush. Conway was able to hire 25 white labourers only by promising them ten days' bonus pay. He also hired 25 Chinese.

By mid-May, Big Bend had fizzled and the labour situation eased; by June 1, Conway had 150 men at work, 86 of them in construction camps north and west of Quesnel, 26 packers and 160 mules and horses transporting supplies, and 38 men in bateaux bringing supplies up the Fraser to Yale. Over the winter, Conway had hired men in Quesnel to build four bateaux in the Hudson's Bay Company style—clinker built, 35 feet long, seven-foot beam, three or four feet deep, sharp at both ends and with a capacity of 5,000 to 6,000 pounds of freight. These boats could be used to carry supplies up the Fraser River and its tributaries to Fraser Lake. Fearing he would not be able to find boatmen in Quesnel, he hired natives at New Westminster and took them with him to Quesnel. It proved a wise decision, for there were no boatmen to be had at Quesnel. In June, however, the Fraser grew high and swift with the spring runoff, and the bateaux were pulled from the water after only two difficult and time-consuming trips upriver. The remaining supplies were packed north by road.

Despite the problems of labour and supply, work on the line progressed rapidly. Between May and the suspension of work for the winter on October 2, Conway and his men built 440 miles of road, erected 378 miles of line, built 15 log station houses 25 miles apart, constructed innumerable bridges, corduroyed swamps, graded steep hillsides to reduce the slope and cleared timber. The average width of their road was 20 feet through standing timber, 12 feet through fallen, fit for horses to travel from 30 to 50 miles a day. Some 9,246 poles now stood along the route. The telegraph line stretched from Quesnel to Fort Fraser, thence along the Endako River to Burns and Decker lakes, and along the Bulkley River to Hagwilgaet. Here, the line crossed the Bulkley and continued to the village of Kispiox, where the crews built a station they called Fort Stager, named after General Anson Stager, the superintendent of military telegraphs under whom Bulkley had served. By October 2, the line was working to Fort Stager and poles were up and wire strung a further 25 miles up the Kispiox River.

Conway was proud of his line; he reported to Bulkley that "I can assure you, that we constructed in every respect, a first class line, omitting nothing, that would help in making it a good working, and durable line. It runs through an extremely favourable country, and is constructed in such a manner, that it can be kept in repair with but little difficulty, and at not a very great expense."[9]

Conway next turned his attention to the country north of the Skeena and south of the Yukon. He was an old enough hand in this country to realize how crucial it was to establish his supply routes. While in San Francisco in January, he had persuaded Bulkley that he would need a new steamer to bring supplies from Victoria up the coast and along the rivers to supply depots as close as possible to the construction and exploration parties. He specified exactly how the steamer should be built, noting that half the boats built for British Columbia rivers proved useless, being totally unable to fight the river current up to Yale. The boat must be able, he told Bulkley, to get as far as Yale or as far as the village of Shakesville on the Stikine.

The sternwheel steamer *Mumford* was built on Puget Sound, but according to the instructions of the company directors rather than those of Conway. James Butler, apparently completely recovered from his accident north of Quesnel, was named to command the group that would travel north on the *Mumford*. Among the crew that he picked to accompany him was a Victoria "lad of 22" named Charles Frederick Morison.

"In 1865, things were getting very dull indeed in British Columbia," Morison recalled in a memoir, explaining why he jumped at the chance of a job with the exploring expedition. In 1861, he had emigrated to B.C. from England to join his brother, a colonial government official. He worked on the Cariboo Road, then found himself in New Westminster in 1865, working 16 hours a day in an office and snatching meals when he could. He hired on to go with Butler, whom he described as "one of Chinese Gordon's officers . . . a splendid man for the work, exactly the man for the job which he certainly filled to a 'T',"[10] a description that may owe more to the chronically positive approach Morison reveals in his writing than to the intrinsic qualities of Butler. Some fine chaps were part of the group, he added, and some of the rough and ready sort—not that the latter weren't absolutely fine chaps as well.

Assigned to the *Mumford*, the crew waited at New Westminster for the arrival of the company ship *George S. Wright*, bringing from San Francisco the telegraph supplies and provisions they had been ordered to deliver to supply points along the northern rivers. Morison found it more difficult to be as positive about the captain of the *Wright*, which arrived shortly after the *Mumford*. The captain was a brutal man who hung a crew member by his thumbs for some trivial misdeed. The scene grew ugly as the entire populace of New Westminster gathered at the dock to save the man and, in all likelihood, savage the captain. The arrival of a government official saved the day; he informed the captain that such things would not be tolerated in a British port. The captain cut the man down as he was told to, then reversed out of harbour and anchored in mid-river, fearing further action from the still-grumbling citizens.

Once loaded, the *Mumford* steamed out of port, headed for the north coast. She stopped at Fort Rupert at the north end of Vancouver Island for coal, but this fuel was soon consumed by her hungry engine. The captain was forced to anchor offshore at a number of places, while men went ashore to cut wood for fuel.

Morison wasn't impressed by the food: salt horse and salt pork were the main dishes. Yet when Captain Coffin shot a deer from the boat, there were those who wouldn't taste a morsel. Venison, after all, was no food for a white man.

The *Mumford's* drawbacks showed vividly once the ship entered the Skeena. "Captain Coffin wedged the safety valve down we had a line out and heaving on the windlass, I was busy with a bucksaw sawing short lengths of wood to feed the furnace, they threw a five-gallon tin of tar into the furnace, all the cook's slush and several sides of fat bacon, the steam gauge had gone to 'No Man's Land', the line parted and we gave up, dropped down a few yards and tied up, the Chief Engineer knocked away the lever, opened the valve, threw the fire overboard and we were at peace."[11]

As Morison noted, the ship could make no headway at all against the strong current, and Coffin and Butler had to hire a fleet of canoes manned by natives to freight the supplies upriver. Half the supplies were unloaded into a shelter to await the second trip of the fleet, and Morison volunteered to stay behind to guard them. He soon regretted his hasty decision. Alone for days in the pouring rain, with only a tin plate to serve as frying pan and serving dish, he quickly grew tired of north-coast isolation. After two weeks, he was overjoyed to see Captain Butler return; Butler was less content, for his native freighters had quit after just one trip up the river. Convinced that Butler was financing this giant project by himself, they had decided they would never get paid for their work.

Hoping to find other Indians who would work for the telegraph expedition, Butler set out for Metlakatla, a model mission established on the coast by lay preacher William Duncan. Duncan was at first opposed to the procedure; he had worked long and hard to bring the local Tsimpsean Indians into the fold and isolate them from their old beliefs and from the evil influence of other white men. Eventually, though, Duncan relented and Butler was able to hire Tsimpsean and Kitselas Indians to help the 35 men already in his party.

Butler, Morison, the Tsimpsean workers and the rest of the exploring party then set out upriver once more. Camped one night just downriver from the narrow rock-walled canyon called Kitselas, they received an envoy from Kitselas chief Kit-Horn, who informed them they would be killed if they tried to pass through the canyon. Butler discovered from the envoy that the natives thought the telegraph men were traders who were trying to take over the lucrative trade the Kitselas tribe carried on as middlemen between the coast and the interior. Butler tried to reassure the envoy about their intentions—and made sure the envoy saw the arms the men carried.

The next morning, the telegraph men loaded their canoes and pushed off into the river current. As they entered the narrow canyon, they looked up to see the 500 Kitselas Indians who lived on either side of the canyon lining the canyon walls, seeming just an arm's length away. The telegraph men stopped breathing—then started again as the natives seized the tow ropes on the canoes and hauled the craft up through the canyon, a feat that took a full day of fighting the July floodwaters that coursed between the steep rock walls.

Morison was given responsibility for a fleet of 25 canoes, but had to abdicate when he cut his foot badly and was unable to continue the journey. Once more, he was left behind to guard freight left on the riverbank. Fed up with the agonizing pain of his infected foot, he sharpened his penknife on a stone, soaked his foot in the icy cold river, and slashed the infected part open, releasing about a cup full of "infected matter". He applied salve and bandage, soaked the foot frequently, and rapidly got well. "I knew nothing of germs, microbes or blood-poisoning," he later recalled, "in those days these luxuries came afterwards with civilization."[12]

Alone again and bathing nude in the river one morning, he was surprised by an interested group of onlookers, a hundred Hagwilgaet Indians gazing curiously from the riverbank. Eschewing modesty, he leapt out of the river and led a parade to his camp, where he put the kettle on the fire and threw a few handfuls of rice into the kettle with the water. Then and only then, he put on his clothes. He added molasses to his impromptu stew and distributed the results, thereby acquiring friends for life.

Once Morison's foot healed, he rejoined the main party, continuing upriver to the native town of Kispiox. By now, Conway's party, working from the south, had completed the line as far as the Skeena. The Kispiox shaman declared that if the wire crossed the river, no more salmon would come upriver and birds and beasts would be killed crossing the river. Conway, who had just arrived at the Kispiox, sent a man to parlay and Morison went with him. The two talked and gave out tobacco; after some anxious moments the villagers decided to accept the telegraph and banish the shaman.

Butler and his crews left 240 miles of wire, insulators and brackets and 12,000 daily food rations at Fort Stager before they backtracked to the coast. They then returned to the *Mumford,* and the steamer and crew chugged south to Victoria to reload, then northward to Wrangell, Russian America, at the mouth of the Stikine, where they stored 200 miles of material and 20,000 rations in a large log building formerly used by the Hudson's Bay Company.

Morison did not go north with the *Mumford.* Instead, Butler assigned him and bookkeeper R.A. Brown to travel by canoe, inspecting the coast en route and stopping at Metlakatla and Fort Simpson. Morison was greatly impressed by the Tsimpsean settlement outside the fur-trading post at Fort Simpson, with its boldly carved and coloured totem poles standing beside the larger native houses, and the Tsimpsean in their bright blankets. He was equally impressed by the canoes that lined the beach, some of them 60 feet long. The canoes had been bought from the Haida in return for oolichans, the tiny fish highly valued by North Coast natives for its high oil content, used for both food and light. The gates in the 22-foot high stockade around the fur fort were open all day long, Morison reported, and a steady stream of traffic passed between them.

Morison and Brown rested two days at Fort Simpson, then paddled north 165 miles to Wrangell, where the supplies left by the *Mumford* had been stored. Morison and a Tsimpsean/Stikine crew convoyed up the Stikine River by canoe with 4,500 rations. They planned to leave the provisions at the head of navigation for the use of exploring parties expected over the winter.

This trip was the most miserable of all Morison's experiences in the region. For ten days, he was constantly wet, wading in cold water under teeming rain or soggy snow. He arrived at his destination, the miners' settlement known as Buck's Bar, now renamed Telegraph Creek in honour of the planned telegraph line, to find just two or three shacks and a dozen miners washing gold. They were the last holdouts of the hundreds who had flocked here in 1862. Most had returned down the coast on the *H.M.S. Devastation,* sent to rescue them from hunger, cold and despair.

His task accomplished, Morison headed back to Wrangell, where he was given a choice. He could return to Victoria with the *Mumford* and spend the winter on half pay, or he could stay in Wrangell for $50 a month, plus bread and bacon. He chose Wrangell.

He spent the winter with another company employee, Charlie Timpson, the best all-round two-fisted user of profanity it had ever been Morison's lot to meet, but a decent chap for all that, who made excellent bread. Morison and Timpson passed the time putting out cabin fires, since the stone and plank fireplace in the cabin they built caught fire an average of five times a day, and eating bacon and beans for breakfast and beans and bacon for the other two meals. They were soon joined by two other telegraph employees, then a third who arrived aboard the *Otter*. This man, George Chismore, was a great friend of Morison's from the previous year on the Skeena. He spent much of his time trying to teach Morison the rudiments of medicine, but his own health grew steadily worse because of a kidney abscess. Late one night, the abscess broke, but Chismore survived, and he and the rest of the party saw out the old year together.

Over the season between April and October, Conway had sent other exploring parties into the country north of the Skeena. He dispatched seven men to Shakesville, on the Stikine, and others from Kispiox up towards the Stikine, in search of the best route between the Skeena and the Yukon. One man travelled some 1,500 miles in the seven months, working back and forth between the Skeena and the Stikine. Conway himself tried to work his way inland from the head of the Portland Canal, just north of the Nass River, but he started too late in the season and could not find a good guide.

"Too much cannot be said in praise of these men," he wrote to Bulkley in his summary of the year's work, "the hardships which they had to encounter were fearful; being compelled to pack their blankets and supplies on their backs, and this through a country covered with underbrush, fallen timber, swollen rivers, and numerous other obstacles."[13]

Although the onset of winter put an end to line construction in October, Conway still had some men active. He sent men to spend their winter exploring from the Stikine south towards the Skeena, and north towards the Taku and the Chilkat Rivers, Dease Lake and the Yukon. The moment winter gave way to spring in 1867, Conway wanted to be ready to carry the line yet farther north.

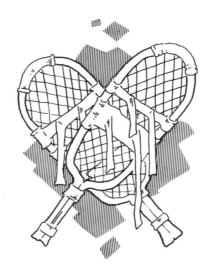

**CHAPTER 16**

# Siberia, 1866: Reunion

As 1865 gave way to 1866, four groups of telegraph explorers contemplated their next moves in the snowy expanses of eastern Siberia. Somewhere west of the Okhotsk Sea, James Mahood and Richard Bush sought a way out of the anonymous mountains that enclosed them. At Gizhiga, Serge Abasa wondered where his men were and what he could do next. On the featureless steppes between the Okhotsk and the Anadyr, George Kennan and J. Dodd rushed northward behind their dog teams. And at the mouth of the Anadyr River, Collins Macrae and his men sat frustrated in their inadequate burrow.

On January 2, 1866, the temperature in the little camp at the mouth of the Anadyr sank to its lowest point yet, −53° F., and still Macrae and his men saw no sign of transport upriver. Four days later, the wandering Chukchi O-Cargo-Cray returned, with just six light sleds. He would really like to take Macrae and his party to Anadyrsk, he said, but the snow was too deep and the weather too severe. Everyone would freeze to death on the journey. Why didn't Macrae come with him to see the Great Deer Chief, and then the group could travel to Anadyrsk with the chief by way of the mountains, where they would be protected from the cold?

Macrae decided that he and Arnold would take O-Cargo-Cray up on the offer, leaving Robinson, Harder and Smith behind at the river mouth. Although Harder was the only one of the group who spoke Russian, "I did not take Lt. Harder with me," wrote Macrae in his report to Charles Bulkley, "because I thought him too young and inexperienced to deal with the rough people, into contact with whom we might be thrown"[1]—an ironic comment considering Macrae's demonstrated difficulties in dealing with these same people. The little group set off for the Deer Chief's camp, with a letter written in Russian by Harder explaining their purpose in Siberia.

Meanwhile, 200 miles to the southwest, Kennan, Dodd and their exploring party were following the winter road north in search of Anadyrsk, and, they hoped, the Americans who were said to have landed at the mouth of the Anadyr. The great cold was teaching them the rules of travelling in a Siberian winter: eat plenty of fat food, avoid over-exertion and night journeys, and never take violent exercise for the sake of temporary warmth, for the perspiration thus created will freeze to the skin and death will surely follow.

The trip was monotonous, with four hours' travel a day and 20 hours in camp, huddled by the side of the fire. Since leaving Petropavlosk, Kennan and Dodd had talked over every subject known to man—their lives, their ancestors' lives, love, war, politics, science, religion—and even devoted, according to Kennan, 20 or 30 nights to the size of the army with which Xerxes invaded Greece and the extent of Noah's deluge. Now they had run short of topics and were increasingly bored. Kennan decided to give the benefit of his North American scientific knowledge to his Korak drivers. He chose as his first topic astronomy, and took frozen tallow to represent the earth, black bread the moon and pieces of dried meat the lesser planets. The lectures were very popular, but the listeners could not be convinced the object was "astronomical, not gastronomical." They ate a solar system every night; as planetary material became scarce, Kennan substituted stones and snowballs, with the result that no one attended his lectures at all.

Twenty-three days after they left Gizhiga, the party arrived at

Anadyrsk, the collective name given to Markovo, Crepast and two other villages within a ten-mile radius of the point where the Mayn River flowed into the Anadyr. The villages had been founded by Cossacks in the 18th century and were rarely visited by foreigners. When the Russian Cossacks first entered the territory, they fought with the Chukchi for control of the region. Some years later, the Russians set up military bases in Kamchatka, and the Cossacks moved south. The Chukchi then took revenge on any tribes that had sided with the Russians, killing many of their members. The remnants of these tribes had settled at Anadyrsk with the few remaining Russians, and established a trading post at Markovo. Though the Chukchi came here to trade, they emphasized their continuing wariness by offering their trade goods—furs and walrus teeth—on the point of a spear.

In winter, most of the natives left the villages and travelled over the snow to trade with neighbouring tribes. Kennan and Dodd took up temporary residence in Markovo, in one of the small log houses with winter windows cut from the thick river ice. On January 6, they attended the Russian Christmas service, in Old Slavonic, and watched the bands of singers that afterwards went from house to house. Three days later, 40 people gathered in the priest's house for a special ball in their honour. The men were in furs, the ladies in muslin. They sat down to a meal of frozen cranberries, thin shavings of raw frozen fish—today still

*Markovo. (From Bush,* Reindeer, Dogs. . . . )

considered a Siberian delicacy—white bread and butter, cranberry tarts and tea.

After the eating came the dancing, to the music of violins, balalaikas, and comb and paper. The men threw themselves about in a frenzy, down on the floor to dance on the tips of their toes and their elbows. Waltz followed waltz, the tempo ever increasing, and Dodd and Kennan soon discovered it was a grave breach of etiquette to sit down before asking each and every lady to dance. After an hour or two, they returned to the sidelines, exhausted, but the dancing and games went on for a total of nine hours, until two in the morning. The social whirl of masquerades, tea parties, sleigh riding and ball games continued through New Year's Day, 12 days after the North American New Year by the Julian calendar still used in Russia.

Revelry was all very well, but Kennan's thoughts were more and more on the party said to have landed at the mouth of the Anadyr. Information from visiting Chukchi suggested that the men had built a subterranean hut with smoke and sparks flying out through an iron tube stuck in the snow. This must surely be a stovepipe, reasoned Kennan. Yet if this was part of the telegraph expedition, why had the group not come upriver by whaleboat, as Bulkley promised they would? Kennan wanted to go and find out, but he had no idea exactly where they were, and no good navigational instruments. Was it 200 or 500 miles to the mouth of the river? No one could tell him. The longer the trip, the more dogfood they would need, and the less the chance of survival in the bitterly cold winter. The natives told him the journey would be impossible, since they would be beset by cold and storms, and no wood or food was available en route. A Cossack and the priest, who had both travelled along the river, said the journey was possible. Kennan threatened the natives with the governor's disapproval if they did not attempt the trip, and got, grudgingly, 11 men with dogs and sleds.

Then a Cossack named Kozhevin returned from a trip toward the river mouth. There were five men a day's journey above the river mouth, he said, and one tame black bear. Kennan gave a shout of joy—the bear must be Cook, Robinson's Newfoundland dog. He and Dodd started out at once, with their men and dogs, a fur tent and equipment including Siberian snowshoes, dogfood and provisions piled five feet high on the sleds. Kennan and Dodd were now experienced enough to drive their own sleds.

In ten days, they covered 125 miles of snow and steppes. On the tenth day, they left behind any vestige of vegetation and continued through the half-light of a Siberian winter along the mile-wide frozen river, through plains bereft of all life. On February 1, when they had made camp, Dodd cried out as he took his first sip of water—salt water, and therefore tidewater. The river mouth must be near. The expedition broke camp at midnight, and set out across the silent, lifeless plain.

Kennan, ever susceptible to mood, was daunted by the unearthliness of the scene: "Far as eye could pierce the gathering gloom in every direction lay the barren steppe, like a boundless ocean of snow, blown into long wave-like ridges by previous storms. . . . All was silence and desolation. . . . We seemed to have entered upon some frozen, abandoned world, where all the ordinary laws and phenomena of nature were suspended, where animal and vegetable life were extinct, and from which even the favor of the Creator had been withdrawn."[2] A blood-red full moon rose and changed shape from a long ellipse to an urn to a bar to a triangle, increasing the otherworldly feeling. Even the drivers, accustomed to sing, shout and halloo as they raced their dogs through the snow, fell utterly silent.

They paused only for food and drink. By midnight the next night, they were exhausted and 15 miles past the place where the Americans were supposed to be. Anything might have happened in the two months since the men had last been sighted and Kennan estimated now there was one chance in 100 of finding them. The feet of the sled dogs were swollen and cracked. The nearest wood for a fire was 50 miles away. Exhaustion, cold and depression finally overwhelmed Dodd. Despite Kennan's best efforts, he gave up his driving stick and lay down on his sled to sleep—and, Kennan knew, to die.

Trying to revive the man who had become his close companion, Kennan called a halt to the search and ordered one of the drivers to break up a sled and build a fire. Then, through the night, came the sound of a halloo. They harried the dogs into life and rushed in the direction of the call. The drivers found an overturned whaleboat, then footprints in the snow.

"Thank God, thank God," muttered Kennan—but he could not find any entrance to a shelter. He found the stovepipe and shouted down it for directions. The door was located and in seconds, Kennan had brought Dodd inside, from a temperature of −40° F. to +70° F.

The men huddled over cups of tea. Harder, Robinson and Smith told their story, little knowing how close to fainting their new guests were. Although the group at the river mouth had no means of leaving their camp, they had been reasonably comfortable. Wandering Chukchi regularly brought them meat and blubber for lamp-oil. But they had heard nothing of Macrae and Arnold from the day they had left camp with O-Cargo-Cray, a month previously.

Dodd, Kennan and their native guides rested in the underground shelter for three days, then loaded the provisions that remained at the river mouth onto the sleds, and made an uneventful trip with Robinson, Harder and Smith to Markovo. They hoped to find that Macrae and Arnold had also reached the settlement. But, 45 days after they left the camp at the mouth of the Anadyr, there was still no sign of the two missing men. All were pessimistic: Macrae and Arnold could simply have disappeared forever into the wilderness, the first known deaths on the overland telegraph expedition.

The five took up residence at Markovo, and waited out the winter writing up their journals and preparing reports to be forwarded by Cossack courier to Abasa. On February 26, the night sky was slashed by a magnificent display of northern lights: a broad arch of colours trailed by crimson and yellow streamers and wide luminous bands rapidly rising and rolling across the sky, followed by a kaleidoscope of shattered rainbows.

It was a temporary diversion: still no word from Macrae, Arnold or Abasa. Early in March, Kennan decided to act on his own, and set out to find a better route for the telegraph than the one he and Dodd had followed on their way north to Anadyrsk. In many places on this route, there were neither poles nor means to transport poles from elsewhere. He found that the river system of the Anadyr was separated from that of the Penzhina only by a low mountain ridge, so that almost unbroken water communication was possible between the Bering Strait and the mouth of the Penzhina River. Now a good route, with abundant timber for poles—or where there was no timber, rivers along which poles could be rafted—could be established from Gizhiga on the Okhotsk Sea to the Bering Strait.

Kennan returned to Markovo March 13—to great jubilation. Macrae and Arnold had finally straggled into town the day before, 64 days after they left the camp at the river mouth, bearded and destitute with only a quart of whiskey and an American flag as their baggage. The Americans raised the flag and drank the whiskey in celebration as they listened to Macrae's story.

On January 13, he and Arnold had arrived with O-Cargo-Cray at the tents of the Deer Chief. The chief, of course, had never received Macrae's gift of a rifle, had not arranged to furnish deer or sled, and had no intention of going to Anadyrsk in any case. Oh well, said O-Cargo-Cray, Macrae and Arnold can travel with me and my family; we're going to Anadyrsk for tobacco, though en route we plan to go through the woods and get timber for new sleds.

Macrae was adamantly opposed. The journey with wives and children would take at least a month, and he and Arnold would have to live in what Macrae considered would be indescribable conditions in the camp of the Chukchi family. But O-Cargo-Cray held all the aces. He simply refused to take Macrae and Arnold back to the Anadyr River camp. The two could choose between staying alone where they were or travelling with the Chukchi family. On January 29, they left camp, with 15 days' provisions, and were swallowed up by forest and tundra.

For six weeks, they wandered with the Chukchi family. Their daily journeys were short, since the Chukchi were in no hurry: sometimes as they made camp at night they could see the spot that they had left that morning. In good weather they travelled an average of eight miles a day. In poor weather, they stayed in camp. They occupied a *polog* in O-Cargo-Cray's tent, and once their own rations were gone—O-Cargo-Cray helped consume them—they ate Chukchi meals of half-cooked deer meat and soup made from the contents of the deer's stomach. The family took them to the grand rendezvous of the Chukchi, where they were met with great suspicion, since some of the Chukchi feared that the Americans were spies, and that helping them would bring conflict with the Russians. Though Macrae could not understand the language, he did understand that some of the Chukchi wanted to abandon the Americans in the wilderness; by showing them the expedition uniforms, the letters they carried to Russian officials and their guns, they were able to persuade the gathering that they should be allowed to continue.

Nine weeks after they left the mouth of the Anadyr, they arrived in Markovo. Despite their uncertain relations at the beginning of the trip,

*The telegraph expedition's headquarters at Markovo. (From Bush,* Reindeer, Dogs. . . . )

the Americans parted good friends with their Chukchi family, O-Cargo-Cray not excepted.

The group spared little time for celebration. Soon after Macrae and Arnold arrived at Markovo, they set off with Kennan and Dodd for Gizhiga.

*   *   *

Far to the south, on the first day of 1866, the Okhotsk coast exploring party of Bush, Mahood, Swartz and their Cossack Ivan were trying to find their way out of the morass of mountains west of the Okhotsk Sea. That New Year's Day, they stumbled with their deer into a Tunguse camp. The nomadic family confirmed what the Americans had suspected: they were lost. Heading west from the coast, they had crossed the divide at the wrong place, and must now backtrack to find an easier route. One of the Tunguse offered to guide them back across the mountains and show them the way to Ayan.

They celebrated the new year by changing the clothing they had worn since Oudskoi—a task for the brave considering the −30° F. temperature—and by opening a can of roast turkey they found in their remaining supplies. Well into their meal, they were halted by Swartz's sudden look of consternation. Holding up a bone, he announced it was the tail bone of a cat. But Ivan reassured them by suggesting it was only the neck bone of some fowl.

The next day, the group began to retrace its steps to the southeast, back along the route they had originally taken through the mountains. The easier going did not lessen the appetite of the three Tunguse who now accompanied them. Bush watched in wonderment at one meal as they swallowed a gallon of tea, a pail of boiled fish and soup, two pails of boiled beef and a pail of mush, then snacked on dried fish and fishskins they broiled in the fire. Bush went to sleep to the sound of the Tunguse cracking the beef bones for the marrow.

They regained the point where they had started their ascent up the eastern slopes of the mountains. Their guide now took them northwest again through a different pass across the range, into a severe wind and blowing snow. The drifting snow made it impossible to see more than a few feet ahead, and the group had to stay close together or risk being lost. No sooner did a deer raise its hoof from the snow than the track was filled, leaving no trail behind to guide anyone following.

They reached the height of land and began to make their way down the western side of the pass. At one point, Bush and his deer crashed through the ice and dropped through five feet of air. When the river was high, ice had formed on its surface; when the river fell, the retreating water left an ice roof five feet above the riverbank.

They followed the valleys into the camp of Ephraim Caramsin, an old Tunguse bear hunter, who traded them supplies and made them a present of spoons carved of mountain-sheep horn—a welcome gift since their wooden spoons had long since worn out and they had been reduced to trying to drink their soup with their knives.

On the trail again, Bush somehow neglected to check his nose at regular intervals. One of the Tunguse informed him it was frozen; fearing it would crack and break off, Bush hurriedly rubbed it with the hard, sharp snow—completely removing the skin and leaving him with an enormous scab that disfigured his face for 20 days.

Their days slipped into a routine:

Fifteen minutes from camp—beard and furs cemented together by a solid mass of ice. About 11 A.M., frozen noses and sometimes fingers. At noon, break the ice off beards enough to allow us to eat a dried fish and smoke, usually accomplished on the backs of deer. The afternoon was devoted to scratching our noses and guarding them from freezing until dark, when camp was prepared, beards thawed, and tea and venison soup disposed of, after which came our only enjoyment—pipes, followed by the most disagreeable task of all—journalizing. This was succeeded by sleep, from which to awake and repeat the performance. The only variety we had was in shifting from the backs of our deer to snow-shoes, and vice versa; and the only gratification, the knowledge that at the end of each day's journey, we were so many versts nearer the end of our task.[3]

The routine made it difficult to take scientific observations, some-thing their lack of maps and instruments had never made easy. Though it was Bush's task to keep a record of temperatures as they travelled, he soon realized he could not do so on reindeer back, nor could the group stop repeatedly for long enough for proper observations to be made. Compass directions were noted in their journals, together with rough estimates of distances, computed from points their native guides could name.

Despite the monotony, they exulted in it all, especially in a feeling of perfect freedom and total absence of all restraint that exhilarated them and bound them together. Here existed no cords of custom and eti-quette, no fear of being thought undignified. "Many times a party of bearded men might have been seen tumbling about in the deep snow, or making the woods ring with hideous howls and noises without fear of odious comparison. . . . Often at night. . . have we stepped out into the clear, still atmosphere, and, from overflowing feelings of un-restraint, whooped and shouted, pausing after each to listen to the echo as it bounded from mountain to mountain, and finally lost itself among the loftiest peaks."[4]

After dark on January 17, they reached the post road that linked Ayan and Yakoutsk. The narrow trail through the forests had been cleared by the Russian-American Company in 1848. Some 800 miles long, it was now used mainly for transporting the mail. Bush, Mahood and Swartz quickly descended along it to Ayan, which they found all but deserted after the departure of the whalers from its storehouse, well-built log houses, chapel and bath houses. Only a few people remained, including an old acquaintance of Swartz's, Popoff, who was the commandant of the post. Popoff immediately wrote a letter for the mail, which was on the point of leaving, instructing Tunguse 125 miles away to bring deer down to Ayan for the telegraph explorers.

The Americans had now reached what they expected would be the most difficult part of their trip. They could easily have followed the post road to Yakoutsk, then dropped back down to Okhotsk in a long triangular route that quadrupled the direct distance between the two points, but avoided an unknown region that no white man had ever traversed. Their instructions from Abasa, however, were to find a more direct route. Popoff advised against it, saying when he tried the journey he had been forced back on the second day by horrific weather and impossible terrain. But Bush, Mahood and Swartz considered the route could be no worse than the one they had already travelled. As soon as the reindeer arrived, they would be off.

The few remaining inhabitants of Ayan went all out to entertain the group at teas and dances. At one of the latter, Bush resolved to outdance a Cossack widow, 46 years old, 175 pounds and proud of both. Exhausted after 40 minutes of continual leaping about the floor, he gave way as the lady still tripped on, making note that "[I will] never again try and outdance a Cossack widow, though she should be as old as Methuselah and weigh ten tons."[5]

Never cowed for long, Bush decided to climb the mountain behind the town to see the view, a feat never before attempted in winter. Insouciant, he left behind his mittens, an omission he soon regretted as he clawed at the frozen rocks that marked the steeply angled ascent. At the top, he looked out over the wide expanses of the Okhotsk Sea, the icefields veined by the black cracks of open water, to mountains and islands in the distance. He descended quickly and without regret, with frozen and blistered hands that plagued him severely over the next few days. His adventure gave him the idea that they might be able to travel by dogsled along the shore ice he had seen. Then he recalled a story told by Swartz, of an ordeal in a previous winter, when Swartz and his companions had been swept out to sea on just such ice. In any case, there were no dogs available.

On February 5, they started out again with new deer, new guides, new furs, new snowshoes and renewed provisions. Their Tunguse drivers raced their reindeer sleds wildly inland along the frozen river ice, providing a memorable experience for the group. They reached the camp of a Tunguse chief who provided them with new guides and deer, then went ahead on snowshoes. Here the Dzhugdzhur range curved close to the coast and had to be crossed once more to reach the tributaries of the Lena River. They made stumbling, weary progress through wind and clouds of snow—then reached the summit where, with 20 strides, they crossed from snow that would eventually find its way to the Okhotsk Sea to snow that, melted, would travel thousands of miles to the Arctic.

They made a rapid descent, camping when possible with Tunguse groups. At one camp, they noted that reindeer found the scent of human urine incredibly attractive, knowledge that their drivers used to good effect to catch any deer that escaped and resisted capture. So familiar were the deer with the gesture, noted Bush, that the "mere feint" was all that was necessary to attract them.

The remaining route presented surprisingly few difficulties. By mid-February, they reached the midpoint of their trip to Okhotsk, and their guides returned home. A Cossack sent by Abasa crossed their route, bringing them news of the rest of the party under Abasa's command. They hurried on through temperatures that descended to −45° F., noting again the false suns and haloes that sometimes surrounded the sun, back across the Dzhugdzhur Mountains and down the Ul'ya River towards the sea. Once there, they were provided with dogs for the final 60-mile dash north to Okhotsk.

On February 22, they arrived at Okhotsk, after 130 days on the road, 78 spent travelling and the remainder waiting—for weather, guides, dogs or reindeer. Of the total distance of 800 miles, 600 had been spent on the backs of reindeer, the rest behind dogs.

Arrival at Okhotsk, the goal of their trip, was a great letdown. Okhotsk had once been the most important Russian post on the shore of the Okhotsk Sea, the starting point for major exploring expeditions including that of Vitus Bering. But when Nicolaevsk was established on the Amur to the south, soldiers and traders alike had left Okhotsk, leaving just two or three traders and a few dozen settlers and natives behind. The town was not impressive, a collection of low and dirty log houses, and the meeting with Abasa, who had made his way to Okhotsk the previous month, so anticlimactic that Bush did not even mention it in his book. All he could think of was his desire to be back on the trail again, away from this depressing town.

Mahood reported to Abasa that the route they had travelled between the Amur and Okhotsk should present no insurmountable difficulties for a telegraph line. The line should go far enough inside the coast range of mountains, he suggested, to avoid sea fogs and winds. Where possible the line should follow tributaries of rivers that ran to the sea, making it possible to bring stores upriver in flat-bottomed canoes. Transport by reindeer and dogs would be easy in winter.

Mahood recommended construction on the route that he had traversed should start with the northern and southern sections. The most difficult, centre section could be left for last. Since few Tunguse lived in any part of the region, and those who did so were poor and owned few reindeer, the company must establish its own depots for stores and reindeer stations, especially between the Amur and Ayan. Tunguse herders should be hired to look after the hundred or more deer that would be needed. These people, said Mahood, were very honest, and would be useful as herders, though, nomadic by nature, they would not be good as labourers on the line. Abasa would be better advised to get men from Yakoutsk—a conclusion Abasa had already reached.

It would be too expensive, Mahood thought, to bring Americans to work on the line; in any case, American workers would cause trouble. The company did need to hire American foremen to supervise the native labourers. The company could get horses and cattle from Yakoutsk. For transport, they should use whaleboats, flat-bottomed canoes and some horses—but should depend mainly on reindeer for most packing and sled-drawing. Dogs were too expensive and too scarce in most regions to be of great use.

Abasa himself had arrived at Okhotsk early in February, a month after he left Gizhiga. Preoccupied with the overall problems of the line, Abasa made few notes on his experiences or the people he met, preferring to include in his written reports to Bulkley recommendations for the telegraph route, supplies and manning. He noted that near the Villiga River, he was forced considerably into the interior to avoid high mountains, and that he had to choose between four or five different and dangerous paths at this point. But for the most part his journey passed without major incident.

Nonetheless, he arrived at Okhotsk ill and exhausted, with business to finish, correspondence to write and no help at hand. Rather than chase after Bush and Mahood somewhere en route from Ayan, he sent off a messenger to them and settled in to plan the remainder of the year's work. He first examined the *ispravnik's* archives, where he found information on Bering's expedition from Okhotsk, maps and other information on the region. He drew a map based on the information he found. Then, between February 16 and February 24, he wrote his long report to Bulkley, two dozen pages of information and recommendations about the telegraph line.

He selected ten points on the coast between Gizhiga and Okhotsk where ships could discharge supplies. He would need a working party for each location selected, he told Bulkley, a house and store built at each and boats and canoes available there. Several of these work stations could later be used as telegraph stations. He also wanted horses and reindeer at each point, with the reindeer to be guarded by Tunguse. The houses and stores would cost from 35 to 50 roubles each, canoes and boats from three to 30 roubles, depending on size. Abasa wanted to go to Yakoutsk to hire labourers and buy horses and cattle but the old and nagging problem stopped him: he had no money.

Broke, he needed 8,000 to 10,000 roubles. It was simply taking too long for the mail to travel through Siberia for him to use the credits available to him through an American merchant at Nicolaevsk. If I had had the money in time, he told Bulkley, I could have gone to Yakoutsk and been back with men and beasts by the beginning of June; now, it cannot be done before September, so we have lost most of another year.

He was careful to give due credit to the Russian government and its agents. "I must say," he wrote, "that had the expedition in Eastern Siberia been placed under different circumstances [i.e. without Russian co-operation] the Company's expenses, only for the work of exploration of this immense territory, would have tripled, to say the least."[6]

His recommendations complete, Abasa set out by dog team to reconnoitre more of the country himself, but starvation forced him back after 60 miles. On February 22, when Mahood and Bush arrived in Okhotsk, Abasa heard their reports and recommendations and considered his next steps toward building the overland telegraph.

**CHAPTER 17**

# Siberia, 1866–67: Year of Famine

Richard Bush found Okhotsk boring, dirty and depressing. Fortunately for his state of mind, he was soon on the road again. Serge Abasa, Vushine and Bush would leave immediately for Gizhiga. Abasa put Mahood in charge of construction from Okhotsk south and, much to Mahood's dismay, told him that he and Swartz must wait at Okhotsk, making out a detailed report on their travels together with Mahood's recommendations for building the telegraph, and accepting any letters that arrived addressed to Abasa "in expectation of the much-needed funds."[1]

Abasa, Vushine and Bush set off in *pavoskas*, the long narrow, enclosed sleds that Kennan had likened to coffins. Bush was quite content with this mode of travel, where the passenger rode warm, dry and smothered in furs—perhaps because the Yakouts were more considerate drivers than Kennan's Koraks. For the first half-day, the group progressed along the seacoast between ice boulders up to 40 feet high and broad, slowed by melting snow that made sled travel sluggish.

The cliffs once more barred their way along the beach, and the group turned inland. At first, they travelled rapidly through fine weather. Then a *poorga* struck, and Abasa began to fear their food supply would not last the trip. He hurled Russian threats and epithets at the drivers to urge them onward, but at length the driving snow forced them to a halt. Abasa and Bush took shelter in the *pavoskas*; the drivers waited out the storm in the open, sheltered only by their furs.

The weather cleared that same afternoon, and the group continued on. Bush whiled away the journey by considering the character of the sled dogs. Some, he concluded, were reserved and dignified; to them fell the honour of leading the team, setting a good example to the young rattlebrains behind. Behind these youngsters were the knaves of the team, who pulled when watched and slacked when unobserved, stole food and picked fights with the other dogs. The lazy and the stupid brought up the rear, within reach of the driver's staff. The leaders, intelligent, active and discreet, fetched up to 80 roubles ($60). Ordinary dogs cost five to 15 roubles. Every three years or so, distemper ran through the teams, killing off many of the dogs. In those years, no amount of money sufficed to buy the survivors from the natives, who depended upon them for their livelihood and, in many cases, their lives.

The route the explorers followed led from Okhotsk on the seacoast across the neck of a peninsula to Tausk, also on the coast, then across a second peninsula to Yamsk. When the sleds drew into Yamsk, on the coast, Bush was mightily impressed by the houses whose interiors were bravely painted with bright colours obtained from the whaling ships that now no longer called at the village. Labourers Abasa had hired on his way south had been hard at work, and piles of poles lay cut. Abasa paused to consider the routes the line could take from here to Gizhiga. Nothing he heard locally changed his mind: the telegraph must be detoured inland, to avoid the dangerous and difficult Villiga Mountains that swept down to the shore. He and Bush continued along this inland route, completing the more than 1,200 miles between Okhotsk and Gizhiga.

On the morning of April 7, Bush, Abasa and Vushine sledded into

Gizhiga. Waiting for them there were Arnold, Kennan, Dodd and Macrae. The achievements of the Siberian exploring parties in that time had been remarkable. With almost no support from Bulkley or Western Union, fewer than a dozen members of the expedition, aided immeasurably by Cossacks and natives of Siberia, had covered and recommended a telegraph route over some 3,000 miles of sparsely inhabited and virtually uncharted land. In their reports, they had evaluated the natural resources of the land, detailing where telegraph poles could be cut and how they could be transported, where cattle could be pastured, where food must be brought in, where and how labourers could be hired and what animals should be obtained for which portions of the line. Bulkley summed up the achievement in his report to the executive committee of the Western Union Extension Company: "The energy and determination displayed by all members of the first parties landed upon those, then unknown, shores, is worthy of the highest commendation. Against all obstacles they have struggled faithfully and bravely, and accomplished more than the most sanguine could have anticipated."[2]

The work was far from over, for still not a pole had been erected nor a mile of wire strung in Siberia. Abasa now planned his next year's work. He set out with Bush, Macrae and the local *ispravnik* for Anadyrsk. He planned to hire labourers and supervise the start of station-house construction along the Anadyr. He would return to Gizhiga just before the roads thawed in May, leaving Bush in charge of the northern section. Bush, Macrae and the men still at Anadyrsk were to move downriver by canoe as soon as the ice broke up, wait for the company ships at the river mouth and see that the men, material and supplies in those ships were dispatched along the projected route of the telegraph.

Kennan and Dodd were instructed to wait at Gizhiga for the company ships that were to bring materials for the telegraph line along the Okhotsk Sea. Once Abasa returned from Anadyrsk and the ships arrived, Abasa would head for Yakoutsk, where he would buy horses for transport and cattle for food, and hire more Yakouts to cut and transport poles.

The Yakouts continued to impress all members of the expedition. Kennan commented that they were the most industrious natives in all of Asia. You could take a Yakout, said Kennan, strip him, put him in the middle of a desolate steppe, then come back in a year, and find him in a large comfortable house, surrounded by barns and haystacks, owning horses and cattle.

Early in May, Abasa returned to Gizhiga from Anadyrsk, crossing Penzhinsk Bay on the cracking ice of breakup. True to his laconic nature, he reported only that "many adventures occurred."[3] As 1866 wore on with little accomplished, the continuing problems of transport and communication gnawed away at Serge Abasa. No ships had arrived, and therefore no work was being carried out. Worse, he had received no money, so he could not go to Yakoutsk to buy animals and hire men. He had been unable to hire men at Anadyrsk, for "influenced by some ill-disposed persons (their names are known and steps have been taken to commit them for trial), they declined under different unfounded pretexts to be employed by us."[4]

As he had in 1865, he pleaded with Mumford, head of the telegraph executive committee and far distant at the company's headquarters in Rochester, New York, to send money to the Imperial Bank of St. Petersburg, where it could be converted to Russian paper money and sent to a branch of the bank in Irkutsk. The money could be held there at Abasa's disposal; the governor-general could send Abasa money as needed, since he preferred not to carry $20,000 around with him. Curbing his language as much as his annoyance allowed, Abasa told Mumford that the power of attorney Bulkley had sent was not legal, since it was not on legal paper and had not been certified by a Russian government official. Through the polite words filtered Abasa's frustration at American company officials who would not listen to the one man in their employ who knew how to deal with the Russian bureaucracy.

Having written off much of 1866, Abasa made his requests for 1867. He needed a small steamer for the Anadyr and its tributaries, three shallow-draft sailing ships, two steamers for the Penzhina and Aklan rivers, five large whaleboats able to withstand heavy weather for posts on the Okhotsk Sea, and later, when work was more advanced, a steamer for the Amur.

Kennan and Dodd, waiting at Gizhiga for company ships, found the boredom of enforced inactivity far more irksome than the rigours of the road. They passed their time in a little rented house overlooking the river valley, "furnished it as comfortably as possible with a few plain wooden chairs and tables, hung up our maps and charts over the rough log walls, displayed our small library of two books—Shakespeare and the New Testament—as advantageously as possible in one corner, and prepared for at least a month of luxurious idleness."[5]

Ever restless and inquisitive, Kennan threw himself into religious research, investigating Siberian spiritual trances. There was little else to occupy his time: week after featureless week, no ship appeared in harbour. In mid-June, an American trading brig arrived, but it brought no telegraph news or instructions. It did have some use: from its captain, Abasa bought 10,000 pounds of tea and 20,000 pounds of white loaf sugar to use as wages for his native labourers, who looked askance at letters of credit or cash.

Beleaguered by mosquitoes, afflicted by boredom, distressed by the continuing lack of news from Western Union, Kennan and Dodd began to question whether the line would ever be built. Bulkley had promised ships, men, material and supplies, but by August still nothing had arrived. Were the ships lost? Was the enterprise abandoned? They had no idea.

Then, on August 15, a year after they had arrived at Kamchatka, the company barque *Clara Bell* sailed into harbour at Gizhiga bearing supplies that included brackets and 50,000 insulators. Commissary supplies, wire, instruments and men to supervise construction of the line were on board the *Palmetto* and *Onward*, still presumably somewhere west of San Francisco. The *Clara Bell* also brought American workers, to serve as foremen and technicians in building the line.

The next day, the Russian naval corvette *Variag* arrived at Gizhiga, under Russian government orders to assist with construction of the line wherever possible. Bulkley had wanted the corvette to help lay the line across the Bering Strait, but that cable had not yet arrived from England. Instead, Bulkley had sent the ship to the Okhotsk, where it was to be under Abasa's orders. The thought was good—but the ship of little use: it could not approach within ten miles of most of the coast because its draught was too deep.

Abasa sent some of the men from the *Clara Bell* to Yamsk, to hire workers to cut poles and build station houses along the southern part of the telegraph route. The *Variag* Abasa dispatched to Okhotsk, where for five months, Mahood had been awaiting news, money and provisions.

By mid-September, there was still no sign of the *Palmetto* or *Onward*. Abasa fumed in his dispatches to Bulkley, dispatches that he now knew might not reach his chief for yet another year, that the summer lost was the year lost. He had delayed his trip to Yakoutsk for weeks now, unable to plan ahead until he received news from Bulkley.

On September 18, frustrated, angry and depressed, Abasa decided to send a messenger to Irkutsk, to telegraph for instructions. Before the messenger could start, the *Palmetto* finally arrived, along with the Russian supply steamer *Saghalin*. The two ships anchored offshore. On September 23, under the onslaught of gale-force winds, the heavily laden *Palmetto* broke its heaviest anchor cable and began to drift towards the rocks. Luckily, it grounded on a sandbar with little damage done. Low tide canted the ship at 45 degrees. High tide righted her and all available hands worked furiously for four days using boats of both ships, transporting the boxes, crates and flour barrels in its hold to shore.

Winter ice now threatened and the *Palmetto's* captain wanted to be gone before his ship was frozen in for the winter. But the black American crew went on strike: they would not sail the Pacific, they said, at this stormy season, in a badly damaged ship. The captain of the *Saghalin* examined the ship and pronounced it sound, but the crew still refused to sail. Abasa sentenced the leader of the revolt to the ship's "black hole", to no avail. Finally, as ice began to form on the edges of the bay, the crew relented. The ship floated free on October 11 and put out to sea on October 12.

The land party, expanded by the dozen men brought by the *Palmetto* and equipped with the tools and provisions rescued from the ship, broke into action, trying to recover some of the time lost waiting for the ships. Abasa left for Yakoutsk even before the *Palmetto* departed. By December, he reported to Kennan, he had hired 800 Yakout labourers for three years at 60 roubles each, $40 per year per man. He bought 300 horses, saddles, materials and provisions for the next year. He discovered via communications from Bulkley that the *Onward* had been delayed first at Victoria, British Columbia, and again by calm and contrary winds on the Pacific. It had arrived too late in the season to venture into the Okhotsk, and was anchored at Petropavlosk. He sent a courier to ask that the *Onward's* officers be sent by land to Gizhiga, to supervise the men he had hired.

Once the *Palmetto* had gone, Kennan dispatched natives to Yamsk, to deliver axes, provisions and orders to the men from the *Clara Bell* who were cutting poles and building station houses near there. He also sent the men from the *Palmetto* into the woods near Gizhiga by dogsled, to cut poles and build station houses that would later be distributed between Gizhiga and Penzhinsk Bay.

As soon as the temperature dropped enough to freeze the land, Kennan himself set out for Anadyrsk, travelling by sled with his camp equipment, extra fur clothing, tea, tobacco, sugar and provisions, but for the first time without his by-now boon companion Dodd. Five Cossacks accompanied him for the first few days, but they turned back at the native village of Koeel, and Kennan travelled on with some of his least favourite people, settled Koraks, on a dismal and lonely expedition. He had to threaten his Korak drivers with his revolver to make them go at all, and could not convince them that they should do the camp work of cooking and other chores. When they did cook, the results were not to Kennan's liking: "Tomatoes they brought me fried into cakes with butter, peaches they mixed with canned beef and boiled for soup, green corn they sweetened, and dessicated vegetables they broke into lumps with stones. Never by any accident did they hit upon the right combination, unless I stood over them constantly, and superintended personally the preparation of my own supper."[6]

He got some measure of revenge by having them taste a cucumber pickle. The first tasted, then looked up with "blended surprise, wonder and disgust", a look quickly disguised as he handed the pickle to the next Korak, All six took a bite, each saying the taste was good before handing the pickle on. Only when the last had tried the novelty, did they give vent to "vehement spitting, coughing, and washing out of mouths with snow"; the experiment proved to Kennan "that the taste for pickles is an acquired one."[7]

Early in the spring, Abasa had placed Bush in charge of building the line from Gizhiga to the Bering Strait, with Collins Macrae under his command to oversee construction of the section from Anadyrsk east to the mouth of the Anadyr River. The two were spared the long wait for ships and news; they left Gizhiga April 18, headed for Markovo, one of the Anadyrsk villages. Their progress was slow. Their dogs were exhausted from their winter's journeys. The first days of the journey were brightly sunny and brilliant reflections off the hard-polished spring snow caused snowblindness and blistered faces. A severe *poorga* followed the sunny days. Bush was as unhappy with the Koraks as Abasa and Kennan had been. He too longed for the day when he could teach these "impudent, independent and cowardly" natives a lesson.

They planned to get dogfood at the native villages on their route, so they carried no dried fish with them. At their first stop, they found an indication that all was not well in the region between Gizhiga and Anadyrsk: only one day's food was available. The story was repeated at Penzhina: the natives would trade them only 150 fish, enough for three teams for five days. Nor could they obtain fresh dogs.

Lack of dogfood and dogs forced Bush to revise his plans. He had planned to explore the Mayn River, south of Anadyrsk, and assess it as a possible telegraph route. That was now impossible. Instead, he sent the native drivers and a Cossack on to Markovo with the worst of his dog teams. He and Macrae took the best dogs and went in search of wandering Koraks. Though dried fish was better food for the dogs—since 20 pounds of fish fed as many dogs as 70 pounds of deer meat—they would now be more than happy to settle for any deer the Koraks would trade them.

They crossed the plains towards the mountains, the monotony of travel broken by an unending display of castles, turrets, palisades and columns that formed and reformed in marvellous mirages high on the peaks before them. They found a party of Koraks, and were able to trade tea, tobacco and needles for deer. On May 1, they headed north towards the Mayn, in howling winds and drifting snow. Try as they might, they could find no resemblance between this Siberian May Day and the ones they remembered at home. "Macrae and I tried to picture to ourselves," wrote Bush, "joyous parties robed in light summer costumes, decorated with gay ribbons, and wearing wreaths of freshly-plucked flowers, picking their way over green meadows and through shady groves to the rendezvous at the May-pole." The picture would not form in their minds. "Blast followed blast in rapid succession, wailing, shrieking, and roaring as if bent upon the destruction of every living thing that came its way."[8] Bush raised himself from his bearskin and peeped out of his *polog* in the tent, to see a chaotic mass of snow whirling by. The only object visible through the snow was a silent and motionless fur-clad driver, with a large snowdrift piled on his windward side.

The *poorga* prevented them from moving on or from making a fire. They divided what remained of their dried fish and determined to stay awake all day lest they could not sleep at night. At nightfall, they prepared to sleep, eliciting bewildered looks from their drivers, now ready to start off in what was really the dawn of another 24-hour day of light.

At their next camp, Macrae tapped the experience he had gained crossing the Rockies "in the early days" to roast a side of deer on a spit over the fire, pouring the escaping juices back over the savoury meat. The group named the spot Roast Rib Camp, in commemoration of the feast. "Though 'sans' salt, 'sans' pepper, 'sans' plates, and, in fact, 'sans' everything except the roast and our sheathknives, I think I never before enjoyed a more delicious morsel," Bush confided.[9]

They now travelled over snow rapidly softening under the strong spring sun, to a river they decided was the Mayn. Bush was more than content with this river valley as a telegraph route. "Mr. Kennan had found the banks of the Anadyr River perfectly barren of trees, but here were poles enough to supply a line from Ghijiga to Behring's Sea," reported Bush, "and to keep it in repair for any length of time."[10] There was enough water in the river to make rafting poles to other locations entirely possible. Bush and Macrae also noted that the line could cross the river at a narrow stretch surmounted by a bluff they named Telegraph Bluff.

The group followed the Mayn on to Crepast, one of the four villages of Anadyrsk, then to Markovo. There, they met up again with Abasa, Dodd, and the remaining members of the Anadyr mouth party. Abasa, Dodd, the *ispravnik,* Robinson and the dog Cook left on May 9, bound for Gizhiga. Each had a sled to himself—even Cook, whose feet were sore from the trip from the Anadyr mouth to Markovo. "Cook's driver didn't relish the idea of being a dog's driver," noted Bush.[11] Cook had had a weary time of things, fighting the native dogs to get some respect, but had now become Siberianized, and had been put to work hauling wood and casks of water from the river to the village.

Food, for themselves and for the dogs, was an increasing problem. On May 10, Bush sent a Cossack and a group of natives off with tobacco to try to buy deer from the Koraks; he sent a second Cossack off in the opposite direction on the same mission. The Cossacks were also to order any Koraks they found to bring their herds of deer to the camp. Bush and Macrae went 20 miles upriver to buy summer fishing huts that could be transported along the route of the telegraph to be used as winter shelters.

The first Cossack sent back 12 deer and set out again. The second was able to get 20 deer. The Koraks refused to bring their herds to the telegraph camp: the deer were about to deliver young and could not be moved. The first Cossack returned from his second trip with no deer, travelling the last four days nourished only by gnawing on a piece of sealskin thong. His dogs had been without food for five days.

Plagued all along by delays and difficulties, the Siberian telegraph expedition had now met one more obstacle. Every four or five years, the fish failed to come upriver on the Anadyr; the result was famine throughout the region. The summer of 1866 would be a summer of famine. Until the snow began to melt, the natives could live on the grouse and ptarmigan they trapped on top of the snow. After that, they would be reduced to chewing on their deerskin bedding in the hopes of extracting some small amount of nourishment. In years like this, the wandering Chukchi stayed well away from Anadyrsk. They knew the residents would probably have no goods to trade for reindeer. The Chukchi would have to give their deer away to the starving people of Anadyrsk.

Bush railed against the natives for their lack of foresight and failure to store food against the famine, conveniently forgetting that the telegraph expedition had likewise failed to protect its men against starvation. He and his companions must now survive on the tea and sugar, plus a little rye flour, that they carried with them, plus whatever geese they could shoot or deer they could buy from the Chukchi. They returned to the Mayn, and began to cut poles. When the river ice began to crack and break, they feared they would be stranded deep in the wilderness, so they returned once more to Markovo, having piled 1,500 of the 1,800 poles where the rising waters should not reach them and leaving the rest to chance.

By now the snow was heavily saturated with water and dog-team travel was next to impossible. As the expedition tried to cross the rivers, the dogs were forced to swim from one cake of ice to the next, while the men threw driftwood and brush into the river to support the sleds. Markovo afforded a poor welcome: there was no food available. Even the waterfowl had deserted the town. So had most of the inhabitants, who had left for the mouth of the Mayn River, hoping against hope to find fish there. Bush and his men set to work bringing the fishing huts he had bought earlier in the year down to Markovo, and linking them in a raft-train so they could be towed downriver and erected as telegraph station houses.

On June 6, the ice on the Markovo River broke with a rending crash and roar. "The wildest race ensued among the ice-blocks, each apparently striving to pass the other, and crowding, squeezing, or trying to force its neighbor beneath the boiling flood. The river was strewn with tree-trunks and logs, writhing in the mad tumult, and tossing their scarred and twisted arms in the air as if imploring assistance."[12] The few remaining inhabitants of the town stood on the riverbanks shooting off old flintlocks and crossing themselves religiously in a yearly ritual.

The water level rose with astonishing rapidity. The land around Anadyrsk was a vast level tundra cut through by channels, dry most of the year, for miles inland from the river. Twelve hours after breakup, most of the land within sight of the river was underwater. People climbed on to the hummocks that jutted out of the water, on to their cabin roofs or into boats, waiting for the waters to subside. Until the river returned to normal, they had to live on hoarded provisions plus any rabbits that had taken refuge on the same hummock. "One native came to me with tears in his eyes, and told me he was in a fearful state of want. He and his family had been subsisting for several days upon dog-harness which they had boiled into soup. Others were eating their deerskin bedding."[13] Bush could spare only a little deer meat which had spoiled as soon as the warm weather came; he gave this to the natives.

The waters began to subside 12 days after they had risen. Bush, Macrae, their Cossacks and a group of natives set out aboard their rafts along the Mayn, bound for its mouth on the Anadyr and eventually the mouth of the Anadyr itself. The river still coursed 15 feet above its normal level; the rafts were drawn along by a six-knot current but buffeted by a strong cross-wind. Just two miles downstream, the raft was thrown violently against an island and swept into a narrow channel. Held prisoner in the channel by a strong current, they had to send back to the village for help. It took 15 men two hours to move the raft 100 feet back to the main channel. Their speed now checked by a strong headwind, they floated downriver through the continuous daylight between two rows of treetops poking out from the water to mark the riverbanks. As the water slowly revealed the tundra, the men were able to shoot waterfowl that were building their nests along the river and steal eggs from the nests. Native hunters speared wild deer that attempted to swim the river and traded the meat to Bush and Macrae.

Tormented by mosquitoes, they wore nets night and day, to little avail. Their hands and faces puffed up until the men were unrecognizable. A new foe appeared, a small fly with spotted legs whose bites caused greater pain and torment than did those of the mosquitoes. They "almost have to suffocate themselves with smoke to have any peace," wrote Bush.[14] The dogs were even worse off, tearing the hair off their backs with their teeth, and neither eating nor sleeping.

Nonetheless, work continued. As they floated downriver, Bush selected sites for his station houses every 60 miles. Macrae and Harder, with native helpers, were left with the first cabin, to roof it with logs, sod and bark, chink the walls with moss and build a clay-plastered fireplace. Once they completed this cabin, they were to continue downriver, stopping at the site of each of the cabins.

On July 13, Bush and his remaining men arrived at Macrae's old camp near the mouth of the Anadyr. They found it in chaos; among the items missing were a can of arsenic, intended to preserve natural history specimens, and a jug of liniment containing sulphuric acid, sugar of lead and vinegar. When a Russian priest arrived from Markovo July 22,

*Going down the Anadyr River. (From Bush,* Reindeer, Dogs. . . . )

Bush asked him to tell any Chukchi he met about the theft and vandalism, and to threaten that Bush would chastise them if any more trouble occurred. Bush later discovered that two Chukchi from farther north had entered the cabin and drunk something, probably the liniment. One of the two was not expected to live.

Bush and Macrae now settled in for their own long, tedious wait for the arrival of company ships. On August 15, far too late in the year to be of use on the river, the steamer *George S. Wright* arrived, with Colonel Bulkley on board, to pick up a load of coal left the previous summer. Bulkley had planned to leave a notice for Macrae or any other telegraph man who might visit the site, and was astonished to find Bush, who had travelled 2,500 miles from Nicolaevsk to the mouth of the Anadyr. It was, suggested expedition artist Frederick Whymper, also aboard the *Wright*, surely the most remarkable trip of the many undertaken by the members of the expedition.

Bush left with the *Wright*, bound for Plover Bay and a rendezvous with other ships of the expedition, to get men, telegraph material and provisions that would be brought back to the mouth of the Anadyr. The *Nightingale* and *Rutgers* were in harbour when the *Wright* arrived; the *Golden Gate* did not appear for a further two weeks. The two ships had brought a large number of men from San Francisco to erect a post to be known as Kelsey's Station, named after the man in charge. Bulkley left 15 men at Plover Bay, with provisions for 300 days and enough material to build 40 miles of line—ten of which were complete before the colonel left the bay.

The *Wright* stayed a month at Plover Bay, amidst whalers pursuing their prey. She left August 20, bound for St. Michaels, Russian America, with Bulkley and Whymper aboard.

Bush returned to the mouth of the Anadyr on the *Golden Gate*, with materials, men and supplies on board and the sternwheel steamer *Wade*, intended for use on the river, in tow. They arrived at the Anadyr September 19. Almost immediately, the *Golden Gate* ran aground. The crew erected the *Wade's* smokestack, fired up the ship's engines and tried to tow the *Gate* off, with no notable success. They then began unloading the *Gate*, chugging back and forth on the *Wade*. That effort soon turned into failure: the *Wade* consumed so much fuel that the crew had to stop the ship several times in an hour's run to build up more steam pressure.

# Siberia, 1866–67: Year of Famine

On September 24, high tides and an easterly wind floated the *Gate* off the sandbar and unloading speeded up. The next day, the scow being used to carry cargo dragged anchor and was swept into the bay, where it and its ten tons of coal sank.

On October 2, large fields of ice formed across the bay almost instantly. The *Gate* tried to escape to open water, but grounded once more, this time at high tide. There was little hope of setting her free. Breaking through the ice with difficulty, crew members chivvied the *Wade* to the lee side of the *Gate*, hoping to protect the bigger ship from the sharp ice that was already tearing copper from her hull. By low tide, the *Gate* was almost on her beam ends; then ice struck her with such force that she was hurled upright and crashed over onto her other side. The crash sounded as if it had broken every timber in the hull, but in fact little damage was done. Then the captain of the *Gate* announced that his ship was sinking under the ever-increasing weight of the clinging ice.

By morning, the whole bay was frozen over and ice cut through the hull of the *Wade* as she made for shore. The crew had to run the steamer in reverse and use the sternwheel to cut a passage. It took all day to get the *Wade* close to shore; there, a moving field of ice struck her and threw her more than ten feet up onto the beach.

*Hauling supplies off the* Golden Gate. *(From Bush,* Reindeer, Dogs. . . . *)*

163

*The steamer* Wade *beached by the ice. (From Bush,* Reindeer, Dogs. . . . )

By the next day, the *Gate* was sinking rapidly. Twenty-five men had been landed to spend the winter ashore, together with their provisions. Now it seemed certain that an additional 21 crew members were doomed to spend the winter at the river mouth. Every man of the 46 saw the need to unload as many supplies as possible from the *Gate* before she disappeared beneath the ice. All day, four of the ship's boats zigzagged back and forth from ship to shore. Each carried tacks, zinc and canvas, so the sailors could repair the inevitable cuts slashed by the sharp ice. It was a dangerous day, for the ice was not yet strong enough to bear the men's weight if the boats sank. By nightfall, almost all the supplies on board the *Gate* had been hauled to shore. At first, the crew feared the shifting ice would slice the *Gate* to pieces, but in fact it formed a huge bulwark that protected the ship, at least until the heavy ice swept downriver in the spring. Whatever remained aboard the *Gate* could be removed over the winter by sled.

On its stopover at Plover Bay, the *Gate* had loaded aboard 500 poles brought from British Columbia for the telegraph line in Siberia. At the time, Bush had ridiculed the idea, citing the huge quantity of timber available in Siberia. Now the load seemed providential. The ship's crew set to work using the poles to build winter quarters, which they quickly made comfortable with large mirrors, chairs, tables, berth curtains and swinging lamps salvaged from the ship. A hundred volumes of poetry, travel and romance that Bush had acquired for the station library promised to break the monotony of the dark winter days and nights. The men set up a ration system to ensure that their supplies lasted through the winter, and the days soon lost their original names to become bean day, sugar day, bacon day, molasses day and soft bread day.

The party could send no message back to Bulkley about the fate of his ship. Bulkley reported to his superiors that he was sure the *Gate* had arrived safely at Anadyr, and was probably frozen in. "The Party are well supplied with everything necessary for their safety," he declared with unintended irony, "besides being at one of our stations, and the country in which they are wintering is well supplied with game and inhabited by friendly natives."[15]

Bush and three companions left the camp November 5, headed for Markovo. They fought their way through snowstorms and winds, arriving in Markovo minus four dogs that died en route. Famine was epidemic in the settlement. Dogs were eating other dogs that had died of starvation and disease. Some native families faced a classic dilemma. They could let their dogs starve and feed their children with their small remaining supplies of food, but in this case, the children would eventually die as well, for the dogs provided the only means by which the natives could travel elsewhere in search of food. Or they could save the dogs and let the children die.

Bush had enough provisions to feed himself and his men for three months. However, he could not assign his men to work, since he could not obtain food for the dogs that were needed to transport men, supplies and poles along the telegraph route. Leaving D.C. Norton, his interpreter, at Markovo to make what arrangements he could, Bush set out November 20 for Gizhiga, where he hoped he could obtain food for the natives and their dogs. Three days out, he met Kennan, on his way north to Markovo. Bush sent Kennan back to Gizhiga for food; Bush returned to Markovo.

He saw no point in trying to bring his workmen up from the mouth of the river, for he could not feed them. He sent two Cossacks off to buy deer from the Chukchi, but they returned with empty sleds. As 1866 drew to a close, Bush faced the fact that there would be no work done on the Anadyr until the following spring.

The early months of 1867 brought no end to the famine that had stalked the Anadyr region throughout 1866. In January of 1867, Kennan arrived at Markovo with dried fish from Gizhiga, finally enabling Bush to send 11 dog teams and sleds to the mouth of the river to bring upriver any man who wanted to leave the crowded camp and set to work on the Mayn. On February 5, the sleds returned with six men from the river mouth; the rest preferred to remain where they were.

Bush then sent a further five sleds downriver, with instructions for Macrae that any of the *Golden Gate* officers who wanted to work for the telegraph company should be hired immediately. The first officer and five seamen took up the offer, and, led by Macrae, worked their way toward Anadyrsk.

On the way upriver, one of the men, John Robinson, (not the original Robinson who had come with Macrae, but a later arrival) began to complain of stomach pains. Despite doses of Jamaica ginger, laudanum and opium pills, Robinson's condition worsened. Macrae tried to dispatch him back to the mouth of the river, but a severe storm and temperatures of −68° F. prevented this. Robinson died in the snowswept camp as Macrae lamented the lack of some stimulant to give him. He was sewn into blankets and buried five feet deep in a snowbank, to await proper burial when the ground thawed in the spring. The Siberian section of the line had suffered its first casualty.

Bush now sent Macrae and the men who had come upriver from the camp at the Anadyr mouth to cut poles on the Mayn section of the line. Hunger, and snow five feet deep, made work almost impossible. They had no snowshoes, so they spent almost two-thirds of their time travelling from tree to tree, cutting only about 30 poles per man per day. Since they lacked proper food, they became weak from hunger and diarrhea, which Macrae blamed on a complete absence of grease in their diet. The sun glared off the white snow, causing snowblindness, and they froze their feet in the chilling temperatures. Worn out and ill, they did less and less.

In early April, the fish traps set by the Cossack accompanying the men failed. As fish disappeared from their table, they subsisted on the most meagre rations, supplemented at last when Harder arrived at their camp with deer, flour, beans, bacon and tea. But the food was soon consumed, and they ran short of everything but tea. Macrae offered any native 30 roubles to go in search of the wandering Koraks and their reindeer, but they replied that they would happily go without pay if there existed the slightest chance of finding anyone in the driving snow-storm that now engulfed them. They went anyway, but turned back the next day, out of food, unable to defeat the storm and pulling their own sleds because the dogs were too exhausted and starved to work.

This failure marked the end of work on the Mayn. Day after day, the men huddled in camp, living off their rapidly dwindling supplies and the few poor, skinny birds and rabbits they could kill.

On the first of May, the mercury began to rise. The birds left the riverbanks for the tundra and the rabbit traps failed. With only seven rabbits and 20 pounds of beans left for ten men, Macrae adopted desperate measures. Weak, sick and worn out by the winter's deprivations, he set out for Markovo, where he found the villagers still hungry but drinking tea and dancing out Easter week. He succeeded in buying a horse from the priest, but could get no other food.

He sent the horse back to camp, with instructions that it should be killed only if absolutely necessary, since it would be useful in hauling poles to make rafts. Necessary it was; the 500 pounds of horse meat lasted the ten men on the Mayn six days.

By the morning of May 18, there was still no sign of the sleds Abasa was supposed to be sending from Penzhina. A steadily weakening Macrae collected the "frames of eight animals that might have been called dogs"[16] and traded a fishnet and horses' tails for 40 grouse for dogfood. He also bought another horse and sent it off to the Mayn. Meeting Illia, their Cossack guide, he was able to trade his poor team for Illia's stronger dogs. The two set off together for Penzhina with four small fish, a piece of spoiled deer meat and a piece of horse meat. Macrae was fortunate to meet the sleds coming north with provisions for the Mayn; he turned back "so unwell I could scarcely keep my feet."[17]

The famine ended with breakup, when the men could spear deer as they crossed the rivers. Bush and his companions left Markovo June 6, travelling downstream by raft, hoping to find news and supplies at the mouth of the Anadyr.

## CHAPTER 18

# Russian America, 1866: Arctic Heartbreak

On the shores of Norton Sound in Russian America, 1866 dawned cold and stormy. The new year brought little promise of brighter prospects for the Yukon River exploring party headed by Robert Kennicott. Plagued by bad weather, food shortages, the failure of his river steamer and problems with sled dogs, Kennicott refused to fail at his task for lack of trying. On January 2, he sent George Adams and Fred Smith out once more from Unalakleet with 20 dogs, four sleds and provisions, instructing them to travel 30 miles inland to the Indian village of Ulukuk, to try to obtain more dogs and sleds they could use to move up to the Yukon River.

Successful in their mission, they set out for Unalakleet, but fierce storms drove them back. They returned to Ulukuk, and were surprised to meet up there with Kennicott and Ennis who were pushing overland to Nulato with two sleds and just four dogs. They spent several days discussing their plans, arguing with the natives over the high price of dried fish and, eventually, obtaining enough fish to feed 25 dogs for a short time. They also obtained 350 pounds of bear meat.

Kennicott and Ennis sledded on to Nulato, reaching the Russian post in nine days, then returning in four days with dogs lent to them by the Russians. The group spent the next weeks travelling back and forth between Unalakleet and Ulukuk, either transporting provisions and supplies or seeking additional dogs and provisions. The temperature dropped to −58° F.; most of the time the men were cold, hungry and tired, though still easily cheered when anything went right. They were successful in obtaining fish, grouse, rabbits and partridges; by early February, they could trade with the Indians for large quantities of small black fish that the Indians caught and froze into cakes four feet by 12 feet by six inches. Their efforts now were directed to sustaining themselves, though, on occasion, they attempted a task connected with the telegraph line or with their scientific studies. On February 27, for example, they measured the Yukon River south of Nulato and found it to be almost 7,776 feet wide.

In March, as Ennis hauled provisions and prepared for spring explorations that would take him westward toward the Bering Strait, a new disaster struck. Most of his dogs fell ill with a disease similar to hydrophobia and had to be shot; those that survived were so poor and thin they could hardly stand. Nonetheless, Ennis was determined to begin exploring the telegraph route from Unalakleet overland to Grantley Harbor, starting early enough that he could tackle a second route if the one he intended to use turned out to be unsuitable. He worked his way back from Nulato to Unalakleet even though the new dogs he had obtained were starving and his men were forced to carry the loads themselves. With commendable restraint, Ennis commented tersely that he thought it would be difficult to explore 500 miles of unmapped terrain and barren wastes with no food for man or dog.

On March 14, messengers arrived at Unalakleet, from Kennicott at Nulato, saying the major had abandoned his plans to go by dogsled to Fort Yukon, for it had become increasingly obvious that only severe hardship and loss of life would result from a trip made in soft snow and cold weather, without sufficient dogs or food. Kennicott's message shook Ennis: "The Major wrote," he noted, "in a most dispiriting condition and the failure to penetrate to Fort Yukon preyed greatly on his mind." Kennicott also informed Ennis that "in case of my death before the arrival of Col. Bulkley or orders superseding those given me," Ennis should consider himself in charge of the Russian-American expedition.[1] Ennis sent the messenger back to Kennicott, saying that the major should cheer up, that open water was the right and only season in which to travel to Fort Yukon.

Ennis himself set out again on April 3, with ten men, three sleds and 21 dogs, and dried fish, reindeer meat, tea and sugar for two months. He sent two men eastward from Norton Bay to explore for a shorter telegraph route between the bay and Nulato, and to check on whether he would be able to get food for his men and dogs, and native labour for building the line, during the summer. He himself headed west along the coast, into the teeth of a three-day blizzard that hurled snow into the faces of the slow-moving men and dogs. Leaving a small party to survey and sound Norton Bay for possible anchorages, he and his remaining men had to snowshoe along the seacoast beside their dogs, over snow too soft and deep to permit dogsled travel. He then con-

*Travelling by dogsled. (From Dall,* Alaska and. . . . )

tinued west across the mountains that rimmed the bay, to Golovin Sound.

It seemed likely that their first stop, at an Indian village on Golovin Sound, would mark the end of their trip. The guide who had brought them this far refused to continue, and no man from the village volunteered, because all considered the trip to the Bering Strait too long and dangerous: there were no villages on the way, and thus no chance of getting food for the dogs or for themselves. When the dogs died from starvation, they said, the men would also die.

Finally, seeing a momentary glint in one chief's eye, Ennis offered him his single-barrelled shotgun in return for guide services. The offer was accepted; the man proved to be the best guide and helper Ennis had yet acquired. Seven days later, with no misadventures along the way, Ennis and his men arrived by dogsled at the whaling station of Port Clarence, on the Bering Strait.

They spent just one day there, for spring was rapidly approaching. They raced back eastward, hoping they could beat breakup and cross Norton Bay to Unalakleet before the bay ice melted. They reached Norton Bay just at breakup, and had to load themselves, their dogs and their sled onto a skin boat to cross the bay.

Ennis reported back to Bulkley with recommendations, and maps and charts he had drawn. He wrote that the route surveyed from Norton Bay to Golovin Sound was good for telegraphic purposes, having good timber for poles, Indians who were willing to work on the line, fish available year round and game present in the spring. The line should follow the seacoast, leaving the water only to cut across headlands and save distance, for the interior was barren of both wood and game. For some 85 miles westward from the sound, the land and its resources would support the construction party.

West of that point, the country was the most desolate, treeless expanse that Ennis had ever seen. "Many a night," he reported, "we could scarcely secure sufficient sprigs to boil a pot of tea."[2] Since no trees grew anywhere nearby, the company would have to land poles at Grantley Harbor, near Port Clarence, and raft them up the Fish River to points as close as possible to the route of the telegraph line. They could then be taken overland to the line.

He suggested the company bring in oxen for this land work, claiming that the idea was practical rather than preposterous. The oxen could

*St. Michaels redoubt. (From Dall,* Alaska and. . . . )

work through the summer, then be killed to add to the supply of winter provisions.

To the east, Kennicott's explorations up the Yukon River toward Fort Yukon were continuing to flounder. George Adams returned to St. Michaels from Unalakleet to check on the company's provisions that had been left at the redoubt, and spent his birthday there on March 21. "Do not much feel in high spirits the living here is high-toned and do not much feel like leaving here," he wrote to his family back home. "Am not much 'stuck after' going back to the hardships of which I have seen so much."[3] Go back he did, however, over snow so soft the dogs could travel only at night when the temperature dropped and the surface froze hard enough to support their weight. Kennicott and two other members of the expedition joined him at Unalakleet, and the group arrived at Nulato on April 23. There, to his astonishment, he was ordered to return at once to Unalakleet. Kennicott, ever worried about his diminishing provisions, had decided that he did not have enough food to support the men now at Nulato if he took them all to Fort Yukon with him. If they could not all go to Fort Yukon, those who stayed behind might as well spend their time on the coast.

Kennicott's previous travels in the north had been very different from those on which he was now embarked. On that earlier trip, he had only himself to answer to; his mission was to collect natural history specimens, and his success or failure would be measured only in the most general terms. He depended largely on Hudson's Bay Company men for his travel arrangements, and had to find provisions only for himself. On his return, his colleagues hailed him as a marvel, both for what they considered his heroic travels and for his successful natural history collections.

His job for the telegraph company had turned out to be a much different proposition, for he was expected to turn in concrete results both in planning and in building the line. The difficulties inherent in this, and in providing food and transportation for men under his command, had unnerved and depressed him to the point where he changed plans again and again, ever unsure of the correct path.

This last change in plans exasperated both Adams and his good friend Fred Smith. Adams wrote little in his diary, but Smith was more direct. "Mr. Kennicott has made another change in his plans (nothing unusual)," he wrote. "I don't know what to make of the man I begin to think he is crazy, he has succeeded in making himself generally disagreeable and has disgusted us all this [to?] such an extent that hardly one will remain in the country another year, at least to be in any way connected to him."[4]

Despite his misgivings, Adams started out for Unalakleet as ordered. On May 1, still dispirited, he cast his memory back a year to happier times, a picnic he had gone on with one male and two female friends across San Francisco Bay. Now, 12 months later, he had reached the height of misery, for he had no food for his dogs, spring was coming fast, the snow was melting and the route soft. He had been so unhappy when his face froze five times in one day in January that he could never have imagined that four months later he would have given anything for freezing weather. Rain began to fall and the snow turned to quicksand; Adams was forced to retreat towards Nulato.

He bought a canoe to journey up the rapidly melting river, but it leaked and stranded its occupants on a cake of ice that swept downriver in the direction they had just come from. They had been seen, however, and a *bidarka* was dispatched to rescue them and bring them to Nulato. The following day, the river rose a further six feet.

On the evening of May 12, Adams sat in his quarters writing about his experiences. Kennicott came in and stood behind Adams for a few minutes, watching the movement of his pen, then said he was tired and would turn in early. When Adams looked in on him later, Kennicott was asleep. "That is good," wrote Adams, "he will forget his troubles for a time, at least. He has been a great deal troubled about the way things have gone since we were landed at St. Michaels and seems to take to heart our many disappoints and failures which though it has been impossible to remedy has taken a severe hold on him and seems to have entirely broken him down."[5]

When Adams went for breakfast the next morning, Kennicott was missing. Someone said he had arisen at three in the morning, written for a few minutes, then gone outside. Adams went to look for him. A native woman came running up the beach, saying she had found the major. Adams followed her and came upon Kennicott 500 yards south of the post, lying on his back, dead. A compass was at his side, and scrawled in the sand beside his body were three unintelligible marks.

"There is a gloom cast over the whole party which will take a long time to efface," Adams wrote in his diary.[6] As each member of the expedition learned of Kennicott's death, each reacted with shock and sorrow, for he had been "more than a brother" to many. In the company's papers, his cause of death was listed as heart failure, and reference was made to his early ill health and an "episode" he had suffered in San Francisco early in 1865. Perhaps his constitution had been further weakened, Bulkley among others suggested, by his long trips to the north. Even in death, he said, Kennicott had been at work, taking observations with his compass.

But, writing a memoir on the expedition some 40 years later George Adams penned a different account:

> There were no marks of any kind on his body and it looked as if he died from some natural cause, a stroke of paralysis or heart disease. Late that evening, a white froth came from his mouth, and then we realized our commander Major Robert Kennicott had committed suicide by taking strychnine.
>
> We knew he had strychnine to poison wild animals for their skins for the Smithsonian Institute at Washington. We could not find

any of the strychnine about him or among his personal effects and concluded he had taken the poison and thrown the balance into the river thinking he could cover up the cause of his death and to further mystify us, he had made some meaningless marks on the sand nearby a circle of a foot in diameter, placed his small pocket compass in the centre, and made some lines from the compass toward the river as if he was taking some kind of an observation.

We found on the table of our quarters, a letter written that morning, directing that in case of his death, Ketchum the oldest member, forty years of age, should be in charge of the party.[7]

Did Kennicott, just 31 years old in 1866, die of disappointment and heartbreak, or did he commit suicide? Did his friends and the telegraph company conceal the cause of his death, both to save Kennicott's memory and to whitewash the company? Was Adams telling the truth in his diary or in the memoir he wrote years after the death? Smith might have told us the truth, for he was the only one of the group who indulged in no elegies for the man who had so exasperated him.

Smith's diary, along with Adams', was found in a San Francisco secondhand store in the 1930s. The diary pages for May 12 to 18, 1866, had been ripped out. Kennicott died on May 13.

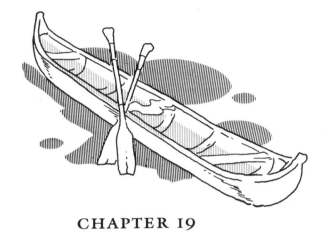

## CHAPTER 19

# Russian America, 1866–67:
# Yukon and Bering Strait

They sewed the major into a deerskin shroud and built a coffin strong and tight. Until breakup, they laid him in a temporary grave, next to the Russian commander who had died the previous fall. They could not bear the thought of leaving Kennicott forever in the country that had witnessed his failure. On May 21, the ice in the Yukon River began to move. Four days later, with the river running free, they brought the coffin to the riverbank and placed it in the bow of a sail- and oar-equipped *baidara*. Smith, Adams, two other expedition members and three Nulato Indians started downriver in the *baidara* and two canoes.

Smith, as always, was unsentimental. He declared himself much relieved that the coffin seemed to be airtight, for he had feared "the corpse would be so offensive that we would be obliged to leave it."[1] As those remaining on shore fired a salvo out over the river and dipped the post flags, the *baidara* slid off into the river current.

They shared the river and the suddenly warm spring sunshine with a variety of Indian canoes and skin boats, passing native villages on shore, cheered by the realization that the land had once more come alive with the arrival of spring. They were young, had survived a miserable winter and could not be sad for long. As they sailed downriver on May 29, their lusty choruses of "Marching through Georgia" attracted a young Indian boy, who followed them by canoe until they finished their song. The current was swift and it would take the lad all night to battle against it upriver to his home village, Adams remarked. If the song had had four more verses, it would have taken him two full days.

They checked their bearings against Zagoskin's map as they headed downstream, readily adapting to his system of identifying the many islands and sandbars by number rather than by name. At one point they were halted by a wind that blew so strongly upriver that, using both

*An Indian fishing camp on the Yukon River. (From Whymper,* Travel and Adventures. . . . )

oars and sail, they could still make no headway. Once the wind abated, they continued downriver day and night, since "we are afraid to stop any wheres for fear that the mosquitoes should carry us of[f] bodily."[2] On June 6, 12 days from Nulato, they entered Norton Sound. Three days later, they arrived at St. Michaels.

Here, they subsided into idleness, for there was "no amusement no excitement of any kind in fact nothing to do but eat sleep and *wait wait wait*".[3] What they awaited was the arrival of the company ships with the year's supply of provisions, supplies to begin building the telegraph line and new orders for their next year's work. They put Kennicott's coffin in a small building reserved for that purpose, and cast around for something to do. So bored were they that they tried once more to fire up the *Lizzie Horner*. The pipes leaked so badly that the steamer had to anchor a few miles offshore to get up enough steam to return to harbour. "So endith the steamer," commented Smith wryly, "a rather costly try for the company, costing $3000 in New York, the expense of bringing her round the Horn, her engineer's salary for over 18 months then fail at last to do anything with her."[4] The engineer, Green, made one more try five days later, but admitted final defeat when the ship almost blew up.

They expected the ships to arrive as soon as the bay was clear of ice. Breakup came two weeks earlier than normal, but the weeks came and went with no sight of a sail or sound of an engine. The men passed their days by eating, smoking, sleeping, playing cribbage, and walking to the neighbouring Indian village to watch the natives bring in herring caught in seine nets. On June 26, the men put on their boiled shirts and paper collars to practise being civilized. They celebrated the fourth of July with a 35-gun salute, one for each state of the union, but still without the ships.

On July 11, Frank Ketchum and Mike Lebarge, two telegraph employees who remained behind at Nulato when the flotilla left with Kennicott's body, arrived at the redoubt. Following Kennicott's last instructions, they and the Russian Ivan Lukine had left Nulato May 26, as soon as the river ice was clear, bound for Fort Yukon. They travelled by *baidara,* accompanied by two Indians and their provisions in a large canoe. Alongside was the Russian factor from Nulato, who was making his spring trip upriver to trade for furs. Driftwood crashing downriver holed the canoe not far from Nulato: the provisions were transferred to the factor's boat and the two boats continued on.

*A halt beside the Yukon River. (From Dall,* Alaska and. . . . )

For 25 miles upstream from Nulato, the right bank was high; for the next 60 miles, the banks were low and level. On May 31, they paddled past the Meloyekagut River and saw in the near distance the Mushotilla Mountains, according to the Indians the only range of mountains between Nulato and Fort Yukon. All the way to the fort, Ketchum noted, plenty of spruce trees suitable for telegraph poles grew close to the river.

The factor stopped to trade at an Indian village, and Ketchum and Lebarge continued on in their skin boat, accompanied by Indians in a canoe bought at the village. At the village of Nuklukayet, a hundred friendly men, women and children rushed out to greet the two boats. Their native companions decided to stay here, but Ketchum and Lebarge pushed on, chasing a missionary who had just left the village on his way to Fort Yukon and finding him 15 miles upstream. The missionary, who was based at Fort Yukon, had been for some time carrying letters for Colonel Bulkley and for the chief telegraph officer of the region; in the letters were pictures of Bulkley and Pope, sent from company offices in New York in the fall of 1864. The letters, presumably, were intended to test communication via the interior of the country; the pictures would serve to identify Bulkley and Pope to Hudson's Bay Company officers and natives in the region.

Ketchum and Lebarge travelled on with the missionary, completing with anticlimactic ease the trip that had stymied Robert Kennicott. They reached Fort Yukon on June 21, to find that the H.B.C. men, alerted to their presence in the region by the letters from New York, had expected them for many months. The factor was now away on his annual trip to other H.B.C. posts in the region. Those remaining at the fort welcomed the telegraph men, though they were too short of food to produce a banquet. Ketchum inquired about the course of the river and nature of the country from Fort Yukon to Fort Selkirk, the most southerly H.B.C. post on the river, and was told a boat drawing more than four feet could go upriver to Fort Selkirk.

Eager to meet with Colonel Bulkley, who they assumed had by now arrived at St. Michaels aboard the company ships, and to find out what orders he might have for the remainder of the year, Ketchum and Lebarge turned around and headed back downriver, taking just eight days to run back down with the swift spring current to Nulato, and a further eight days to St. Michaels.

All the men were now gathered back at St. Michaels, where they waited day after day, week after week, for ships that did not arrive. So little of interest took place that Adams and Smith abandoned diary-keeping altogether; Ennis' diary for the summer has not survived.

*Fort Yukon. (From Whymper,* Travel and Adventures. . . . *)*

On September 22, two months after the men at St. Michaels expected to see it draw into harbour, the steamer *George S. Wright* arrived with Bulkley on board. Two days later, the clipper ship *Nightingale* emerged from driving snow and hail in Norton Bay. It brought workmen who would help build the telegraph line through Russian America, naturalist William Dall and artist Frederick Whymper.

Continuing execrable weather kept the *Nightingale* lying 12 miles off St. Michaels. The ship's commander was understandably nervous since he had been told a strong north wind such as that now howling over the ship greatly diminished the volume of water in the bay. Since the *Nightingale* could not venture closer to shore, the *Wright* hove to beside the *Nightingale* and expedition members came aboard bearing news, including that of Kennicott's death. Dall was horrified.

"So he was gone, that noble, impetuous, but tender-hearted man, who has been to me and many others as more than a brother," he lamented. "During the past two years many had had bitter controversies with him, but all felt and expressed their grief at his untimely death. He was one who made enemies as well as friends, but even enemies could not but respect the purity of motive, the open-handed generosity, the consideration, almost too great, for his subordinates, and the untiring energy and lively spirits which were the dominant characteristics of the man."[5]

Dall's tremendous admiration for Kennicott had impelled him to join the telegraph expedition in the first place, back in the summer of 1864. At that time, just 20 years old, he was earning $27.50 a month working for the Illinois Central Railroad selling railway land to Mississippi settlers and studying botany, zoology and geology in his spare time. Seeking greater adventure than he could find in the United States, he signed on with Kennicott's Scientific Corps, for board, transportation and $13 a month.

Since that time, he had been travelling aboard company ships around the North Pacific, making scientific observations along the way. He had proposed to return to Siberia to make further scientific investigations, but news of Kennicott's death changed his plans. Bulkley named him the new head of the Scientific Corps, and Dall decided that he would complete Kennicott's studies in North America. Information on the American north was far more important than that on Siberia.

Dall made hurried plans, based on Kennicott's earlier decisions, and had them approved by Bulkley. He would first explore the region from Nulato to Fort Yukon, then that from Nulato to the sea, then the area that bordered on Norton Sound.

Since the *Nightingale* could not put in to shore, Dall and Whymper, who had likewise decided to travel through Russian America, left the ship and were taken to shore at St. Michaels aboard a large scow loaded with coal and towed by the *Wilder*, one of two steamers built in San Francisco and shipped north on the deck of the *Nightingale*. The workmen shared their ungainly conveyance.

Dall was no more impressed by the *Wilder* than his friends had been by the *Lizzie Horner*. It was, he said, shaped like an old-fashioned flatiron and "just about as valuable for the purposes required, being unable to tow anything, or to carry any freight, while in a breeze of any strength it is no easy matter to steer them."[6] Dall and Whymper sat pensively on the scow, in a cold, penetrating rain, wondering what they would do when the tow line broke and disabused of any romantic notions they might have held about their long-awaited arrival in Russian America.

"We bore more resemblance," said Dall, "to a party of slaves en route for the galleys. . . than to a party of young and ardent explorers, defying the powers of winter, and only anxious for an opportunity to exhibit our prowess."[7]

The night ashore was no better than the day afloat, for the Russians at the post were celebrating the arrival of the liquor brought by the ships, the dogs howled all night and the roof leaked fine gravel.

They spent the next week preparing for the year ahead and getting acquainted with the Russian steambath and the diverse inhabitants of the fort: Russians, Finns, Yakouts, Aleuts, North American Indians and every variation thereof. Whymper was not impressed by the inhabitants, a "not very satisfactory body of men"; the steambath, though at first astonishing, was more to his liking. The transition from the intensely hot sauna-style steam room to the freezing cold outer room "made us rub with great vigour, but we found ourselves much refreshed."[8]

On October 1, the *Nightingale* sailed for San Francisco, leaving behind the 27 disconsolate expedition members who would not see another company ship for a year or more. The next day, Ennis and most of the men set off for Unalakleet, some in an overloaded *baidara*, the rest on the steamer *Wilder*. The *baidara* was almost swamped and its load of flour ruined, but the steamer reached Unalakleet without major incident. The men set to work expanding the winter headquarters built the year before. The two sod-walled houses they constructed would be the only permanent home for 40 men and their provisions over the winter.

Whymper learned quickly. "This writer soon became au fait at building sod walls, and was consequently allowed to follow the natural bent of his genius," he wrote, "and each man, as far as possible, did that which he could do best. In consequence, we soon had a double-roomed house, well-earthed around, and with a large open fire-place in one chamber." The other room served as a kitchen; the men used an American cooking-stove, "one of those excellent little institutions which will bake, boil, stew, fry, and broil, in the best manner, with the smallest possible expenditure of fuel."[9]

The expedition officers shared with the cockroaches every corner of the post that was not already occupied by the Russians, making several small rooms cozy by lining them with deerskins.

With the ice gradually taking over the bays, they hauled the *Wilder* up on shore, beaching her for the season. Within a week, the little steamer was iced over from bow to stern and the river was almost completely frozen over. Ennis sent a messenger to St. Michaels, telling the men who remained at that post that they must leave soon or be trapped on the island by the ice. The next day, those remaining at St. Michaels set out, Ketchum and Dall in one skin boat, the astronomer Westdahl and two Indians in a second.

The spreading ice soon sliced through one of the *bidarkas*, and Ketchum sent out four men from his boat with needles, deer sinew, a piece of deerskin and grease—all the items necessary to repair skin boats. Stalled by bad weather for one day at a temporary camp, Dall and Ketchum started out again the next. Ten miles from Unalakleet, the fast-forming ice caught up with them, and they had to stave off large cakes of ice with their paddles.

Dall was less than satisfied with his quarters in a cockroach-infested Russian building when he arrived at Unalakleet, and betook himself to a tent, where he installed his scientific equipment and raised the ensign of the Scientific Corps atop a hastily erected flagpole, pledging "to carry the blue cross and scallop, before the year was out, where no other flag had yet floated, if that were possible."[10]

Though the snow was still soft and travel difficult, Ketchum was impatient to be on his way to Nulato, and Dall and Whymper eager to go with him. Dall and Whymper, neophytes in this land, outfitted themselves in native clothing of deerskin parkas, Eskimo boots, deerskins for the beds and a deerskin blanket to supplement their woollen blankets.

Though still doubtful that the rivers were frozen hard enough to permit easy travel, Ketchum and his party of six telegraph officers and three natives set off from Unalakleet October 25, bound for Fort Yukon and encouraged onwards by a grand volley from those remaining of blank cartridges fired from an odd assortment of revolvers, muskets and old battered cannons. Before they left, Ketchum divided his minuscule assortment of medicines with those who would be staying at Unalakleet. "The liberal scale on which everything was purchased," Dall commented sourly, "allowed of no excuse for the inefficiency and red tape which left fifty men for a year, in a country where nothing of the kind was available, with a supply of medicines which could be packed into a Manila cigar box."[11]

Dogs hauled the four sleds, each packed with some 350 pounds of provisions including bacon, biscuit, dried salmon and molasses, while the men ran alongside, sweating horribly in their heavy skin clothing. The newcomers soon learned that it was better to sleep under the sky, for in winter, tents quickly became coated with ice from the breath of the sleepers inside. They were introduced to telegraph stew, a dish invented the previous year by Kennicott's men, that combined white grouse, fresh reindeer meat and the backfat from reindeer, cut into small cubes, and simmered in a little water for an hour with pepper and salt. Broken biscuit from the bottom of the provisions bag was then stirred in until all the gravy was absorbed.

Open water barred their way on the first day, forcing them to make a wide detour around the riverbanks and ensuring they would not reach their destination, an Indian village, that first night. Since they carried no dogfood, their dogs went hungry. They had acquired these Eskimo dogs, surly and unwilling beasts, with great difficulty. During the night, four of the 20 gnawed off their harnesses and headed for home. The men reached the village nonetheless, where Whymper passed his time sketching and making notes on the local tribe, and arguing with Francis, one of the new telegraph arrivals who had recently travelled in China, the relative merits of beans versus rice. Whymper cited the great variety of ways beans could be cooked and insisted they were the most nourishing and inviting food. Francis pointed out that rice took little time to cook and sustained millions of Chinese.

Such philosophical considerations aside, the group tried to keep its mind on telegraph business. While they were at the village, sleds from Unalakleet, bringing up provisions from that village for Nulato, arrived. Ketchum sent back his heavy sleds, keeping the light ones for the rest of the journey, and dispatching Dall and Francis to find the deserting dogs.

On arrival at Unalakleet, they discovered the dogs had already been sent back by the telegraph men remaining at the village—but Dall and Francis could not return, because the weather had turned suddenly warm and stormy. Dall struggled back as soon as he could, fearful that Ketchum would leave without him. On his own and with little knowledge of how to travel in the country, he got lost, fell into the river to his knees and froze his socks—but to no avail. By the time he reached the next village, Ketchum had already left, and Dall was forced to return once more to Unalakleet to wait for the next convoy of provisions sleds headed for Nulato. Understandably, his subdued return after he had set out with such confidence caused considerable amusement among the "pioneers", as last year's veterans were called.

Ketchum had bought a small skin boat at an Indian village—one that

*The Yukon River in winter. (From Whymper, Travel and Adventures. . . . )*

was to last for 1,200 miles of river travel—and loaded it and his provisions aboard dogsleds. He and Whymper started out through deep, thick snow that buried the dogs to their bellies. Men and dogs crossed half-frozen streams, the men in water to their waists. They cached the skin boat and some provisions for later use, amazing Whymper by the perfect safety with which they could do so. "It would require some faith in one's species to do the same in St. James's Park," he commented.[12]

Soft wet snow continued to impede their progress. With each step, the soft snow glued itself to the bottom of their snowshoes, until they lifted an extra 12 pounds with each foot. Making only ten miles a day, they at last reached the Yukon River on November 11. The sight both impressed and depressed Whymper. "Neither pen nor pencil can give any idea of the dreary grandeur, the vast monotony, or the unlimited expanse we saw before us."[13]

They worked their way upriver, fighting wind and snow, and encountering a Russian-native sled train transporting supplies on November 15. They travelled with the train to Nulato, entering the village with much noise and fun, and lunching on raw salt fish and bread at the house of the post commander.

Lebarge now left Nulato to return to Unalakleet in yet another of the interminable journeys to transfer provisions from one point to another. When he arrived on the coast, Dall joined up with him, and the two returned to Nulato together. Dall soon learned the delights of "chai", the Russian tea that made it possible to face strong winds and sleet, though there were times when the tin teacup burned his hand on one side while the winter wind gnawed at the other.

They arrived at Nulato on November 26; Lebarge started back again three days later. Dall put his meteorological instruments in order, and Whymper and Dall discussed the future, deciding to ascend to Fort Yukon and beyond as soon as the ice went out in the spring, to collect specimens, make scientific observations and sketch the surrounding countryside and its occupants. On December 5, Dall recorded a temperature of −58° F. Both Whymper and Dall were fascinated by the deep cold, and recorded their attempts to deal with it. Whymper went out to sketch though the temperature was −30° F., running about or going back to his quarters for warmth after every four or five pencil strokes. He skinned his fingers and froze his ear so badly it swelled up to the top of his head. Water colours were an impossibility outside un-

Aurora borealis *at Nulato in December 1866. (From Whymper,* Travel and Adventures. . . . )

less he kept them warm over a fire. Even in the house, the temperature was freezing; on one occasion, he mixed water colours with warm water, but the paint-laden brush froze before it touched the paper. Their dried apples were rock hard and had to be smashed with an axe; molasses formed a thick paste; ham could not be cut from the bone. Meat could be kept for months without going bad.

The group celebrated a wilderness Christmas trying to be jolly, though it took great effort. In rooms decorated with flags, trade goods and spruce boughs, they ate *soupe à la* Yukon (ingredients unspecified), roast Arctic grouse, reindeer, Nulato cranberry sauce, California preserved peas and tomatoes, dried-apple pudding, pies, gingerbread *à la* Dall, iced cheese, coffee, tea—and iced water. Rum punch and pipes wound up the festivities.

They had set their sights on an imposing New Year's celebration—the raising of the first telegraphic pole in the division of the Yukon. They sent two men out to find a fine spruce, and peel and trim it. On December 31, they saw the old year out by hailing the prospect of successful explorations in 1867, amidst hopes that everyone would be present for the pole-raising ceremony the following day.

On January 1, 1867, they raised the telegraph pole, along with the flags of the United States, the telegraph expedition, the Masonic fraternity and the Scientific Corps. They then fired a salute of 36 guns.

Those who had been left behind at Unalakleet had little to occupy their time. Nothing could be accomplished until the snow hardened sufficiently to permit winter travel. "Half dead with ennui," reported Adams. "Since I got back from St. Michaels, there has been nothing to do except eat, sleep and color our 'Murshaums'. The consequence is the disappearance of large quantities of provisions for which we have nothing to show but empty barrels, boxes and bags and the line seems no nearer completion than it did three months ago."[14] Adams was pleased, however, that Bulkley had promoted all the telegraph men who had been in Russian America since 1865 to the new rank of Pioneers: a pioneer captain was to get $125 a month, the same as a major, and a pioneer lieutenant would receive the same as a captain, $100 a month.

Adams singled out the obvious cause for the hiatus: the failure yet again of the company ships to arrive at the beginning, rather than the end, of summer. But, he concluded philosophically, "if they can stand it, I can."

He was far less philosophical about the stocks of provisions left by the ships, blaming the shortage on some "brass mounted officers" who had doubtless lined their own pockets by taking a commission from the fraudulent dealers they bought from and who were now "living at the first class Hotels in San Francisco."

> We have had left here about half the provisions we will need this year and I am afraid there will be 'tall skirmishing for hash &c' before the ships arrive again. Our sugar is most gone and what we have left is to be kept until we get to work. We have a barrel of molasses. . . . We have very little tea and this is also put away until we commence work. We are now living on Coffee without sweetening, and of course no Milk. (The cows have all died.) Bacon once a day, very little bread, (soon we will have none) now and then a mess of grouse, and beans most every meal. . . . There has been left here a potatoe powder, it is first made into a mush and then baked in the oven. . . and is when cooked perfectly

tasteless, but we flavor it up with pepper, sald and greese and manage to stow away a small quanity of it at each meal. On Sundays we have canned Meat, Tomatoes, & Peas of which we have a small quanity. And the other day we 'astonished our stomachs' with a little 'blamonge'. Mss. Seaminon gave to Mr. Chappel a small paper of 'gellatin' and he made it up according to directions substituting for 'eggs' 'milk' and 'wine' a little more water and instead of 'white sugar' used 'molasses'. The only thing that saved this delightful mess was 'Nutmeg' of which he was not at all stingy. . . . 'Alas' the effect was tremendous being unused to such luxuries, we left the table but to retire to our beds, near the region where our unaccustomed desert had gone there was a sever pain in all probability the 'bacon' kicked up a row with the 'Blamonge' for intruding on the premisus where the 'bacon' had ruled supreme for over a year. [15]

Feeling somewhat aggrieved by the lack of provisions, the men at Unalakleet passed resolutions that anything that could be made into blancmange should be made into it at once and eaten by the entire mess as punishment for past sins—and that the resolution should be conveyed to Colonel Bulkley by telegraph, to reach him at Christmas dinner. Someone resolved that the large quantity of spoiled sauerkraut should also be sent to Bulkley, together with the empty sugar barrels and tea chests. Small obstacles such as sending sauerkraut over a yet unbuilt telegraph line did not deter the protestors.

Ennis took stock and decided that the provisions would be exhausted before the ships arrived the following season. He restricted officers and men to two meals a day while lying idle in winter quarters. An exception to the tight rations was made for Christmas dinner: the men enjoyed vegetable soup made from preserved vegetables and boiled all day, stewed grouse, stewed tomatoes and peas, and two huge and noble puddings weighing between 50 and 75 pounds each, made from flour and dried apple sauce, together with two pounds of the remaining sugar. Concluding the meal were two giant pies, made from unnamed berries; they proved a total failure, since no sugar could be spared for them. "I never knew what Alum or vinegar pie would taste like but I think I know now," wrote Adams. "What merry times there are in Frisco now. What I am loseing, but I hope it will come out all right in the future. If my life is spared and all goes well with me I will be far better in both 'Body & Pocket' for my vanishment (self-imposed) I do not expect to see San francisco until two years from now. I hope I shall spend many a Christmas at home with the dear ones I love so much."[16]

Late in the summer of 1866, far to the west at Port Clarence, Bulkley had landed 39 men, nearly a year's supply of provisions, 3,100 telegraph poles, 125 miles of wire and other telegraphic material and supplies to build a frame house and two log houses. The party, under E.B. Libby, who had worked on the line in British Columbia, built their winter quarters, then rafted poles to the head of Grantley Harbor. Before the year ended, they were able to set up 15 miles of line from Port Clarence to a small shelter station they erected before the weather turned bad and they were forced to retreat to Port Clarence—the first actual line construction and the most westerly part of the line in Russian America. They tried again in November to extend the line, but made little progress. After three weeks, they withdrew once more to their winter headquarters to wait out the season of storms and snow that lasted until the end of 1866.

Libby soon discovered that life just below the Arctic Circle bore little resemblance to that in British Columbia. Severe cold and howling storms that thrashed his base near the Bering Strait cancelled his plans to continue work on the line through the winter of 1866–67. Instead, he and his men tried to explore some of the nearby territory, to establish the route both for the line and for transporting telegraph supplies, poles and provisions.

Between November and March, they managed to travel twice between Port Clarence and Golovin Sound. The first section of the coast, some 60 miles east along the north shore of Grantley Harbor and Innarzook Bay, Libby thought would be good for the distribution of materials and supplies, with numerous bays that could probably accommodate ships that drew up to 12 feet.

The second section lay east southeast for 80 miles across low swampy land and mountain divides. It was very difficult country, especially in winter, with stormy weather and temperatures as low as −68° F. The company must provide lumber to build shelter stations along this route, wrote Libby, and arrange better transport for the men. What sort of transport Libby could not decide; perhaps Siberian ponies would best meet the expedition's needs. The third section lay down the rivers that led 65 miles to Golovin Sound. Prospects picked up here: there was good timber for poles, probably enough to supply the rest of the route.

By March, the weather seemed to have eased, and Libby moved all his men to the head of Grantley Harbor, where they built shelters and began work on the line. Despite cold as deep as −55° F. and bitter storms, the men finished 23 miles of line, pounding their crowbars and shovels with extreme difficulty into the frozen earth. Some of the men on the line had only tents to protect themselves from the storms; fortunately, Libby wrote to Bulkley, none were frozen.

Just as the weather began to ease in April, Libby's party ran out of provisions. Forced to quit work so they could seek their own food in order to survive, the men were justifiably unhappy and morale in the Grantley Harbor camp quickly deteriorated. Libby berated Bulkley in his letters, saying his men refused to stay and work for a company that made such a fundamental mistake as not leaving its employees the necessities of life.

The country in which they were stationed was not productive, and the natives reasonably enough refused to give up any of their meagre winter provisions to the telegraph party. Libby sent men out to fish and hunt, reporting it as a miracle that some were not lost in the wilderness.

*Spearing walrus. (From Bush,* Reindeer, Dogs. . . . )

Fish became the staple diet of the camp, supplemented by seal and walrus when hunger was extreme. On May 1, Libby sent men to Cape Prince of Wales to intercept one of the whalers that sailed those seas, but the men were not successful.

"We lived and dragged along," reported Libby,[17] but no more work was attempted. The group was short of even such necessities as flour; though they had 17 boxes of bread, much of it was old and mouldy. Hardworking men in this country eat more than soldiers in the United States, complained Libby; the company's failure to recognize this fact and provide properly for the men "is an injustice to the men and a disastrous thing for the interests of the company."[18]

There was little about the company's arrangements that pleased Libby. He considered that those who had supplied the party obviously had no idea of the weather in Russian America. For the next year, Libby demanded heavier tents to withstand the winter gales, better kettles, tools stronger than the ones supplied that were poorly made and bent or broke easily, and a portable forge to sharpen the tools. He also wanted better clothing: what was available was poorly made, small in size and limited in supply. Army coats were useless in Arctic weather; what was needed was fur clothing. Libby also needed different kinds of trade goods; he could not progress without native help and the natives were not interested in what the company offered. Libby appended a list, unfortunately lost, of the trade goods he preferred.

Libby told Bulkley the company simply could not depend on the men living off the country, for the country was barren and inhospitable. Send us cornmeal, hominy, split peas and coffee, in addition to the regular provisions, he begged. Hoping to raise the men's spirits, he promised to increase their salaries April 1 to $60 a month from $45 if they would promise to stay on for another year. Not one agreed.

CHAPTER 20

# "They Have Chained the Lightning and Laid It Low"

Through the summer, fall and winter of 1866, the men of the Russian-American Telegraph expedition continued to battle the elements, the terrain and the failings of their superiors. Isolated in northern lands, hearing only rarely from home, they were not aware of events a hemisphere away, in the North Atlantic.

Cyrus Field had refused to accept the failure of the 1865 attempt to lay a trans-Atlantic telegraph as the final word on the submarine cable. Despite the financial blow the failure struck him and his colleagues, he was now more convinced than ever that a trans-Atlantic cable could succeed. "This last attempt at ocean-cable laying proved conclusively that all the principal difficulties had been overcome in the way of carrying the grand enterprise to successful completion," he wrote. "The *Great Eastern* as a cable ship had proved herself admirably fitted for the service on which she was employed. The cable itself could hardly be improved. The paying-out apparatus was almost perfect. . . . "[1]

He and the directors of the telegraph company immediately agreed not only to launch another trans-Atlantic attempt but also to try to pick up the end of the cable that now lay on the ocean floor.

The new venture would, of course, require additional money— £600,000, according to conservative calculation. They decided to issue shares, but found themselves stymied when the British attorney general declared the company had no legal right to do so. Field and his friends decided to start a new company that would issue its own shares to raise capital and take over the job of laying the cable. The new Anglo-American Telegraph Company raised the entire £600,000 in just two weeks, almost all of it from British sources.

It was now March of 1866. If the cable were to be laid in 1866—and Field was determined that it should be—it must be manufactured in just four months. Work began at once. The *Great Eastern* was scrubbed and scraped, and her engines modified. Once more, day by day, cable piled up at the manufacturing works and was towed aboard a barge to fill the holds of the great ship.

On June 30, 1866, the *Great Eastern* steamed out of port, bound once more for Valentia. A business-like, sober atmosphere prevailed, in contrast to the cheers and excitement of previous attempts. The shore end of the cable was laid and spliced to the cable aboard the ship, and the *Great Eastern* set out on a course 30 miles south of that taken in 1865.

The seas were calm, the winds light. The cable reeled out serenely and disappeared beneath the waves. On July 18, the cable fouled and twisted back over itself on the deck—but two hours of work unravelled the tangle. The aft tank was emptied, and cable began to unroll from the forward tank. Mid-ocean came and went, and still signals passed back and forth along the cable between the *Great Eastern* and Valentia. The forward tanks were emptied and the crew drew cable now from the tanks amidships.

On July 26, the ship encountered welcome fog—welcome because it meant they had entered shallower seas. Seabirds and floating debris confirmed that their long journey was coming to an end. At 8 A.M., Saturday, July 28, the fog lifted to reveal the shores of Trinity Bay, New-foundland, and Heart's Content, the tiny fishing village where the cable would be brought ashore. Just as they prepared to splice the cable to the shore-end line, a message arrived, a quote from the morning's editorial in the London *Times*: "It is a great work, a glory to our age and nation, and the men who have achieved it deserve to be honoured among the benefactors of their race."[2]

The long-awaited finish was almost anticlimactic. Eager to send news of the triumph to New York, Cyrus Field discovered that the cable from Newfoundland across the Gulf of St. Lawrence, broken in 1865, had not been repaired. News could now travel from Europe to Newfound-land by telegraph; from Newfoundland to New York, it had to go by ship.

In New York, at last, it received the reception it deserved. Leaders from around the world sent their congratulations. "They have chained the lightning and laid it low," declaimed a writer to *The Telegrapher*[3]; quoth another poet, in his Cable Hymn:

From world to world His couriers fly,
Thought-winged and shod with fire;
The angel of his stormy sky
Rides down the sunken wire.

And one in heart, as one in blood,
Shall all her peoples be;
The hands of human brotherhood
Are clasped beneath the sea.

Throb on, strong pulse of thunder! beat
From answering beach to beach;
Fuse nations in thy kindly heat,
And melt the chains of each![4]

Field and the Anglo-American Telegraph Company were not yet content. Still two miles beneath the Atlantic was the tattered end of the cable laid in 1865. The break had occurred in calm, sunny weather, and the ship's navigator had been able to pinpoint the location where the cable presumably still lay. Just 12 days after the *Great Eastern* arrived in

Trinity Bay, she steamed back out to sea, to rendezvous with two smaller ships that had already located the cable end 600 miles from the Newfoundland shore.

Grappling began at the spot the smaller ships had marked with buoys. On August 17, the cable was hooked. The grapnel brought the cable almost to the surface, but the weight was too great and the cable sank slowly out of sight once more. Winds and rising seas hampered efforts over the next two weeks, and on the last day of August, the captains of the ships decided they would make one final attempt, their 30th. At ten minutes after midnight Saturday morning, the grapnels hooked the cable. Slowly, painfully, the machinery on board the ships creaked the cable toward the surface. On Sunday morning, the cable was brought aboard.

With trepidation, the telegraphers aboard tried to send a message to Valentia. The cable worked. Field could hold back his emotion no longer. "I left the room, went to my cabin and locked the door; I could no longer restrain my tears—crying like a child."[5]

The Atlantic submarine cable was a success—but it had been a success before, in 1858. It had failed then after a month of operation; the new cable could also fail. The directors of the Western Union Extension Company were understandably concerned, but they were not yet ready to concede the race. Only time would tell whether the cable would continue to work, and there were many who said it would not. Throughout the autumn of 1866, Western Union directors continued to make optimistic speeches about their overland line, claiming, without great reference to the truth, that it would soon be finished.

Finished it was, but in the metaphorical rather than the literal sense. On September 15, 1866, Western Union directors covered themselves and their friends by announcing that the holders of extension company stock could exchange it for bonds in the parent company, Western Union. Yet, as late as March of 1867, *The Telegrapher* still carried descriptions of the ongoing overland expeditions.

On March 9, 1867, the directors announced that they were abandoning the Russian-American overland line. "It was decided at a meeting of Directors of the Western Union Telegraph Company last week that in view of the successful working of the Atlantic cable, it is not advisable to expend any more money on the Russian extension at present."[6] Wrote the Western Union vice-president to Secretary of State William

Seward, "All doubts concerning the capacity and efficiency of ocean cables, are now dispelled, and the work on construction on the Russian line, after an expenditure of $3,000,000 has been discontinued."[7]

Suspension of the project brought severe criticism of Western Union. By allowing the shareholders—most of them also directors of Western Union—to exchange their shares for Western Union bonds, the Western Union board of directors transferred the debts and losses incurred on the overland line to the shareholders of Western Union itself. "To say the least," commented the editor of *The Telegrapher*, "this must look—to the original shareholders who were not interested in the Extension Line—like remarkably sharp practice.

"We would like to inquire if there was any warrant for the issuance of these bonds whereby the shareholders of the Western Union are compelled against their will to accept the gigantic expenses of the huge failure? Mr. Collins made money, and the directors of the company have saved themselves a great loss, but what do the stockholders of the Western Union Company gain?"[8]

The editor then castigated the company and its directors for gross mismanagement and such complete lack of foresight and prudence that the failure of the line was inevitable. Inexplicable and fatal delays in the field and at sea, lack of resources and incompetence in Russian America, inefficiency in British Columbia: the editor laid about him, assessing blame and excoriating the company directors. He was particularly unhappy with published—and untrue—reports about the progress of the overland line and with the fact that the directors had bailed themselves and their friends out. But indignation could not save the project or change the new shape of the telegraphic world.

## CHAPTER 21

# 1867: End of the Race

The race was over, but no one had told the runners. Bulkley's men had fanned out around the North Pacific. Two years in the field had already proven that communication in these regions was sporadic at best. New York and London celebrated the success of the Atlantic cable in August 1866. The directors of Western Union had cancelled the Russian-American telegraph project early in 1867. Yet on the coast of British Columbia, on the tundra of Siberia and along the frozen rivers of Russian America, the men of the telegraph expedition continued to toil.

The men at work extending the line north from the Skeena River in British Columbia learned that the Atlantic cable was successful in August 1866, by means of their own telegraph line. However, no order came to stop work until October, when Conway wound down operations, not forever, but simply for the winter. Conway planned to continue construction as soon as he could in the spring of 1867. Meanwhile, exploring parties continued to probe northern British Columbia, seeking the best route to the Yukon. By spring, some had returned to Wrangell, while others had settled in at Telegraph Creek.

Charles Morison spent his winter at Wrangell, looking after the supplies the company had deposited there in 1866. Sometime in April, an Indian came by with word that the United States had bought Alaska. Seeking news, Morison and Thomas Elwyn, one of the telegraph explorers who had returned to Wrangell after his winter's activities, set out by canoe for Fort Simpson. Not far to the south, they sighted a large American flag on shore; they drew in, and found company paymaster Charles Burrage with his flag, his safe and a parcel of mail for the men at Wrangell.

Morison and Elwyn returned with Burrage to Wrangell, where they received their payout—more than expected in Morison's case, since Conway had increased his pay retroactively in tribute to the fine job Morison had done. Burrage then went up the Stikine to bring the remaining men back from Telegraph Creek; the supplies were left there, just in case construction resumed one day. Then almost everyone set out for Fort Simpson, where they would meet up with the men Burrage had brought down from Fort Stager and make their way south.

Morison stayed behind. "Things were awfully dull down south,"[1] he confided, and agreed to remain behind to look after the company stores at Wrangell. Little happened until mid-summer: on July 29, 1867, an American gunboat pulled in to harbour, the American flag was hoisted, and the Russians at Wrangell handed over to the Americans with the customary Russian ceremony of "ten drops" (15 drops usually—but perhaps they were short of spirits). Then an American customs officer arrived, and bunked in with Morison since there was nowhere else to stay. Several American miners also showed up, and built cabins along the shore. Morison gussied up his cabin with curtains made from gunny sacks and curtain rings of telegraph wire.

Morison was still in residence in the spring of 1868, together with American troops who had arrived to man a new military depot. With the troopship came orders from San Francisco, that the telegraph wire was to be loaded aboard the ship and sent back down to San Francisco. But the Western Union officials who dispatched the orders forgot to send money, and Morison had none with which to pay Indians to take the tons of wire by canoe from the beach to the ship. The steamer sailed, leaving the wire behind. Morison also had no orders to dispose of the company stores at Wrangell, so, sorrowfully, he saw them slowly decompose in the wet climate. Once his duties with the company were complete, he accepted a job with the Hudson's Bay Company, and sailed south with the *Otter* to receive his new orders.

On the opposite side of the Pacific, it was no business as usual at the mouth of the Anadyr River where telegraph workers and *Golden Gate* crew waited out the winter. The original Robinson, who spent the winter in the camp, apologized to Bush via letter for his failure to investigate the effects of the *aurora borealis* on the telegraph line but, he excused himself, "a house 25 ft square occupied by from 30 to 60 men leaves but little room for experiments."[2]

Clerk M.J. Kelly went out lightly dressed to visit a Chukchi encampment, although he had been warned repeatedly not to venture outside without skin clothing. Losing his way on his return journey, he wandered for some time, and froze two fingers. Dixon, the surgeon, amputated the fingers with a hand saw, a jack knife and rusty old tweezers to pick up the arteries. Mr. Kelly, concluded one of the group, not at all sympathetic, "has learned a lesson that will benefit him in future."[3] With the exception of Kelly, they survived the winter in good health, "except Charles Geddes has died of fevers."[4] The second casualty in Siberia was buried at Golden Gate Bay.

When the ice broke up in mid-June, the crew repaired and launched the *Wade*. On June 24, shortly after Richard Bush and his companions reached the camp at the river mouth, the *Golden Gate* drifted free but grounded again, badly damaged by the spring ice grinding against her hull.

The Anadyr party learned that the telegraph project had been abandoned when the *Clara Bell* arrived in July. With surprise and regret, Bush sent the *Wade* upriver to collect men and property. Harder, who had resigned from the company three months earlier, (no reason is given, nor do we discover what he planned to do in Siberia) was told to get himself on board the *Clara Bell* if he wanted to go home. Instead, he decamped and disappeared into Siberia while the *Clara Bell* set course for Plover Bay.

## 1867: End of the Race

Far to the south, on the coast of the Okhotsk Sea, George Kennan had spent the early months of 1867 travelling to Yamsk to meet Abasa, then returning to Gizhiga while Abasa returned to Yakoutsk to make sure his labourers would be available for work over the upcoming season. On June 1, Kennan was still at Gizhiga, waiting for company ships and orders. On that day, to amuse himself, he boarded a whaling ship, the barque *Seabreeze*, out of New Bedford, Massachusetts.

What in tarnation, inquired the captain of the *Seabreeze*, were Kennan and his companions doing here? Building a telegraph line, said Kennan. He explained the overland project, then asked whether anything new had happened on the Atlantic cable.

"Works like a snatch-tackle," said the captain. "The Frisco papers are publishing every morning the London news of the day before. I've got a lot of them on board I'll give you."[5]*

Back on shore, Kennan read the papers and realized the Russian-American telegraph line was dead. Though they might well build the line, "there was no company in the world which would undertake to sustain and work it a single year in competition with the cable." He then proceeded to sell off all the telegraph supplies on hand. Wire, pick-axes, shovels, frozen cucumber pickles, glass insulators that could serve as teacups, telegraph brackets for kindling: all went to anyone who wanted them at the best price Kennan could get. Soap and candles were offered as a bonus to anyone who bought salt pork and dried apples. He taught the natives how to make biscuits and limeade, so he could get rid of lime juice and baking powder. He sold everything on hand, much of it "of no more use to the poor natives than iceboats and mouse-traps would be to the Tuaregs of the Saharan desert."[6]

In mid-July, the company barque *Onward* arrived at Gizhiga with orders to discharge all employees and bring the American workers back to the United States. Kennan and Mahood declined. They concocted a new adventure with two other telegraph workers, to wait for winter and go home through Siberia and Russia, "across Asia and Europe,

---

* Interestingly enough, Kennan did not include this information or indeed any information about the days that followed his visit to the *Seabreeze* in the original, 1870, version of his book. Nor was it present in new editions published in 1871 or 1903. It finally appears in the 1910 edition of Kennan's book, where he adds 15,000 new words to his original manuscript.

around the world." When the *Onward* sailed for Plover Bay, it left the four behind.

While E.B. Libby and his party huddled near their camp at the western edge of the Bering Strait in Russian America, William Ennis, George Adams, Fred Smith and a work party of a dozen men tried to make a start on the line that would lead west from Norton Bay toward Libby's section of the line. Between January 21 and the end of April, they built 28 miles of line, suspending work only when spring thaw came, and water filled each hole as soon as it was dug. It was boring, backbreaking work. Short of food, short of dogs to haul provisions and supplies, they soon found that the frozen ground defied their efforts to work quickly. It took the best digger in the party two hours to sink a single posthole, and steel crowbars split in the cold as if they were made of tin. The ground was as "hard as Pharaoh's heart,"[7] the snow blew into their frozen faces and the men were hungry.

By late March, Smith reported "the Indians have been eating boot soles and old fish nets since we have been here and we fell to discussing how soup 'a la boot sole' would go,"[8] and Adams cursed the company for its criminal act of leaving the expedition members with only half the provisions they needed. On April 28, he wrote, "Most of the men are unable to work. Hard work and no grub or very little has completely played them out. We are almost entirely out of provisions. Only a little tea and bran is all we have to depend on—our bacon has given out. Sugar is all gone two weeks since—and bread and tea is all we will have to live on unless we can get reindeer meat."[9]

On June 26, they were clustered at a house they had built on the shores of Norton Bay, waiting for the water to dry up and the ground to become solid enough for them to resume their work when they sighted a Russian boat hove to offshore. Adams and Smith rowed out to the boat and asked the Russian commandant from the post at Unalakleet what news he brought. He told them the race was over: "Company has suspended operations. Reason; the Atlantic Cable is a success. We are all ordered home (much joy)."[10]

Together with that news came the announcement that the United States had bought Russian America for seven million dollars. Intensely excited, the group at Norton Bay erupted into fevered discussion. Would they get paid for the work they had completed? When could they go home? What would happen next? Adams went on to the second camp on Norton Bay to announce the news, and all the party travelled together by boat back to St. Michaels.

At Nulato at the beginning of 1867, Frank Ketchum was as vexed as the rest of the Russian-American party. From the beginning, the expedition had been sabotaged by lack of provisions and a shortage of sled dogs. The Russians could provide little; what they did, was expensive and given grudgingly.

Nonetheless, Ketchum was eager to continue his explorations. On March 2, Mike Lebarge arrived from Unalakleet, bringing 22 dogs and enough dried salmon to feed them for a month. Unwilling to use any of the salmon before they left on their trip, Ketchum and the men with him made a soup for the dogs of every edible thing that remained in their stores: oil, fish, meat scraps, bran, rice, even the last of the camp beans. They cooked up the melange and poured it into a trough, whence the dogs licked up every last drop.

Ketchum also made final plans for a telegraph station that was to be built a mile from Nulato near the Klatkakhatne River as the headquarters of the Yukon division, and hired a Russian to construct the log building that would be known as Fort Kennicott. The four telegraph employees at Nulato set to work cutting the 30 telegraph poles needed to link Fort Kennicott to Nulato, had a Russian workman clear the route, and erected the poles.

On March 11, Ketchum, Lebarge, and four natives of what Whymper called the Co-Yukon tribe left Nulato bound for Fort Yukon by dogsled, sped on their way by the dire predictions of the Russians and natives, who were convinced the journey was doomed by the shortage of dogfood and provisions, and the soft snow that would make travel difficult.

Snow fell constantly for 18 days, and travel was indeed difficult. It took Ketchum almost two months to reach Fort Yukon overland, arriving with just eight of the 14 dogs he had set out with; the others, starving or exhausted, had been left behind at Indian villages or had died en route. He and his companions had been able to shoot enough game to feed themselves. There was no food available for them at Fort Yukon, so they continued on up the Rat River to shoot geese, returning to the fort on May 21.

By then, Fort Yukon factor McDougall had returned from his trip. Although he had no orders to help the telegraph explorers and was doubtful about the effort, he did agree to supply an interpreter and some pemmican. Bolstered by these additions, Ketchum and Lebarge continued upriver by boat, arriving June 25 at Fort Selkirk after an uneventful journey.

Ketchum noted that Fort Selkirk marked the point where the Pelly and Lewis rivers merged to form the Yukon. Though the current at the mouth of the Pelly was rapid, rocks and debris could be cleared and the river made safe for navigation. Natives in the area told Ketchum they thought the Pelly would be navigable for a small steamer of light draft for more than 450 miles upriver. This country was more fruitful than that farther north. Moose and deer were abundant, and could be used to supply fresh meat, dried meat and mooseskin clothing. The country was well timbered with trees suitable for telegraph poles.

Their initial explorations successful, Ketchum and Lebarge set out once more on the Yukon River. In four days, they drifted back down to Fort Yukon.

There, they met up with Dall and Whymper. The artist and the scientist had spent the winter at Nulato, each engaged in his own activities. Dall was well content with two large boxes of natural history specimens he had collected and prepared for transport back to St. Michaels. The two waited at Nulato through the first thaw in early

*Fort Yukon. (From Dall,* Alaska and. . . . *)*

April until the breakup of the Nulato River on May 5, the first appearance (far from the last) of mosquitoes on May 12, the arrival of swallows on May 13, and, finally, the key event: the breakup of the Yukon River which began on May 19 and continued for a week.

Breakup was the signal for activity. Dall and Whymper planned to go upriver in the *baidara* they had bought the previous fall and cached for later use. The Russians at the post prepared for their spring trading trip and one of the telegraph men at Nulato prepared to go down the Yukon to meet Everett Smith, captain of the steamer *Wilder,* who had been instructed to sound the various channels at the mouth of the Yukon River and determine the best route for steamer traffic.

Dall and Whymper headed out on the river with the Russians through pouring rain on May 26. Floating ice and driftwood made navigation difficult, and both craft had to keep near the banks to avoid the swifter and more dangerous current in the centre. One man stood at the bow of the boat, pushing away wood and ice with an iron-tipped pole. Great trees rolled through the current under the Russians' large canoe, lifting it out of the water before they slid on down the river. Only a thin piece of sealskin separated the men from the water; they felt each ice cake and log as it scraped its way under the *baidara's* keel. The telegraph group and their native companions were exhilarated by the battle, and overjoyed when the Russian boat was forced into shore while they battled on against current and hazard to take the lead.

The group continued on upriver, starting each day very early in the morning and camping soon after noon to avoid the worst of the summer heat. On the 31st, they passed an Indian village that marked the furthest extent of Zagoskin's map; from here on Whymper kept a constant survey of bearings and distances. As he had since he began his trip, Dall kept a diary in which he recorded every aspect of natural history, geography and geology that met his eye. Both men took exhaustive notes on the natives they met and their customs.

While the Russians traded for beaver, marten and other furs, Dall bargained for dried deer (pemmican), moose meat and fat, and an extra canoe that could carry their new supplies. "We were not well provided with trading goods," noted Whymper, and they had to trade off their own personal property. "Spare shirts, socks, pocket or sheath knives, and other possessions, gradually melted from our gaze." Whymper gave up his towel and soap, but baulked at trading off his toothbrush. "The

*The Yukon River during the spring breakup. (From Whymper,* Travel and Adventures. . . . )

future traveller," he warned, "should either cut down his own kit to the lowest standard, or take all the little luxuries of life by the dozen."[11]

By early June, the spring runoff had passed and the water level began to fall. Their native companions tracked the boat through the shallows, floundering through slimy mud and over rocks, hauling on lines attached to the skin boat to move it and the men and cargo aboard slowly up the river. On June 8, they arrived at the native village of Nuklukayet, the furthest point inland reached by Russian traders and the furthest village down river reached by the traders of the Hudson's Bay Company. They set off again accompanied by natives in birchbark canoes, paddling and tracking ever northeastward toward Fort Yukon.

The shortest night of the year, June 21/22, only 45 minutes long, found them just downstream from the fort; 29 days after they left Nulato, they paddled up to the Hudson's Bay Company post. A week later, Ketchum and Lebarge arrived at Fort Yukon from Fort Selkirk.

Their explorations complete, the foursome set out downriver once more on July 8. They lashed their three canoes together, and let the current sweep them along at a rate of 100 miles in a 24-hour day, for they went ashore only once or twice a day to boil tea and fry fish. After the exertions of the upriver trip, it was a holiday excursion. They arrived at Nulato five days and 20 hours after they left Fort Yukon.

Awaiting them there was a peculiar message. Everyone was to go as quickly as possible to St. Michaels, taking with them everything portable that belonged to the telegraph expedition. Amid rumours that the United States had purchased Russian America, Ketchum bought a large *baidara* from the Russians and loaded aboard all the company's goods. On July 15, they set out for the Russian redoubt, "full of anxiety, not knowing what changes were at hand."[12]

On July 25, nearing St. Michaels, they pulled ashore to don clothing more suited to the civilized company they soon expected to join. That afternoon, they climbed ashore at the redoubt, to find the rest of the telegraph expedition gathered together to meet them.

They received the news that the telegraph project had been cancelled with far less jubilation than had the men at Norton Bay. In the country only a year, Whymper and Dall had looked forward to another year's work on their artistic and scientific ventures. Whymper was particularly distressed for the men who had worked so hard to build part of the line that winter:

"They had persevered, and had put up a large piece of the line; and I can sympathize with the feeling that prompted some of them at Unalachleet, Norton Sound, on hearing of the withdrawal of our forces, to hang black cloth on the telegraph poles and put them into mourning!"[13]

On August 18, the *Clara Bell* arrived with the men who had wintered at Grantley Harbor, to carry them all to Plover Bay. All, that is, but one. Dall was by no means ready to go home. Although the Yukon above Nulato and the shores of Norton Sound had been thoroughly explored, little had been done in the Lower Yukon and on the river's delta. Dall wanted to stay behind, to carry out the plans of Robert Kennicott. George Wright, in charge of the men and materials that were to be shipped aboard the *Clara Bell*, acquiesced, though he had no provisions he could give or sell to Dall. He did sell Dall some trade goods, and paid him part of the salary due him. "For the rest," concluded Dall, "I must depend upon the natural resources of the country."[14]

On August 23, the *Clara Bell* sailed, leaving Dall behind.

Six days later, the ship arrived at Plover Bay, on the west side of the Bering Strait, where the men were to await the *Nightingale* to take them home. For the first time since the spring of 1865, all 120 of the men of the Russian-American Telegraph expedition were gathered together, though not for the celebration they had long anticipated.

To house the gathering crowd, Captain Kelsey, in charge at Plover Bay, had the men set up temporary shelters of canvas, sails, poles and planks. On September 6, the *Nightingale*, with Colonel Bulkley aboard, arrived at Plover Bay. Men and materials were loaded onto the ship, and the *Nightingale* sailed for San Francisco, taking with it the last hopes of the telegraph line that was to have ruled the world.

CHAPTER 22

# Aftermath

Along with the depressing news of the death of the overland telegraph project came news of a more upbeat nature. On March 28, 1867, just three weeks after Western Union called a halt to work on the line, the United States government bought Russian America—henceforth known as Alaska—for seven million dollars.

The Russian-American Telegraph project and the purchase of Alaska were closely related. The United States had been interested in Alaska since the days of the Crimean War, but the Russian government had been reluctant to sell. When Perry McDonough Collins and Hiram Sibley visited St. Petersburg in 1864 to work out the details of an agreement for the building of the telegraph line, Sibley talked to the Russian Foreign Minister Gorchacov. Gorchacov questioned whether the Hudson's Bay Company would allow Western Union to have a right-of-way through British Columbia. If they did not, Sibley replied, then Western Union would consider buying the H.B.C.; it shouldn't cost more than a few million dollars.

Gorchacov laughed. For not much more than that, he suggested, Russia would sell all of Alaska. And yes, certainly, Sibley could tell the U.S. government what he had said. Sibley told U.S. representative Cassius Clay; Clay told Secretary of State Seward, suggesting the purchase would not only secure the telegraph line but also help American traders, fishermen and whalers.

Seward, a confirmed continentalist, needed no persuading. But there was sizeable opposition from those who thought that Russia was selling a "sucked orange", that Alaska was an Arctic wasteland that would contribute nothing but drain much from the United States treasury. Seward confronted his opposition with information gathered by the expedition's scientific and exploring parties. Henry Bannister worked with the expedition at Norton Sound. After he returned with the other expedition members to San Francisco in 1867, Bannister, an immediate supporter of the purchase, began to put together the information from the expedition in a form that would bolster Seward's cause.

The purchase treaty called forth a storm of controversy as the senate considered whether to ratify. The *Chicago Daily Journal* considered that "the effect of this cession will also hasten the time when British Columbia will become a part of the United States. . . . Being surrounded by the United States will tend to strengthen and tighten the cords that were already drawing that province into the folds of the American Union."[1] The *New York World*, doubtful of the immediate value of the purchase, was nonetheless equally convinced that it made it inevitable that British Columbia would one day become American, if only because the ragged nature of the map now drawn would offend the country's sense of symmetry.

Collins too weighed in on the side of the continentalists, in prose no less moderate than that of a few years earlier. He cited the valuable fur trade, the fisheries based on myriads of codfish, "unsurpassed in size or delicacy", that would one day result in a population and commerce that would rival that of Newfoundland or Cape Cod, the timber resources of the country, the coal deposits, and even the agricultural potential, as good reasons for the purchase.

"The country of Russian America cannot be considered, as some would have it, a dreary waste of glaciers, icebergs, white bears and walrus, and only fit for Esquimaux and drinkers of train oil," Collins wrote to Seward.[2] He then proposed yet another scheme for exporting the very pure ice from Alaskan lakes to American cities on the Pacific coast.

Other supporters of the purchase suggested that American seamen nurtured off the coast of Alaska would become "a race of hardy adventurers to repeat on the Pacific, softened by Christian civilization, the deeds of the old Norse sea kings on the Atlantic."[3] And a summary report from the Smithsonian, based on notes from Kennicott and Dall, waxed enthusiastic about the climate along the coast (similar to that at the city of Washington), the soil (producing excellent barley and root crops), the abundance of fur-bearing animals, fish in exhaustless numbers, iron ore also exhaustless, and the industrious peaceable inhabitants of the country—to an extent that might have surprised those members of the telegraph expedition whose experiences of frostbite and near-starvation were not quite as positive as the report suggested.

The enthusiasts carried the day and the senate ratified the treaty on June 20, 1867. *The New York Times* applauded ratification in words remarkably similar to those Collins had used a few years earlier to support the Russian-American Telegraph project, suggesting the purchase made it inevitable that the United States would dominate the commerce of eastern Asia.

Though the failure of the Russian-American Telegraph may have left a sour taste in the mouths of many who invested in the project, the results were sweet for some of those who took part in the expedition. Four fat books resulted, by Dall, Whymper, Bush and Kennan. Dall remained in Alaska until late summer, 1868, travelling back and forth between St. Michaels and Nulato, and taking copious notes on events, native customs, natural history, history, geography and resources of the territory. On his return, he penned a 600-page tome, one-third of it devoted to recounting his experiences in Alaska, the rest an exhaustive inventory of the country that stood as the standard reference work for decades. Dall spent much of the rest of his life as an increasingly eminent scientist with the U.S. government and with the Smithsonian.

George Kennan's experiences on the telegraph expedition marked the beginning of a lifelong fascination with Siberia. He returned to the United States after his 5,000-mile journey across Siberia and European

Russia, and sampled various careers. He sold books and worked in banks and law offices. He lectured on his Siberian experiences and published a highly amusing and colourful book about his three years in Siberia. Money from the book bought him a second trip to Russia, this time to the Caucasus; this trip provided more material for lectures and articles.

He was impressed by what he saw, and generally supported the Russian government when others attacked its repressive policies. Then, in 1885, *Century Magazine* sent him back to Siberia to report on the present condition of the country.

This trip depressed him immensely. His book *Siberia and the Exile System*, published in 1891, and his articles in *Century Magazine* revealed the cruelty and oppression inflicted by the Tsarist regime upon its political opponents. His burning indignation converted most who read his reports. The book established Kennan as an authority on Russia and as a superb writer. From 1891 on, he worked as a correspondent for American newspapers and magazines, reporting on the Spanish-American War and the Russo-Japanese War. His unsympathetic writings about Russia made him *persona non grata* there; he was expelled on a visit in 1903 and never returned.

He supported the Provisional Government that took over in 1917 and probably only his age—he was then 72—kept him from an appointment as an American envoy to the revolution-torn country.

Kennan died in 1924, before he could see the use that Russia's government under Josef Stalin made of Siberia and the exile system. In the middle years of this century, George Frost Kennan, a distant cousin of George Kennan's, established himself as a first-rank international journalist and diplomat. In the foreword to the first volume of his autobiography, he acknowledges his debt to his predecessor: "The life of this elder Kennan and my own have shown similarities that give, to me at least, the feeling that we are connected in some curious way by bonds deeper than just our rather distant kinship. . . . I feel that I was in some strange way destined to carry forward as best I could the work of my distinguished and respected namesake."[4]

What became of the other members of the telegraph expeditions? Most slipped back into obscurity. Some continued in the careers set up by the telegraph expedition. Edward Conway went to Utah, where he became superintendent for Western Union. He returned to British

Columbia in 1876 with his wife and children, despite his oft-repeated criticisms of the country, to carry out a contract for rebuilding the line from Victoria to Seattle. He died in 1878, at home in Victoria, of a lung hemorrhage.

Franklin Pope, the leader of explorations in northern British Columbia, became a patent attorney for Western Union and the president of the American Institute of Electrical Engineers. He died, it is said in a story perhaps apocryphal, by electrocuting himself while experimenting in his basement with electrical transformers.

Some found they could not abandon the travelling ways they acquired on the expedition. Charles Bulkley left his wife and two sons behind in California, and went to Guatemala to work; he died there in 1894. William Ennis also married, but left his wife behind in 1868 to ship out to trade in Norton Sound; he sent his wife long fervent love letters from aboard ship. Charles Morison never left his beloved north coast, serving as a Hudson's Bay Company agent for many years, then working as an accountant and merchant. He died at Metlakatla in 1933, at the age of 89, outliving all but two of his seven children.

Perry McDonough Collins refused to give up his ideas for linking continents. In 1869, he was at work again, writing to the U.S. government to suggest a telegraph that would link Japan to the Asian mainland. The idea died, and in 1876, at the age of 63, Collins retired to New York, living in the St. Denis Hotel for 25 years until his death in 1900. He became something of a recluse, albeit one who had a reputation for luxurious living. He left a sizeable fortune; 17 years later, his heir bequeathed $550,000 to New York University for scholarships in arts and pure science and in engineering. The awards were given for ten years before anyone formally recognized the man who had made them possible.

And what of the line itself? In Siberia, the posts remained as mute witnesses to the dream that died until they fell down or were used by the natives to build houses. The poles erected in Russian America were early victims; they were not well set in the shifting ground and quickly fell over. The native people in the region of the line's end in British Columbia soon found uses for the telegraph wire and other supplies left behind. A famous native suspension bridge spanned the river at Hagwilgaet for decades; it was built almost entirely of telegraph wire.

*The Indian bridge at Hagwilgaet, BC (in the foreground). (Courtesy of the Provincial Archives of BC. HP 10451.)*

Western Union manned Fort Stager, at the end of the line, until 1869, then shipped out the last operator with 13 canoes loaded with provisions and clothing. The company maintained the line from New Westminster to the Cariboo—though not particularly well, if newspaper reports of frequent breakdowns are anything to judge by—until 1871, when the British Columbia government leased the line in perpetuity.

That same year, when British Columbia became a province of Canada, the federal government took over the lease, and, over the next ten years, repaired, rebuilt and added to the telegraph system. In 1880, the government bought out all Western Union's remaining property and privileges.

In 1954, Canadian National Railways bought the system from the government. In 1978, CNCP Telecommunications, now owners of the British Columbia telegraph service, closed the New Westminster telegraph office after 113 years of service. That same year, they closed the offices in Quesnel, Smithers and Kitimat, bringing to an end the era that had begun when Edward Conway arrived in New Westminster late in 1864. In British Columbia, as in the rest of the world, satellites, telephones and other forms of modern technology left the telegraph far behind.

It was left to a man who traversed the land along the Bulkley and Skeena rivers in 1872 to pen an epitaph for the hopes and dreams of the telegraph builders. Wrote William Butler:

> Crossing the wide Nacharcole River and continuing south for a few miles, we reached a broadly cut trail which bore curious traces of past civilization. Old telegraph poles stood at intervals along the forest-cleared opening, and rusted wires hung in loose festoons down from their tops, or lay tangled in the growing brushwood of the cleared space. A telegraph in the wilderness! What did it mean?
>
> When civilization once grasps the wild, lone spaces of the earth it seldom releases its hold; yet here civilization had once advanced her footsteps, and apparently shrunk back again, frightened at her boldness. It was even so; this trail, with its ruined wire, told of the wreck of a great enterprise.
>
> Europe spoke to America beneath the ocean, and the voice which men had sought to waft through the vast forests of the Wild North Land, and over the Tundras of Siberia, died away in utter desolation.[5]

# Footnotes

Chapter 1:
1. as quoted in *Voice Across the Sea*, by Arthur C. Clarke (New York: Harper Brothers, Publishers, 1958) p. 22.
2. as quoted in *The Atlantic Cable*, by Bern Dibner (New York: Blaisdell Publishing Company, 1964), p. 34.
3. as quoted in Clarke, *op. cit.*, p. 39.
4. *Ibid.*, pp. 44–5.

Chapter 2:
1. as quoted in "The Foundations of Russian Foreign Policy in the Far East 1847–1867," by John W. Stanton (unpublished PhD thesis, University of California, Berkeley.) Quoted in Charles Vevier's introduction to *Siberian Journey* (Madison: The University of Wisconsin Press, 1962, p. 15.) This is a new edition of Collins' book, *A Voyage down the Amoor,* with an excellent introduction by Vevier, setting Collins' expedition in the context of the times.
2. *A Voyage down the Amoor,* by Perry McDonough Collins (New York: D. Appleton and Company, 1860) p. 3.
3. Collins, in *Harper's New Monthly Magazine,* Vol. 17, No. 98, July 1858, p. 221.
4. Collins, 1860, p. 11.
5. Vevier, p. 6.
6. Collins, 1860, p. 86.
7. *Ibid.*, p. 75.

# Footnotes

8. *Northwest to Fortune,* by Viljhalmur Stefansson (New York: Duell, Sloan and Pearce, 1958) p. 250.
9. Collins, *Harper's,* p. 225.
10. Collins, 1860, p. 180.
11. Collins, *Harper's,* p. 227.
12. Collins, 1860, p. 171.
13. *Ibid.,* p. 199.
14. *Ibid.,* pp. 237–8.
15. Collins to Secretary of State Lewis Cass, March 6, 1858, Washington, House Ex. Doc. 98, 35 Cong., 1 sess., quoted in Vevier, p. 301.

Chapter 3:
1. Collins to Cass, March 6, 1858, Washington.
2. *Ibid.*
3. quoted in "The Collins Overland Line and American Continentalism," by Charles Vevier (*Pacific Historical Review,* August 1959, Vol 28, No. 3) p. 241.
4. quoted in *To the Great Ocean,* by Harmon Tupper (Boston: Little, Brown & Company, 1965), p. 62.
5. Collins to Cass, September 20, 1859 (quoted in Vevier's introduction to *Siberian Journey*), p. 33.
6. Speeches of Hon. Milton S. Latham delivered in the Senate of the United States, . . . and Report from the Military Committee, on Telegraphic Communication between San Francisco and the Amoor River, 1862, p. 29 (quoted in "The Collins Overland Telegraph", by Corday Mackay, *British Columbia Historical Quarterly,* July 1946, p. 192.)
7. Hiram Sibley to P. McD. Collins, October 16, 1861, reprinted in appendix of *Statement of the Origin, Organization and Progress of the Russian-American Telegraph, Western Union Extension, Collins Overland Line, via Behring Strait and Asiatic Russia to Europe* (Rochester: Western Union Telegraph Company, May 1866).
8. *Ibid.*
9. *Wiring a Continent: the History of the Telegraph Industry in the United States, 1832–1866,* by Robert Luther Thompson (Princeton, N.J.: Princeton University Press, 1947) p. 399.

Chapter 4:
1. Quoted in "The Russian or Collins Telegraph: A Defeated Success," *Overland Monthly* Vol. XII, p. 17.
2. *Statement of the Origin* etc., p. 13.
3. *Ibid.,* pp. 77–81.
4. *Ibid.*
5. *Ibid.*
6. *The Telegrapher,* Vol. 1, No. 2, p. 9.
7. *Ibid.*
8. O.H. Palmer to Charles S. Bulkley, December 16, 1864, Rochester, New York, in *Statement of the Origin* etc., p. 82.
9. Bulkley to Palmer, May 2, 1865, San Francisco, *ibid.,* p. 83.
10. *The Telegrapher, op. cit.,* p. 74.

Chapter 5:
1. Diaries of William Ennis, transcribed introduction and notes by Harold F. Taggart (in the *California Historical Quarterly,* 1954), p. 5.
2. *The Telegrapher,* June 26, 1865, p. 118.
3. *Ibid.*

Chapter 6:
1. Frederick Seymour to the Rt. Hon. Edward Cardwell, as quoted in *New Westminster, the Royal City,* by Barry Mather (New Westminster: J.M. Dent & Sons (Canada) Limited and the Corporation of the City of New Westminster, 1958) pp. 78–9.
2. *The British Colonist,* December 8, 1864.
3. *The British Columbian,* January 25, 1865.
4. An ordinance to encourage the construction of a line of Telegraph, connecting the Telegraphs of British Columbia with the Telegraph lines of Russia, the United States and other Countries, and for other purposes. No. 5 of 1865.
5. *The British Columbian,* February 25, 1865.
6. *The British Columbian,* November 26, 1864.
7. Conway to Bulkley, April 28, 1865, New Westminster, *Journal and Letters of Col. Charles S. Bulkley, 1865–1867.*
8. *The British Columbian,* March 25, 1865.
9. *The British Columbian,* April 22, 1865.
10. *The Cariboo Road,* by Mark Wade (Victoria; The Haunted Bookshop, 1979), p. 240.
11. Conway to Bulkley, *Letterbook of Edward Conway,* May 14, 1865.
12. *The British Columbian,* September 16, 1865.

Chapter 7:
1. Franklin Pope (attrib.) unpublished manuscript, p. 7.
2. *Ibid.,* p. 13.
3. *Ibid.,* p. 15.
4. *The Telegrapher,* October 16, 1865.
5. *Ibid.*
6. Pope ms., p. 24.
7. *The Telegrapher, op. cit.*
8. Conway to Bulkley, August 16, 1865, New Westminster, *Bulkley papers.*
9. Conway to Bulkley, December 30, 1865, *Bulkley papers.*
10. *Ibid.*
11. *The Telegrapher,* Vol. 2. p. 74.
12. Pope to Conway, November 6, 1865, Bulkley House, *Bulkley papers.*
13. *The Telegrapher, op. cit.*
14. *The British Columbian,* April 11, 1866 (dated December 26, 1865, signed Q.M.)
15. *Ibid.*
16. Conway to Bulkley, December 10, 1865, *Conway letterbook.*
17. Conway to Bulkley, December 30, 1865, *Conway letterbook.*

Chapter 8:
1. *Tent Life in Siberia,* by George Kennan (New York: G.B. Putnam and Sons, 1870) p. 3.

# Footnotes

2. *Ibid.*, p. 6.
3. *Ibid.*, p. 7.
4. *Reindeer, Dogs and Snowshoes*, by Richard J. Bush (London: Sampson Low, Son, and Marston, 1872) pp. 25–26.
5. Kennan, 1870, p. 20.
6. *Ibid.*, p. 38.
7. *Ibid.*, pp. 40–41.
8. Abasa to Bulkley, August 16/28, Fort Petropavloski, Kamchatka, *Bulkley papers*. Letters written from Siberia often carry both Julian and Gregorian dates.
9. Kennan, 1870, pp. 45–46.
10. Bush, p. 56.

Chapter 9:

1. Bush, p. 83.
2. Mahood to Abasa, March 13, 1866, Okhotsk, Eastern Sibera. *Bulkley papers*.
3. Bush, p. 150.
4. *Ibid.*, p. 154.
5. *Ibid.*, p. 158.
6. *Ibid.*, p. 217.
7. *Ibid.*, p. 223.

Chapter 10:

1. Kennan, 1870, p. 61.
2. *Ibid.*, p. 70.
3. *Ibid.*, p. 83.
4. *Ibid.*, p. 128.
5. *Ibid.*, p. 148.
6. *Ibid.*, p. 232.
7. Abasa to Bulkley, February 15, 1866, Okhotsk, *Bulkley papers*.
8. Kennan, 1870, p. 265.
9. *Ibid.*, p. 268.
10. *Ibid.*, p. 269.

Chapter 11:

1. Macrae to Bulkley, March 28/April 9, 1866, Ghijigha, *Bulkley papers.*

Chapter 12:

1. *Travel and Adventures in the Territory of Alaska*, by Frederick Whymper (London: John Murray, 1868) p. 71.
2. Ennis, p. 7.
3. Whymper, p. 75.
4. *Ibid.*
5. Ennis, p. 149.
6. *Ibid.*, p. 151.
7. *Diary of (Author Unknown, George Adams, attrib.)* September 26, 1865 to March 23, 1866, p. 5.
8. *Ibid.*, October 31, p. 7.

9. *Ibid.*, November 2, p. 8.
10. *Ibid.*, November 9, p. 9.
11. *Ibid.*, November 14, p. 10.
12. *Ibid.*, December 19, p. 17.

Chapter 13:
1. Whymper, p. 92.
2. Bulkley to the Executive Committee, December 18, 1865, *Bulkley papers.*
3. Whymper, p. 103.
4. *Ibid.*, p. 105.
5. *Ibid.*, p. 109.

Chapter 14:
1. as quoted in *The Atlantic Cable*, by Bern Dibner (New York: Blaisdell Publishing Company, 1964), p. 81.
2. as quoted in *Three Miles Deep*, by John Merrett (London: Hamish Hamilton, 1958), p. 120.

Chapter 15:
1. *The British Colonist*, April 25, 1866.
2. Conway to Bulkley, *Conway letterbook*, pp. 303–4.
3. *Ibid.*
4. *"A Snowshoe Trip in B.C."*, by J.T. Rothrock Jan. 22, 1876.
5. *The Telegrapher*, Vol. 2, August 15, 1866, p. 188.
6. *Ibid.*
7. *Ibid.*
8. J.T. Rothrock to E.O.S. Scholefield, Jan. 11, 1913.
9. Conway to Bulkley, February 19, 1867, San Francisco, *Bulkley papers.*
10. "Reminiscences of the early days of British Columbia 1862–1876 by a Pioneer of the North-West Coast," by Charles Frederick Morison.
11. *Ibid.*, p. 16.
12. *Ibid.*, p. 18.
13. Conway to Bulkley, *op. cit.*

Chapter 16:
1. Macrae to Bulkley, March 28/April 9, 1866, Ghijigha, *Bulkley papers.*
2. Kennan, 1870, p. 310.
3. Bush, p. 240.
4. *Ibid.*, p. 245.
5. *Ibid.*, p. 255.
6. Abasa to Bulkley, February 16 to 24, *Bulkley papers.*

Chapter 17:
1. Mahood to Abasa, March 13, 1866, Okhotsk, *Bulkley papers.*
2. Bulkley to the Executive Committee, March 1, 1867, San Francisco, *Bulkley papers.*
3. Abasa to Mumford, August 14/26, 1866, Gijigha, *Bulkley papers.*
4. *Ibid.*

# Footnotes

5. Kennan, 1870, p. 351.
6. *Ibid.*, p. 383.
7. *Ibid.*
8. Bush, p. 374.
9. *Ibid.*, p. 376.
10. *Ibid.*, p. 379.
11. *Ibid.*, p. 387.
12. *Ibid.*, pp. 396–397.
13. *Ibid.*, p. 397.
14. *Ibid.*, p. 413.
15. Bulkley to the Executive Committee, March 1, 1867, San Francisco, *Bulkley papers*.
16. Macrae to Bush, June 4, 1867, *Bulkley papers*.
17. *Ibid.*

Chapter 18:
1. Ennis, March 14, 1866, p. 163.
2. Ennis to Bulkley, June 30, 1866, St. Michaels, *Bulkley papers*.
3. Adams, p. 152.
4. *Diary of Fred Smith*, p. 11.
5. Adams, May 13, p. 6.
6. Adams, May 14, p. 7.
7. Adams, in *Life in the Yukon, 1865–1867* (Richard A. Pierce, ed., Kingston: The Limestone Press, 1982), p. 91.

Chapter 19:
1. Smith, p. 15, May 25.
2. *Ibid.*, p. 19, June 3.
3. *Ibid.*, p. 22, June 15.
4. *Ibid.*, p. 21, June 10.
5. *Alaska and its Resources*, by William H. Dall (Boston: Lee and Shepard, 1870) p. 5.
6. *Ibid.*, p. 7.
7. *Ibid.*
8. Whymper, p. 130.
9. *Ibid.*, p. 145.
10. Dall, p. 21.
11. *Ibid.*, p. 25.
12. Whymper, p. 162.
13. *Ibid.*, p. 164.
14. Adams, 1982, p. 175.
15. *Ibid.*, p. 175.
16. *Ibid.*, p. 184.
17. Libby to Bulkley, June 20, 1867, Port Clarence, *Bulkley papers*.
18. Smith, p. 32.

Chapter 20:
1. as quoted in *Cyrus Field*, edited by Isabella Judson (New York: Harper and Brothers Publishers, 1896), p. 196.

2. Dibner, p. 132.
3. *The Telegrapher*, July 1, 1867, p. 119.
4. Judson, p. 210.
5. Dibner, p. 147.
6. Thompson, p. 435.
7. *Ibid.*, p. 437.
8. *The Telegrapher*, March 15, 1867,Vol. III, 1867, pp. 146, 159.

Chapter 21:
1. Morison, p. 40.
2. J.H. Robinson to Richard Bush, June 27, 1867, Bush's Station, N.E. Siberia, *Bulkley papers.*
3. *Ibid.*
4. *Ibid.*
5. *Tent Life in Siberia*, by George Kennan (New York: G.P. Putnam's Sons, 1910), p. 416.
6. *Ibid.*, pp. 428–30.
7. Smith, p. 35.
8. *Ibid.*
9. Adams, 1982, April 26, p. 29.
10. *Ibid.*, June 26, p. 34.
11. Whymper, p. 204.
12. Dall, p. 118.
13. Whymper, p. 240.
14. Dall, p. 122.

Chapter 22:
1. *The Purchase of Alaska: Contemporary Opinion*, by Virginia Hancock Reid (Long Beach, Calif., 1939) p. 86.
2. Collins to Seward, April 4, 1867.
3. M.C. Meigs to Seward, April 4, 1867.
4. *Memoirs: 1925–1950*, by George Frost Kennan (Boston: Little, Brown, 1967), p. 8.
5. *The Wild North Land*, by W.F. Butler (London: 1874, 4th edition), pp. 333–5.

# Bibliography

*Books:*

Adams, George R. *Life in the Yukon, 1865-1867.* (Richard A. Pierce, ed.) Kingston, Ont.: The Limestone Press, 1982.
Ault, Phil. *Wires West.* New York: Dodd, Mead & Company, 1974.

# Bibliography

Bush, Richard J. *Reindeer, Dogs and Snowshoes*. London: Sampson Low, Son, and Marston, 1872.

Butler, W.F. *The Wild North Land*. London: 1874.

Clarke, Arthur C. *Voice Across the Sea*. New York: Harper Brothers, Publishers, 1958.

Collins, Perry McDonough. *A Voyage down the Amoor*. New York: D. Appleton and Company, 1860.

———. (Charles Vevier, ed.) *Siberian Journey*. Madison: The University of Wisconsin Press, 1962.

Dall, William H. *Alaska and its Resources*. Boston: Lee and Shepard, 1870.

Dibner, Bern. *The Atlantic Cable*. New York: Blaisdell Publishing Company, 1964.

Jackson, Donald Dale. *Gold Dust*. New York: Alfred A. Knopf, 1980.

James, James Alton. *The First Scientific Exploration of Russian America and the Purchase of Alaska*. Evanston and Chicago: Northwestern University, 1942.

Judson, Isabella. *Cyrus Field*. New York: Harper and Brothers Publishers, 1896.

Kennan, George. *Tent Life in Siberia*. New York: G.B. Putnam and Sons, 1870.

———. Revised. New York: G.P. Putnam's Sons, 1910.

———. (Kennan, George Frost, intro.) *Siberia and the Exile System*. Chicago: University of Chicago Press, 1958. Originally published by the Century Company, 1891.

Kennan, George Frost. *Memoirs: 1925-1950*. Boston: Little, Brown, 1967.

Kieve, Jeffrey. *The Electric Telegraph, a Social and Economic History*. Newton Abbott: David and Charles, 1973.

Lavendar, David. *California: Land of New Beginnings*. New York: Harper and Row Publishers, 1972.

Mather, Barry. *New Westminster, the Royal City*. New Westminster: J.M. Dent & Sons (Canada) Limited and the Corporation of the City of New Westminster, 1958.

Merrett, John. *Three Miles Deep*. London: Hamish Hamilton, 1958.

Reid, Virginia Hancock. *The Purchase of Alaska: Contemporary Opinion*. Long Beach, Calif., 1939.

Stefansson, Viljhalmur. *Northwest to Fortune*. New York: Duell, Sloan and Pearce, 1958.

Thompson, Robert Luther. *Wiring a Continent: the History of the Telegraph Industry in the United States, 1832-1866*. Princeton, N.J.: Princeton University Press, 1947.

Tupper, Harmon. *To the Great Ocean*. Boston: Little, Brown & Company, 1965.

Van Alstyne, R.W. *The Rising American Empire*. Oxford: Basil Blackwell, 1960.

Wade, Mark S. *The Cariboo Road*. Victoria: The Haunted Bookshop (Hugh F. Wade), 1979.

Whymper, Frederick. *Travel and Adventures in the Territory of Alaska*. London: John Murray, 1868.


*Articles, newspapers and unpublished sources:*


*The British Colonist*, Victoria, British Columbia, 1864-1878.

*The British Columbian*, New Westminster, British Columbia, 1865-1867.

*Collins Overland Telegraph, General Rules of Organization and Government*. Copy in Provincial Archives of BC (PABC).

"Diaries of William Ennis", transcribed, introduction and notes by Harold F. Taggart. *California Historical Quarterly*, 1954.

*Diaries, Western Union Telegraph Company Alaska Surveys, 1865-1867*. Diaries of Fred Smith and George Adams; unpublished. Copy in PABC.

*Harper's New Monthly Magazine*, Vol. 17, No. 98, July 1858, pp. 221-232.

*Journal and Letters of Col. Charles S. Bulkley, 1865-1867*. Original in the possession of the Library Association of Portland, Oregon; copy in PABC.

*Letterbook of Edward Conway*. PABC.

Mackay, Corday. "The Collins Overland Telegraph", in the *British Columbia Historical Quarterly*, July 1946.

Morison, Charles Frederick. "Reminiscences of the early days of British Columbia 1862-1876 by a Pioneer of the North-West Coast." Unpublished ms. in PABC.

Parker, Jane Marsh. "A Defeated Success." *Overland Monthly*, 2nd series, July 1888.

# Bibliography

Pope, Franklin (attrib.). Unpublished ms. in the Wemple Collection, Western Union Telegraph Company; copy in the special collections division of the University of Washington Library, Seattle.

*Proceedings of the Senate of the United States, 37th Congress, 2d session, February 17, 1862.* Report from Mr. Latham. Public Archives of Canada.

Recollections of Charles Frederick Morison, Vol. 18, McKelvie Papers, PABC.

Rothrock, J.T. to E.O.S. Scholefield. Letter in PABC.

———. "A Snowshoe Trip in B.C." Unpublished ms. in PABC.

*Statement of the Origin, Organization and Progress of the Russian-American Telegraph, Western Union Extension, Collins Overland Line, via Behring Strait and Asiatic Russia to Europe.* Rochester: Western Union Telegraph Company, May, 1866.

*The Telegrapher.* Volume I to Volume III, 1865-1867.

U.S. Department of State. "Communication of Hon. William H. Seward, Secretary of State, upon the subject of an intercontinental telegraph." Washington: Government Printing Office, 1864.

Vevier, Charles. "The Collins Overland Line and American Continentalism," in *Pacific Historical Review*, Vol. 28, No. 3, August 1959.

# Index

# Index

Rosemary Neering is a free-lance writer, editor and researcher who specializes in biography, travel and history. Her many books, for both school-age and adult readers, include *Historic Alberta, Louis Riel, Settlement of the West, Emily Carr,* and *The San Juans;* she also writes frequently for magazines. Ms. Neering undertook *Continental Dash* because she is "fascinated by plans to span continents with railroads or other means of communication."